A Knight Two-in-One Special Edition

FIVE RUN AWAY TOGETHER
FIVE GO TO SMUGGLER'S TOP

The Famous Five are Julian, Dick,
George (Georgina by rights), Anne and
Timmy the dog.

This book brings together their third
and fourth exciting adventures.

Join the Famous Five . . .

FIVE RUN AWAY
TOGETHER

ENID BLYTON

FIVE RUN
AWAY
TOGETHER

KNIGHT BOOKS
Hodder and Stoughton

*This Famous Five Two-in-One Special Edition
was first published in 1987
Revised edition 1993*

ISBN 0 340 59624 4

Copyright © Darrell Waters Ltd.
All rights reserved
Enid Blyton's signature is a Registered
Trade Mark of Darrell Waters Ltd.

Five Run Away Together

First published in a single volume by
Hodder and Stoughton, 1944

First Knight Books single volume
edition 1967

Printed and bound in Great Britain
for Hodder and Stoughton Children's
Books, a division of Hodder and
Stoughton Ltd., Mill Road, Dunton
Green, Sevenoaks, Kent TN13 2YA.
Editorial Office: 47 Bedford Square,
London WC1B 3DP) by Cox &
Wyman Ltd., Reading, Berks. Photoset
by Rowland Phototypesetting Ltd.,
Bury St Edmunds, Suffolk.

British Library C.I.P.

Blyton, Enid
  Five run away together. –
  (Blyton, Enid. Famous Five).
  I. Title
823'.9'1J   PZ7.B629

Contents

1 Summer holidays

'George dear, do settle down and do something,' said George's mother. 'You keep wandering in and out with Timothy, and I am trying to have a rest.'

'Sorry, Mother,' said Georgina, taking hold of Timothy's collar. 'But I feel lonely without the others. Oh I do wish tomorrow would come. I've been without them for three whole weeks already.'

Georgina went to boarding-school with her cousin Anne, and in the holidays she and Anne, and Anne's two brothers, Julian and Dick, usually joined up together and had plenty of fun. Now it was the summer holidays, and already three weeks had gone by. Anne, Dick and Julian had gone away with their father and mother, but Georgina's parents had wanted their little girl with them, so she had not gone.

Now her three cousins were coming the next day to spend the rest of the summer holidays with her at her old home, Kirrin Cottage.

'It will be lovely when they are here,' said George, as she was always called, to Timothy her dog. 'Simply lovely, Timothy. Don't you think so?'

'Woof,' said Timothy and licked George's hand.

George was dressed, as usual, exactly like a boy, in jeans and jersey. She had always wanted to be a boy, and would never answer if she was called Georgina. So everyone called her George. She had missed her cousins very much during the first weeks of the summer holidays.

'I used to think I liked best to be alone,' George said to Timothy, who always seemed to understand every word she said. 'But now I know that was silly. It's nice to be with others and share things, and make friends.'

Timothy thumped his tail on the ground. He certainly liked being with the other children too. He was longing to see Julian, Anne and Dick again.

George took Timothy down to the beach. She shaded her eyes with her hand, and looked out to the entrance of the bay. In the middle of it, almost as if it were guarding it, lay a small, rocky island, on which rose the ruins of an old castle.

'We'll visit you again this summer, Kirrin Island,' said George softly. 'I haven't been able to go to you yet this summer, because my boat was being mended – but it will be ready soon, then I'll come to you. And I'll look all round the old castle again. Oh Tim – do you remember the adventures we had on Kirrin Island last summer?'

Tim remembered quite well, because he himself had shared in the thrilling adventures. He had been down in the dungeons of the castle with the others; he had helped to find treasure there, and had had just as grand a time as the four children he loved. He gave a little bark.

'You're remembering, aren't you, Tim?' said George, patting him. 'Won't it be fun to go there again? We'll go down into the dungeons again, shall we? And oh! – do you remember how Dick climbed down the deep well-shaft to rescue us?'

It was exciting, remembering all the things that had

happened last year. It made George long all the more for the next day, when her three friends would arrive.

'I wish Mother would let us go and live on the island for a week,' thought George. 'That would be the greatest fun we could have. To live on my very own island!'

It *was* George's island. It really belonged to her mother, but she had said, two or three years back, that George could have it, and George now thought of it as really her own. She felt that all the rabbits on it belonged to her, all the wild birds and other creatures.

'I'll suggest that we go there for a week, when the others come,' she thought, excitedly. 'We'll take our food and everything, and live there quite by ourselves. We shall feel like Robinson Crusoe.'

She went to meet her cousins the next day, driving the pony and trap by herself. Her mother wanted to come, but she said she did not feel very well. George felt a bit worried about her. So often lately her mother had said she didn't feel very well. Perhaps it was the heat of the summer. The weather had been so very hot lately. Day after day had brought nothing but blue sky and sunshine. George had been burnt a dark-brown, and her eyes were startlingly blue in her sunburnt face. She had had her hair cut even shorter than usual, and it really was difficult to know whether she was a boy or a girl.

The train came in. Three hands waved madly from a window, and George shouted in delight.

'Julian! Dick! Anne! You're here at last.'

The three children tumbled pell-mell out of their carriage. Julian yelled to a porter.

'Our bags are in the guard's van. Hallo, George! How are you? Golly, you've grown.'

They all had. They were all a year older and a year bigger than when they had had their exciting adventures on Kirrin Island. Even Anne, the youngest, didn't look such a small girl now. She flung herself on George, almost knocking her over, and then went down on her knees beside Timothy, who was quite mad with joy to see his three friends.

There was a terrific noise. They all shouted their news at once, and Timothy barked without stopping.

'We thought the train would never get here!'

'Oh Timothy, you darling, you're just the same as ever!'

'Woof, woof, woof!'

'Mother's sorry she couldn't come and meet you too.'

'George, how brown you are! I say, aren't we going to have fun.'

'WOOF, WOOF!'

'Shut up, Tim darling, and do get down; you've bitten my tie almost in half. Oh, you dear old dog, it's grand to see you!'

'WOOF!'

The porter wheeled up their luggage, and soon it was in the pony-cart. George clicked to the waiting pony, and it cantered off. The five in the little cart all talked at once at the top of their voices, Tim far more loudly than anyone else, for his doggy voice was strong and powerful.

'I hope your mother isn't ill?' said Julian, who was fond of his Aunt Fanny. She was gentle and kind, and loved having them all.

'I think it must be the heat,' said George.

'What about Uncle Quentin?' asked Anne. 'Is he all right?'

The three children did not very much like George's father because he could get into very fierce tempers, and although he welcomed the three cousins to his house, he did not really care for children. So they always felt a little awkward with him, and were glad when he was not there.

'Father's all right,' said George, cheerfully. 'Only he's worried about Mother. He doesn't seem to notice her much when she's well and cheerful, but he gets awfully upset if anything goes wrong with her. So be a bit careful of him at the moment. You know what he's like when he's worried.'

The children did know. Uncle Quentin was best avoided when things went wrong. But not even the thought of a cross uncle could damp them today. They were on holiday; they were going to Kirrin Cottage; they were by the sea, and there was dear old Timothy beside them, and fun of all kinds in store for them.

'Shall we go to Kirrin Island, George?' asked Anne. 'Do let's! We haven't been there since last summer. The weather was too bad in the winter and Easter holidays. Now it's gorgeous.'

'Of course we'll go,' said George, her blue eyes shining. 'Do you know what I thought? I thought it would be marvellous to go and stay there for a whole week by ourselves! We are older now, and I'm sure Mother would let us.'

'Go and stay on your island for a week!' cried Anne. 'Oh! That would be too good to be true.'

'*Our* island,' said George, happily. 'Don't you remember I said I would divide it into four, and we'd all share it? Well, I meant it, you know. It's ours, not mine.'

'What about Timothy?' said Anne. 'Oughtn't he to

have a share as well? Can't we make it five bits, one for him too?'

'He can share mine,' said George. She drew the pony to a stop, and the four children and the dog gazed out across the blue bay. 'There's Kirrin Island,' said George. 'Dear little island. I can hardly wait to get to it now. I haven't been able to go there yet, because my boat wasn't mended.'

'Then we can all go together,' said Dick. 'I wonder if the rabbits are just as tame as ever.'

'Woof!' said Timothy at once. He had only to hear the word 'rabbits' to get excited.

'It's no good your thinking about the rabbits on Kirrin,' said George. 'You know I don't allow you to chase them, Tim.'

Timothy's tail dropped and he looked mournfully at George. It was the only thing on which he and George did not agree. Tim was firmly convinced that rabbits were meant for him to chase, and George was just as firmly convinced that they were not.

'Get on!' said George to the pony, and jerked the reins. The little creature trotted on towards Kirrin Cottage, and very soon they were all opposite the front gate.

A sour-faced woman came out from the back door to help them down with their luggage. The children did not know her.

'Who's she?' they whispered to George.

'The new cook,' said George. 'Joanna had to go and look after her mother, who broke her leg. Then Mother got this cook – Mrs Stick her name is.'

'Good name for her,' grinned Julian. 'She looks a real old stick! But all the same I hope she doesn't stick here for long. I hope Joanna comes back. I liked old fat

Joanna, and she was nice to Timmy.'

'Mrs Stick has a dog too,' said George. 'A dreadful animal, smaller than Tim, all sort of mangy and moth-eaten. Tim can't bear it.'

'Where is it?' asked Anne, looking round.

'It's kept in the kitchen, and Tim isn't allowed near it,' said George. 'Good thing too, because I'm sure he'd eat it! He can't think what's in the kitchen, and goes sniffing round the shut door till Mrs Stick nearly goes mad.'

The others laughed. They had all climbed down from the pony-cart now, and were ready to go indoors. Julian had helped Mrs Stick in with all the bags. George took the pony-cart away, and the other three went in to say hello to their uncle and aunt.

'Well, dears,' said Aunt Fanny, smiling at them from the sofa where she was lying down. 'How are you all? I'm sorry I could not come to meet you. Uncle Quentin is out for a walk. You had better go upstairs, and wash and change. Then come down for tea.'

The boys went up to their old bedroom, with its funny slanting roof, and its window looking out over the bay. Anne went to the little room she shared with George. How good it was to be back again at Kirrin! What fun they would have these holidays with George and dear old Timmy!

2 The Stick family

It was lovely to wake up the next morning at Kirrin Cottage and see the sun shining in at the windows, and to hear the far-off plash-plash-plash of the sea. It was gorgeous to leap out of bed and rush to see how blue the sea was, and how lovely Kirrin Island looked at the entrance of the bay.

'I'm going for a bathe before breakfast,' said Julian, and snatched up his bathing trunks. 'Coming, Dick?'

'You bet!' said Dick. 'Call the girls. We'll all go.'

So down they went, the four of them, with Tim galloping behind them, his tail wagging nineteen to the dozen, and his long pink tongue hanging out of his mouth. He went into the water with the others, and swam all round them. They were all good swimmers, but Julian and George were the best.

They put towels round themselves, rubbed their bodies dry and pulled on jeans and jerseys. Then back to breakfast they went, as hungry as hunters. Anne noticed a boy in the back garden and stared in surprise.

'Who's that?' she said.

'Oh, that's Edgar, Mrs Stick's boy,' said George. 'I don't like him. He does silly things, like putting out his tongue and calling rude names.'

Edgar appeared to be singing when the others went in at the gate. Anne stopped to listen.

'Georgie-porgie, pudding and pie!' sang Edgar, a

silly look on his face. He seemed about thirteen or fourteen, a stupid, yet sly-looking youth. 'Georgie-porgie pudding and pie!'

George went red. 'He's always singing that,' she said, furiously. 'Just because I'm called "George", I suppose. He thinks he's clever. I can't bear him.'

Julian called out to Edgar. 'You shut up! You're not funny, only jolly silly!'

'Georgie-porgie,' began Edgar again, a silly smile on his wide red face. Julian made a step towards him, and he at once disappeared into the house.

'Shan't stand much of *him*,' said Julian, in a decided voice. 'I wonder *you* do, George. I wonder you haven't slapped his face, stamped on his foot, bitten his ears off and done a few other things! You used to be so fierce.'

'Well – I am still, really,' said George. 'I *feel* frightfully fierce down inside me when I hear Edgar singing silly songs at me like that and calling out names – but you see, Mother really hasn't been well, and I know jolly well if I go for Edgar, Mrs Stick will leave, and poor old Mother would have to do all the work, and she really isn't fit to at present. So I just hold myself in, and hope that Timmy will do the same.'

'Good for *you* old thing!' said Julian, admiringly, for he knew how hard it was for George to keep her temper at times.

'I think I'll just go up to Mother's room and see if she'd like breakfast in bed,' said George. 'Hang on to old Timmy a moment, will you? If Edgar appears again, he might go for him.'

Julian hung on to Timmy's collar. Timmy had growled when Edgar had been in the garden, now he stood stock still, his nose twitching as if he were trying to trace some smell.

Suddenly a mangy-looking dog appeared out of the kitchen door. It had a dirty white coat, out of which patches seemed to have been bitten, and its tail was well between its legs.

'Wooooof!' said Timmy, joyfully, and leapt at the dog. He pulled Julian over, for he was a big dog, and the boy let go his hold of the dog's collar. Timmy pounced excitedly on the other dog, who gave a fearful whine and tried to go into the kitchen door again.

'Timmy! Come here!' yelled Julian. But Timmy didn't hear. He was busy trying to snap off the other dog's ears – or at least, that is what he appeared to be doing. The other dog yelled for help, and Mrs Stick appeared at the kitchen door, a saucepan in her hand.

'Call off that dog!' she screeched. She hit out at Timmy with the saucepan, but he dodged and it hit her own dog instead, making it yelp all the more.

'Don't hit out with that!' said Julian. 'You'll hurt the dogs. Hi, Timmy, TIMMY!'

Edgar now appeared, looking very scared. He picked up a stone and seemed to be watching his chance to hurl it at Timmy. Anne shrieked.

'You're not to throw that stone; you're not to! You bad wicked boy!'

In the middle of all this turmoil Uncle Quentin appeared, looking angry and irritable.

'Good heavens! What is all this going on? I never heard such a row in my life.'

Then George appeared, flying out of the door like the wind, to rescue her beloved Timothy. She rushed to the two dogs and tried to pull Timmy away. Her father yelled at her.

'Come away, you little idiot! Don't you know

better than to separate two fighting dogs with your bare hands? Where's the garden hose?'

It was fixed to a tap nearby. Julian ran to it and turned on the tap. He picked up the hose and turned it on the two dogs. At once the jet of water spurted out at them, and they leapt apart in surprise. Julian saw Edgar standing near, and couldn't resist swinging the hose a little so that the boy was soaked. He gave a scream and ran in at once.

'What did you do that for?' said Uncle Quentin, annoyed. 'George, tie Timothy up at once. Mrs Stick, didn't I tell you not to let your dog out of the kitchen unless you had him on a lead? I won't have this kind of thing happening. Where's the breakfast? Late as usual!'

Mrs Stick disappeared into the kitchen, muttering and grumbling, taking her drenched dog with her. George, looking sulky, tied Timothy up. He lay down in his kennel, looking beseechingly at his mistress.

'I've told you not to take any notice of that mangy-looking dog,' said George, severely. 'Now you see what happens! You put Father into a bad temper for the rest of the day, and Mrs Stick will be so angry she won't make any cakes for tea!'

Timmy gave a whine, and put his head down on his paws. He licked a few hairs from the corner of his mouth. It was sad to be tied up – but anyhow he had bitten a bit off the tip of one of that dreadful dog's ears!

They all went in to breakfast. 'Sorry I let Timmy go,' said Julian to George. 'But he nearly tore my arm off. I couldn't possibly hold him! He's grown into an awfully powerful dog, hasn't he?'

'Yes,' said George, proudly. 'He has. He could eat Mrs Stick's dog up in a mouthful if we'd let him. And Edgar too.'

'And Mrs Stick,' said Anne. 'All of them. I don't like any of them.'

Breakfast was rather a subdued meal, as Aunt Fanny was not there, but Uncle Quentin was – and Uncle Quentin in a bad temper was not a very cheerful person to have at the breakfast-table. He snapped at George and glared at the others. Anne almost wished they hadn't come to Kirrin Cottage! But her spirits rose when she thought of the rest of the day – they would take their dinner out, perhaps, and have it on the beach – or maybe even go out to Kirrin Island. Uncle Quentin wouldn't be with them to spoil things.

Mrs Stick appeared to take away the porridge plates and bring in the bacon. She banged the plates down on the table.

'No need to do that,' said Uncle Quentin, irritably. Mrs Stick said nothing. She was scared of Uncle Quentin, and no wonder! She put the next lot of plates down quietly.

'What are you going to do today?' asked Uncle Quentin, towards the end of breakfast. He was feeling a little better by that time, and didn't like to see such subdued faces round him.

'We thought we might go out for a picnic,' said George, eagerly. 'I asked Mother. She said we might, if Mrs Stick will make us sandwiches.'

'Well, I shouldn't think she'll try very hard,' said Uncle Quentin, trying to make a little joke. They all smiled politely. 'But you can ask her.'

There was a silence. Nobody liked the idea of asking Mrs Stick for sandwiches.

'I do wish she hadn't brought Stinker,' said George, gloomily. 'Everything would be easier if he wasn't here.'

'Is that the name of her son?' asked Uncle Quentin, startled.

George grinned. 'Oh no. Though it wouldn't be a bad name for him, because he hardly ever has a bath, and he's jolly smelly. It's her dog I mean. She calls him Tinker, but I call him Stinker, because he really does smell awful.'

'I don't think it's a very nice name,' said her father, in the midst of the others' giggles.

'No, it isn't,' said George, 'but then, he isn't a very nice dog.'

In the end it was Aunt Fanny who saw Mrs Stick and arranged about the sandwiches. Mrs Stick went up to see Aunt Fanny, who was having breakfast in bed, and agreed to make sandwiches, though with a very bad grace.

'I didn't bargain for three more children to come traipsing along,' she said, sulkily.

'I told you they were coming, Mrs Stick,' said Aunt Fanny, patiently. 'I didn't know I should be feeling so ill myself when they came. If I had been well I could have made their sandwiches and done many more things. I can only ask you to help as much as you can till I feel better. I may be all right tomorrow. Let the children have a good time for a week or so, and then, if I still feel ill, I am sure they will all turn to and help a bit. But let them have a good time first.'

The children took their packets of sandwiches and set off. On the way they met Edgar, looking as stupid and sly as usual. 'Why don't you let me come along with you?' he said. 'Let's go to that island. I know a lot about it, I do.'

'No, you don't,' said George, in a flash. 'You don't know anything about it. And I'd never take *you*. It's *my* island, see? Well, *ours*. It belongs to all four of us and Timmy, too. We should never allow you to go.'

'Tisn't your island,' said Edgar. 'That's a lie, that is!'

'You don't know what you're talking about,' said George, scornfully. 'Come on, you others! We can't waste time talking to Edgar.'

They left him, looking sulky and angry. As soon as they were at a safe distance he lifted up his voice:

> *'Georgie-porgie, pudding and pie,*
> *She knows how to tell a lie,*
> *Georgie-porgie, pudding and pie!'*

Julian started to go back after the rude Edgar, but George pulled him on. 'He'll only go and tell tales to his mother, and she'll walk out and there'll be no one to help Mother,' she said. 'I'll just have to put up with it. We'll try and think of some way to get our own back, though. Nasty creature! I hate his pimply nose and screwed-up eyes.'

'Woof!' said Timmy, feelingly.

'Timmy says he hates Stinker's miserable tail and silly little ears,' explained George, and they all laughed. That made them feel better. They were soon out of hearing of Edgar's silly song, and forgot all about him.

'Let's go and see if your boat is ready,' said Julian. 'Then maybe we could row out to the dear old island.'

3   A nasty shock

George's boat was almost ready, but not quite. It was having a last coat of paint on it. It looked very nice, for George had chosen a bright red paint, and the oars were painted red too.

'Oh, can't we possibly have it this afternoon?' said George to Jim the boatman.

He shook his head.

'No, Master George,' he said, 'not unless you all want to be messed up with red paint. It'll be dry tomorrow, but not before.'

It always made the others smile to hear the boatmen and fishermen call Georgina 'Master George'. The local people all knew how badly she wanted to be a boy, and they knew, too, how plucky and straight-forward she was, so they laughed to one another and said: 'Well, they reckoned she behaved like a boy, and if she wanted to be called "Master George" instead of "Miss Georgina", she deserved it!'

So Georgina was Master George, and enjoyed strutting about in her jeans and jersey on the beach, using her boat as well as any fisher-boy, and swimming faster than them all.

'We'll go to the island tomorrow then,' said Julian. 'We'll just picnic on the beach today. Then we'll go for a walk.'

So they picnicked on the sands with Timothy

sharing more than half their lunch. The sandwiches were not very nice. The bread was too stale; there was not enough butter inside, and they were far too thick. But Timothy didn't mind. He gobbled up as many as he could, his tail wagging so hard that it sent sand over everyone.

'Timothy, do take your tail out of the sand if you want to wag it,' said Julian, getting sand all over his hair for the fourth time. Timmy wagged his tail hard again, and sent another shower over him. Everyone laughed.

'Let's go for a walk now,' said Dick, jumping up. 'My legs could do with some good exercise. Where shall we go?'

'We'll walk along the cliff-top, where we can see the island all the time, shall we?' said Anne. 'George, is the old wreck still there?'

George nodded. The children had once had a most exciting time with an old wreck that had lain at the bottom of the sea. A great storm had lifted it up and set it firmly on the rocks. They had been able to explore the wreck then, and had found a map of the castle in it, with instructions as to where hidden treasure was to be found.

'Do you remember how we found that old map in the wreck, and how we looked for the ingots of gold and found them?' said Julian, his eyes gleaming as he remembered it all. 'Isn't the wreck battered to pieces yet, George?'

'No,' said George. 'I don't think so. It's on the rocks on the other side of the island, you remember, so we can't see it from here. But we might have a look at it when we go on the island tomorrow.'

'Yes, let's,' said Anne. 'Poor old wreck! I guess it

won't last many winters now.'

They walked along the cliff-top with Timothy capering ahead of them. They could see the island easily and the ruined castle rising up from the middle.

'There's the jackdaw tower,' said Anne, looking. 'The other tower's fallen down, hasn't it? Look at the jackdaws circling round and round the tower, George!'

'Yes. They build in it every year,' said George. 'Don't you remember the masses of sticks round about the tower that the jackdaws dropped when they built their nests? We picked some up and made a fire with them once.'

'I'd like to do that again,' said Anne. 'I would really. Let's do it each night if we stay a week on the island. George, did you ask your mother?'

'Oh yes,' said George. 'She said she thought we might, but she would see.'

'I don't like it when grown-ups say they'll see,' said Anne. 'It so often means they won't let you do something after all, but they don't like to tell you at the time.'

'Well, I expect she will let us,' said George. 'After all, we're much older than last year. Why, Julian is in his teens already, and I soon shall be and so will Dick. Only Anne is small.'

'I'm not,' said Anne, indignantly. 'I'm as strong as you are. I can't help being younger.'

'Hush, hush, baby!' said Julian, patting his little sister on the back and laughing at her furious face. 'Hallo – look! What's that over there on the island?'

He had caught sight of something as he was teasing Anne. Everyone swung round and gazed at Kirrin. George gave an exclamation.

'Golly – a spire of smoke! Surely it's smoke! Some-one's on my island.'

'On *our* island,' corrected Dick. 'It can't be! That smoke must come from a steamer out beyond the island. We can't see it, that's all. But I bet the smoke comes from a steamer. We know no one can get to the island but us. They don't know the way.'

'If anyone's on my island,' begun George, looking very fierce and angry, 'if anyone's on my island, I'll – I'll – I'll . . .'

'You'll explode and go up in smoke!' said Dick. 'There – it's gone now. I'm sure it was only a steamer letting off steam or smoking hard, whatever they do.'

They watched Kirrin Island for some time after that, but they could see no more smoke. 'If only my boat was ready!' said George, restlessly. 'I'd go over this afternoon. I've a good mind to go and get my boat, even if the paint *is* wet.'

'Don't be an idiot!' said Julian. 'You know what an awful row we'd get into if we go home with all our things bright red. Have a bit of sense, George.'

George gave up the idea. She watched for a steamer to appear at one side of the island or another, to come into the bay, but none came.

'Probably anchored out there,' said Dick. 'Come on! Are we going to stand rooted to this spot for the rest of the day?'

'We'd better get back home,' said Julian, looking at his wrist-watch. 'It's almost tea-time. I hope your mother is up, George. It's much nicer when she's at meals.'

'Oh, I expect she will be,' said George. 'Come on then, let's go back!'

They turned to go back. They watched Kirrin Island

as they walked, but all they could see were jackdaws or gulls in the sky above it. No more spires of smoke appeared. It must have been a steamer!

'All the same, I'm going over tomorrow to have a look,' said George, firmly. 'If any trippers are visiting my island I'll turn them off.'

'*Our* island,' said Dick. 'George, I wish you'd remember you said you'd share it with us.'

'Well – I did share it out with you,' said George, 'but I can't help feeling it's still my island. Come on! I'm getting hungry.'

They came back at last to Kirrin Cottage. They went into the hall, and then into the sitting-room. To their great surprise Edgar was there, reading one of Julian's books.

'What are you doing here?' said Julian. 'And who told you you could borrow my book?'

'I'm not doing any harm,' said Edgar. 'If I want to have a quiet read, why shouldn't I?'

'You wait till my father comes in and finds you lolling about here,' said George. 'My goodness, if you'd gone into his study, you'd have been sorry.'

'I've been in there,' said Edgar, surprisingly. 'I've seen those funny instruments he's working with.'

'How *dare* you!' said George, going white with rage. 'Why, even *we* are not allowed to go into my father's study. As for touching his things – well!'

Julian eyed Edgar curiously. He could not imagine why the boy should suddenly be so insolent.

'Where's your father, George?' he said. 'I think we had better get him to deal with Edgar. He must be mad.'

'Call him if you like,' said Edgar, still lolling in the chair, and flicking over the pages of Julian's book in a most irritating way. 'He won't come.'

'What do you mean?' said George, feeling suddenly scared. 'Where's my mother?'

'Call her too, if you like,' said the boy, looking sly. 'Go on! Call her.'

The children suddenly felt afraid. What did Edgar mean? George flew upstairs to her mother's room, shouting loudly.

'Mother! Mother! Where are you?'

But her mother's bed was empty. It had not been made – but it was empty. George flew into all the other bedrooms, shouting desperately: 'Mother! Mother! Father! Where are you?'

But there was no answer. George ran downstairs, her face very white. Edgar grinned up at her.

'What did I tell you?' he said. 'I said you could call all you liked, but they wouldn't come.'

'Where are they?' demanded George. 'Tell me at once!'

'Find out yourself,' said Edgar.

There was a resounding slap, and Edgar leapt to his feet, holding his left cheek with his hand. George had flown at him and dealt him the hardest smack she could. Edgar lifted his hand to slap her back, but Julian stood in front.

'You're not fighting George,' he said. 'She's a girl. If you want a fight, I'll take you on.'

'I won't be a girl; I'm a boy!' shouted George, trying to push Julian away. 'I'll fight Edgar, and I'll beat him, you see if I don't.'

But Julian kept her off. Edgar began to edge towards the doorway, but he found Dick there.

'One minute,' said Dick. 'Before you go – where are our uncle and aunt?'

'Gr-r-r-r-r-r-r,' suddenly said Timothy, in such a threatening voice that Edgar stared at him in fright. The dog had bared his great teeth, and had put up the hackles on his neck. He looked very frightening.

'Hold that dog!' said Edgar, his voice trembling. 'He looks as if he's going to spring at me.'

Julian put his hand on Tim's collar. 'Quiet, Tim!' he said. 'Now, Edgar, tell us what we want to know, and tell us quickly, or you'll be sorry.'

'Well, there isn't much to tell,' said Edgar, keeping his eye on Timothy. He shot a look at George and went on. 'Your mother was suddenly taken very ill – with a terrible pain *here* – and they got the doctor and they've taken her away to hospital, and your father went with her. That's all!'

George sat down on the sofa, looking paler still and rather sick.

'Oh!' she said. 'Poor Mother! I wish I hadn't gone out today. Oh dear – how can we find out what's happened?'

Edgar had slipped out of the room, shutting the door behind him so that Timmy should not follow. The kitchen door was slammed, too. The children stared at one another, feeling sorry and dismayed. Poor George! Poor Aunt Fanny!

'There must be a note somewhere,' said Julian, and looked round the room. He saw a letter stuck into the rim of the big mirror there, addressed to George. He gave it to her. It was from George's father.

'Read it, quickly,' said Anne. 'Oh dear – this is really a horrid beginning to our holidays here!'

4 A few little upsets

George read the letter out loud. It was not very long, and had evidently been written in a great hurry.

DEAR GEORGE,

Your mother has been taken very ill. I am going with her to the hospital. I shall not leave her till she is getting better. That may be in a few days' time, or in a week's time. I will telephone to you each day at nine o'clock in the morning to tell you how she is. Mrs Stick will look after you all. Try to manage all right till I come back.

Your loving
FATHER

'Oh dear!' said Anne, knowing how dreadful George must feel. George loved her mother dearly, and for once the girl had tears in her eyes. George never cried – but it was terrible to come home and find her mother gone like this. And Father too! No one there but Mrs Stick and Edgar.

'I can't bear Mother going like this,' sobbed George, suddenly, and buried her head in a cushion. 'She – she might never come back.'

'Don't be silly, George,' said Julian, sitting down and putting his arm round her. 'Of course she will. Why shouldn't she? Didn't your father say he was staying with her till she was getting better – and that would be probably in a few days' time. Cheer up, George! It isn't like you to give way like this.'

'But I didn't say good-bye,' sobbed poor George. 'And I made her ask Mrs Stick for the sandwiches, instead of me. I want to go and find Mother and see how she is myself.'

'You don't know where they've taken her, and if you did, they wouldn't let you in,' said Dick, gently. 'Let's have some tea. We shall all feel better after that.'

'I couldn't eat *anything*,' said George, fiercely. Timothy pushed his nose into her hands, and tried to lick them. They were under her buried face. The dog whined a little.

'Poor Timmy! He can't understand,' said Anne. 'He's awfully upset because you are unhappy, George.'

That made George sit up. She rubbed her hands over her eyes, and let Timmy lick the wet tears off them. He looked surprised at the salty taste. He tried to get on to George's knee.

'Silly Timmy!' said George, in a more ordinary voice. 'Don't be upset. I just got a shock, that's all! I'm better now, Timmy. Don't whine like that, silly! I'm all right. I'm not hurt.'

But Timothy felt certain George was really hurt or injured in some way to cry like that, and he kept whining, and pawing at George, and trying to get on to her knee.

Julian opened the door. 'I'm going to tell Mrs Stick we want our tea,' he said, and went out. The others thought he was rather brave to face Mrs Stick.

Julian went to the kitchen door and opened it. Edgar was sitting there, one side of his face scarlet, where

George had slapped it. Mrs Stick was there, looking grim.

'If that girl slaps my Edgar again I'll be after her,' she said, threateningly.

'Edgar deserved what he got,' said Julian. 'Can we have some tea, please?'

'I've a good mind to get you none,' said Mrs Stick. Her dog started up from its corner and growled at Julian. 'That's right, Tinker! You growl at folks that slap Edgar,' said Mrs Stick.

Julian was not in the least afraid of Tinker. 'If you are not going to get us any tea, I'll get it myself,' said the boy. 'Where is the bread, and where are the cakes?'

Mrs Stick stared at Julian, and the boy looked back at her steadfastly. He thought she was a most unpleasant woman, and he certainly was not going to allow her to get the better of him. He wished he could tell her to go – but he had a feeling that she wouldn't, so it would be a waste of his breath.

Mrs Stick dropped her eyes first. 'I'll get your tea,' she said, 'but if I have any nonsense from you I'll get you no other meals.'

'And if I have any nonsense from you I shall go to the police,' said Julian, unexpectedly. He hadn't meant to say that. It came out quite suddenly, but it had a surprising effect on Mrs Stick. She looked startled and alarmed.

'Now, there's no call to be nasty,' she said in a much more polite voice. 'We've all had a bit of a shock, and we're upset, like – I'll get you your tea right now.'

Julian went out. He wondered why his sudden threat of going to the police had made Mrs Stick so much more polite. Perhaps she was afraid the police would get on to his Uncle Quentin and he would come tearing back. Uncle Quentin wouldn't care for a hundred Mrs Sticks!

He went back to the others. 'Tea's coming,' he said. 'So cheer up, everyone!'

It wasn't a very cheerful company that sat down to the tea Mrs Stick brought in. George was now feeling ashamed of her tears. Anne was still upset. Dick tried to make a few silly jokes to cheer everyone up, but they fell so flat that he soon gave it up. Julian was grave and helpful, suddenly very grown-up.

Timothy sat close beside George, his head on her knee. 'I do wish I had a dog who loved me like that,' thought Anne. Timmy kept gazing up at George out of big brown devoted eyes. He had no eyes or ears for anyone but his little mistress now she was sad.

Nobody noticed what they had for tea, but all the same it did them good, and they felt better after it. They didn't like to go out to the beach afterwards in case the telephone bell rang, and there was news of George's mother. So they sat about in the garden, keeping an ear open for the telephone.

From the kitchen came a song.

> 'Georgie-porgie, pudding and pie,
> Sat herself down and had a good cry,
> Georgie-porgie . . .'

Julian got up. He went to the kitchen window and looked in. Edgar was there alone.

'Come on out here, Edgar!' said Julian, in a grim voice. 'I'll teach you to sing another song. Come along!'

Edgar didn't stir. 'Can't I sing if I want to?' he said.

'Oh yes,' said Julian, 'but not that song. I'll teach

you another. Come along out!'

'No fear,' said Edgar. 'You want to fight me.'

'Yes, I do,' said Julian. 'I think a little bit of good honest fighting would be better for you than sitting singing nasty little songs about a girl who is miserable. Are you coming out? Or shall I come in and fetch you?'

'Ma!' called Edgar, suddenly feeling panicky. 'Ma! Where are you?'

Julian suddenly reached a long arm in at the window, caught hold of Edgar's over-long nose, and pulled it so hard that Edgar yelled in pain.

'Led go! Led go! You're hurding me! Led go by dose!'

Mrs Stick came hurrying into the kitchen. She gave a scream when she saw what Julian was doing. She flew at him. Julian withdrew his arm, and stood outside the window.

'How dare you!' yelled Mrs Stick. 'First that girl slaps Edgar, and then you pull his nose! What's the matter with you all?'

'Nothing,' said Julian, pleasantly, 'but there's an awful lot wrong with Edgar, Mrs Stick. We feel we just *must* put it right. It should be your job, of course, but you don't seem to have done it.'

'You're down right insolent,' said Mrs Stick, outraged and furious.

'Yes, I dare say I am,' said Julian. 'It's just the effect Edgar has on me. Stinker has the same effect.'

'Stinker!' cried Mrs Stick, getting angrier still. 'That's not my dog's name, and well you know it.'

'Well, it really ought to be,' said Julian, strolling off. 'Give him a bath, and maybe we'll call him Tinker instead.'

Leaving Mrs Stick muttering in fury, he went back

to the others. They stared at him curiously. He some-
how seemed a different Julian – a grim and determined
Julian, a very grown-up Julian, a rather frightening
Julian.

'I'm afraid the fat's in the fire now,' said Julian,
sitting down on the grass. 'I pulled old Edgar's nose
nearly off his fat face, and Ma saw me doing it. I guess
it's open warfare now! We shan't have a very merry
time from now on. I doubt if we'll get any meals.'

'We'll get them ourselves then,' said George. 'I hate
Mrs Stick. I wish Joanna would come back. I hate that
horrid Edgar too, and that awful Stinker.'

'Look – there *is* Stinker!' suddenly said Dick,
putting out his hand to catch Timothy, who had risen
with a growl. But Timmy shook off his hand and leapt
across the grass at once. Stinker gave a woeful howl
and tried to escape. But Timothy had him by the neck
and was shaking him like a rat.

Mrs Stick appeared with a stick and lashed out, not
seeming to mind which dog she hit. Julian rushed for
the hose again. Edgar skipped indoors at once,
remembering what had happened to him before.

The water gushed out, and Timothy gave a gasp and
let go the howling mongrel he held in his teeth. Stinker
at once hurled himself on Mrs Stick, and tried to hide
in her skirts, trembling with terror.

'I'll poison that dog of yours!' said Mrs Stick,
furiously, to George. 'Always setting on to mine. You
look out or I'll poison him.'

She disappeared indoors, and the four children went
and sat down again. George looked really alarmed.
'Do you suppose she really *might* try to poison
Timmy?' she asked Julian, in a scared voice.

'She's a nasty bit of work,' said Julian, in a low tone.

'I think it would be just as well to keep old Timmy close by us, day and night, and only to feed him ourselves, from our own plates.'

George pulled Timothy to her, horrified at the thought that anyone might want to poison him. But Mrs Stick really was awful – she might do anything like that, George thought. How she wished her father and mother were back! It was horrid to be on their own, like this.

The telephone bell suddenly shrilled out and made everyone jump. They all leapt to their feet and Timmy growled. George flew indoors and lifted the receiver. She heard her father's voice, and her heart began to beat fast.

'Is that you, George?' said her father. 'Are you all right? I haven't time to stay and tell you everything.'

'Father – what about Mother? Tell me quick – how is she?' said George.

'We shan't know till the day after next,' said her father. 'I'll telephone tomorrow morning and then the next morning too. I shan't come back till I know she's better.'

'Oh Father – it's awful without you and Mother,' said poor George. 'Mrs Stick is so horrid.'

'Now, George,' said her father, rather impatiently, 'surely you children can see to yourselves and make do with Mrs Stick till I get back! Don't worry me about such things now. I've enough worry as it is.'

'When will you be back, do you think?' said George. 'Can I come and see Mother?'

'No,' said her father. 'Not for at least two weeks, they say. I'll be back as soon as I can. But I'm not going to leave your Mother now. She needs me. Good-bye and be good, all of you.'

George put back the receiver. She turned to face the others. 'Shan't know about Mother till the day after next,' she said. 'And we've got to put up with Mrs Stick till Father comes back – and goodness knows when that will be! It's awful, isn't it?'

5 In the middle of the night

Mrs Stick was in such a bad temper that evening that there was no supper at all. Julian went to ask about some, but he found the kitchen door locked.

He went back to the others with a gloomy face, for they were all hungry. 'She's locked the door,' he said. 'She really is a dreadful creature. I don't believe we'll get any supper tonight.'

'We'll have to wait till she goes to bed,' said George. 'We'll go down and hunt in the larder then, and see what we can find.'

They went to bed hungry. Julian listened for Mrs Stick and Edgar to go to bed, too. When he heard them going upstairs, and was sure their doors had shut, he slipped down into the kitchen. It was dark there, and Julian was just about to put on the light when he heard the sound of someone breathing heavily. He wondered who it could be. Was it Stinker? No – it couldn't be the dog. It sounded like a human being.

Julian stood there, his hand over the light switch, puzzled and a little scared. It couldn't be a burglar, because burglars don't go to sleep in the house they have come to rob. It couldn't be Mrs Stick or Edgar. Then who was it?

He snapped on the light. The kitchen was flooded with radiance, and Julian's eyes fastened on the figure of a small man lying on the sofa. He was fast asleep, his mouth wide open.

He was not a very pleasant sight. He had not shaved for some days, and his cheeks and chin were bluish-black. He didn't seem to have washed for even longer than that, for his hands were black, and so were his fingernails. He had untidy hair and a nose exactly like Edgar's.

'Must be dear Edgar's father,' thought Julian to himself. 'What a sight! Well, poor Edgar hadn't much chance to be decent with a father and mother like his.'

The man snored. Julian wondered what to do. He badly wanted to go to the larder, but on the other hand he didn't particularly want to wake up the man and have a row. He didn't see how he could turn him out – for all he knew his aunt and uncle might have agreed to Mrs Stick's husband coming there now and again, though he hardly thought so.

Julian was very hungry. The thought of the good things in the larder made him snap off the light again and creep towards the larder door in the dark. He opened the door. He felt along the shelves. Good! – that felt like a pie of some sort. He lifted it up and sniffed. It smelt of meat. A meat-pie – good!

He felt along the shelf again and came to a plate on which were what he thought must be jam-tarts, for they were round and flat, and had something sticky in the middle. Well, a meat-pie and jam-tarts ought to be all right for four hungry children!

Julian picked up the meat-pie and the dish of tarts, and made his way carefully out of the larder. He pushed the door to with his foot. Then he turned to go out of the room.

But in the dark he went the wrong way, and by bad

luck walked straight into the sofa! The dish of tarts got a sudden jerk and one of them fell off. It landed on the open mouth of the sleeping man, and woke him up with a start.

'Blow!' said Julian to himself, and began to back away quietly, hoping that the man would turn over and go to sleep again. But the sticky jam-tart sliding down his chin had startled the man, and he sat up with a jerk.

'Who's there? That you, Edgar? What are you doing down here?'

Julian said nothing but sidled towards what he hoped was the door. The man leapt up and lurched over to where he thought the light switch was. He found it and switched it on. He stared in the greatest astonishment at Julian.

'What are you doing here?' he demanded.

'Just what I was about to ask *you*,' said Julian, coolly. 'What do you think *you're* doing here, sleeping in my uncle's kitchen?'

'I've a right to be here,' said the man, in a rude voice. 'My wife's cook here, isn't she? My ship's in and I'm on leave. Your uncle arranged with my wife I could come here then, see?'

Julian had feared as much. How awful to have a Mr Stick as well as a Mrs and Master Stick in the house! It would be quite unbearable.

'I can ask my uncle about it when he telephones in the morning,' said Julian. 'Now get out of my way, please, I want to go upstairs.'

'Ho!' said Mr Stick, eyeing the meat-pie and jam-tarts that Julian was carrying. 'Ho! Stealing out of the larder, I see! Nice goings-on I must say.'

Julian was not going to argue with Mr Stick, who

evidently felt that he was top-dog. 'Get out of my way,' he said. 'I will talk to you in the morning after my uncle has telephoned.'

Mr Stick didn't seem as if he was going to get out of the way at all. He stood there, a nasty little man, not much taller than Julian, a sarcastic smile on his unshaven face.

Julian pursed his lips and whistled. There came a bump on the floor above. That was Timothy jumping off George's bed! Then there came the pattering of feet down the stairs and up the kitchen passage. Timmy was coming!

He smelt Mr Stick in the doorway, put up his hackles, bared his teeth and growled. Mr Stick hastily removed himself from the doorway and then neatly banged the door in the dog's face. He grinned at Julian.

'Now what are you going to do?' he said.

'Shall I tell you?' said Julian, his temper suddenly rising. 'I'm going to hurl this nice juicy meat-pie straight into your grinning face!'

He raised his arms, and Mr Stick ducked.

'Now don't you do that,' he said. 'I'm only pulling your leg, see? Don't you waste that nice meat-pie. You can go upstairs if you want to.'

He moved away to the sofa. Julian opened the door and Timothy bounded in growling. Mr Stick eyed him uncomfortably.

'Don't you let that nasty great dog come near me,' he said. 'I don't like dogs.'

'Then I wonder you don't get rid of Stinker,' said Julian. 'Come here, Timmy! Leave him alone. He's not worth growling at.'

Julian went upstairs with Timothy close at his heels. The others crowded round him, wondering what had happened, for they had heard the voices downstairs. They laughed when Julian told them how he had nearly thrown the meat-pie at Mr Stick.

'It would have served him right,' said Anne, 'though it would have been a great pity, because we shouldn't have been able to eat it. Well, Mrs Stick may be simply horrible, but she *can* cook. This pie is gorgeous.'

The children finished all the pie and the tarts, too. Julian told them all about Mr Stick coming on leave from his ship.

'Three Sticks are a lot too much,' said Dick thoughtfully. 'Pity we can't get rid of them all and manage for ourselves. George, can't you possibly persuade your father tomorrow to let us get rid of the Sticks and look after ourselves?'

'I'll try,' said George. 'But you know what he is – awfully difficult to argue with. But I'll try. Golly, I'm sleepy now. Come on, Timmy, let's get to bed! Lie on my feet. I'm hardly going to let you out of my sight now, in case those awful Sticks poison you!'

Soon the four children, now no longer hungry, were sleeping peacefully. They did not fear the Sticks coming up to their rooms, for they knew that Timmy would wake and warn them at once. Timmy was the best guard they could have.

In the morning Mrs Stick actually produced some sort of breakfast, which surprised the children very much. 'Guess she knows your father will telephone, George,' said Julian, 'and she wants to keep herself in the right. When did he say he would 'phone? Nine o'clock, wasn't it? Well, it's half-past eight now. Let's go for a quick run down to the beach and back.'

So off they went, the five of them, ignoring Edgar,

who stood in the back garden ready to make some of his silly faces at them. The children couldn't help thinking he must be a bit mad. He didn't behave at all like a boy of Julian's age.

When they came back it was about ten minutes to nine. 'We'll sit in the sitting-room till the telephone rings,' said Julian. 'We don't want Mrs Stick to answer it first.'

But to their great dismay, as they reached the house, they heard Mrs Stick using the telephone in the hall!

'Yes,' they heard her say, 'everything is quite all right. I can manage the children, even if they do make things a bit difficult. Yes, of curse. Well, it's lucky my husband is home on leave from his ship, because he can help me round, like, and it makes things easier. Don't you worry about anything, and don't you bother to come back till you're ready. I'll manage everything.'

George flew into the hall like a wild thing, and snatched the receiver out of Mrs Stick's hand.

'Father! It's me, George! How's Mother? Tell me quick!'

'No worse, George,' said her father's voice. 'But we shan't know anything definite till tomorrow morning. I'm glad to hear from Mrs Stick that everything is all right. I'm very upset and worried, and I'm glad to feel I can tell your mother that you are all right, and everything is going smoothly at Kirrin Cottage.'

'But it isn't,' said George, wildly. 'It isn't. It's all horrid. Can't the Sticks go and let us manage things by ourselves?'

'Good gracious me, of course not,' said her father's voice, surprised and annoyed. 'What can you be thinking of? I did hope, George, that you would be sensible and helpful. I must say . . .'

'*You* talk to him, Julian,' said George, helplessly, and thrust the receiver into Julian's hand. The boy put it to his ear and spoke into the telephone in his clear voice.

'Good morning. This is Julian! I'm glad my aunt is no worse.'

'Well, she will be if she thinks things are going wrong at Kirrin Cottage,' said Uncle Quentin, in an exasperated voice. 'Can't you manage George and make her see reason? Good gracious, can't she put up with the Sticks for a week or two? I tell you frankly, Julian, I am not going to sack the Sticks in my absence – I want the house ready for me to bring back your aunt. If you can't put up with them, you had better find out from your own parents if they can take you back for the rest of the holidays. But George is not to go with you. She is to stay at Kirrin Cottage. That's my last word on the subject.'

'But . . .' began Julian, wondering how in the world he could deal properly with his hot-tempered uncle, 'I must tell you that . . .'

There was a click at the other end of the 'phone. Uncle Quentin had put down his receiver and gone. There was no more to be said. Blow! Julian pursed up his mouth and looked round at the others, frowning.

'He's gone!' he said. 'Cut me off just as I was trying to reason with him!'

'Serves you right!' said Mrs Stick's harsh voice from the end of the hall. 'Now you know where you stand. I'm here and I'm staying here, on your uncle's orders. And you're all going to behave yourselves, or it'll be the worse for you.'

6 Julian defeats the Sticks

There was a slam. The kitchen door shut, and Mrs Stick could be heard telling the news triumphantly to Edgar and Mr Stick. The children went into the sitting-room, sat down and stared at one another gloomily.

'Father's awful!' said George, furiously. 'He never will listen to anything.'

'Well, after all, he is very upset,' said Dick, reasonably. 'It was a great pity that he rang before nine, so that Mrs Stick got her say in first.'

'What did Father say to you?' said George. 'Tell us exactly.'

'He said that if we couldn't put up with the Sticks, Anne and Dick and I were to go back to our own parents,' said Julian. 'But you were to stay here.'

George stared at Julian. 'Well,' she said at last, 'you *can't* put up with the Sticks, so you'd better all go back. I can look after myself.'

'Don't be an idiot!' said Julian, giving her arm a friendly shake. 'You know we wouldn't desert you. I can't say I look forward to the idea of being under the thumb of the amiable Sticks for a week or two, but there are worse things than that. We'll "stick" it together.'

But the feeble little joke didn't raise a smile, even from Anne. The idea of being under the Sticks' three thumbs was a most unpleasant prospect. Timothy put his head on George's knee. She patted him and looked round.

'You go back home,' she said to the others. 'I've got a plan of my own, and you're not in it. I've got Timmy, and he'll look after me. Telephone to your parents and go home tomorrow.'

George stared round defiantly. Her head was up, and there was no doubt but that she had made a plan of some sort.

Julian felt uneasy.

'Don't be silly,' he said. 'I tell you we all stand together in this. If you've got a plan, we'll come into it. But we're staying here with you, whatever happens.'

'Stay if you like,' said George, 'but my plan goes on, and you'll find you'll have to go home in the end. Come on, Timothy! Let's go to Jim and see if my boat is ready.'

'We'll go with you,' said Dick. He was sorry for George. He could see below her defiance, and he knew she was very unhappy, worried about her mother, angry with her father, and upset because she felt the others were staying on because of her, when they could go back home and have a lovely time.

It was not a happy day. George was very stand-offish, and kept on insisting that the others should go back home and leave her. She grew quite angry when they were as insistent that they would not.

'You're spoiling my plan,' she said at last. 'You *should* go back, you really should. I tell you, you're spoiling my plan completely.'

'Well, what *is* your plan?' said Julian impatiently. 'I can't help feeling you're just *pretending* you've got a plan, so that we'll go.'

'I'm *not* pretending,' said George, losing her temper. 'Do I ever pretend? You know I don't! If I say I've got a plan, I *have* got a plan. But I'm not giving it away, so it's no good asking me. It's my own secret, private plan.'

'Well, I really do think you might tell us,' said Dick, quite hurt. 'After all, we're your best friends, aren't we? And we're going to stick by you, plan or no plan – yes, even if we spoil your plan, as you say, we shall still stay here with you.'

'I shan't *let* you spoil my plan,' said George, her eyes flashing. 'You're mean. You're against me, just like the Sticks are.'

'Oh, George, don't,' said Anne, almost in tears. 'Don't let's quarrel. It's bad enough quarrelling with those awful Sticks, without *us* quarrelling too.'

George's temper died down as quickly as it had risen. She looked ashamed.

'Sorry!' she said. 'I'm an idiot. I won't quarrel. But I do mean what I say. I shall go on with my plan, and I shan't tell you what it is, because if I do, it will spoil the holidays for you. Please believe me.'

'Let's take our dinner out with us again,' said Julian, getting up. 'We'll all feel better away from this house today. I'll go and tackle the old Stick.'

'Dear old Ju, isn't he brave!' said Anne, who would rather have died than go and face Mrs Stick at that moment.

Mrs Stick proved very difficult. She felt rather victorious at the time, and was also very annoyed to find that her beautiful meat-pie and jam-tarts had disappeared. Mr Stick was in the middle of telling her where they had gone when Julian appeared.

'How you can expect sandwiches for a picnic when

you've stolen my meat-pie and jam-tarts, I *don't* know!' she began, indignantly. 'You can have dry bread and jam for your picnic, and that's all. And what's more, I wouldn't give you that either except that I'm glad to be rid of you.'

'Good riddance to bad rubbish,' murmured Edgar to himself. He was lying sprawled on the sofa, reading some kind of highly-coloured comic.

'If you've anything to say to me, Edgar, come outside and say it,' said Julian, dangerously.

'You leave Edgar alone,' said Mrs Stick, at once.

'There's nothing I should like better,' said Julian, scornfully. 'Who wants to be with him? Cowardly little spotty-face!'

'Now, now, look 'ere!' began Mr Stick, from his corner.

'I don't want to look at you,' said Julian at once.

'Now, look *'ere*,' said Mr Stick, angrily, standing up.

'I've told you I don't want to,' said Julian. 'You're not a pleasant sight.'

'*Insolence!*' said Mrs Stick, rapidly losing her temper.

'No, not insolence – just the plain truth,' said Julian, airily. Mrs Stick glared at him. Julian defeated her. He had such a ready tongue, and he said everything so politely. The ruder his words were, the more politely he spoke. Mrs Stick didn't understand people like Julian. She felt that they were too clever for her. She hated the boy, and banged a saucepan viciously down on the sink, wishing that it was Julian's head under the saucepan instead of the sink.

Stinker jumped up and growled at the sudden noise.

'Hallo, Stinker!' said Julian. 'Had a bath yet? Alas, no! – as smelly as ever, aren't you?'

'You know that dog's name isn't Stinker,' said Mrs Stick, angrily. 'You get out of my kitchen.'

'Right!' said Julian. 'Pleased to go. Don't bother about the dry bread and jam. I'll manage something a bit better than that.'

He went out, whistling. Stinker growled, and Edgar repeated loudly what he had said before: 'Good riddance to bad rubbish!'

'What did you say?' said Julian, suddenly poking his head in at the kitchen door again. But Edgar did not dare to repeat it, so off went Julian again, whistling merrily, but not feeling nearly as merry as his whistle. He was worried. After all, if Mrs Stick was going to make meals as difficult as this, life was not going to be very pleasant at Kirrin Cottage.

'Anyone feel inclined to have dry bread and jam for lunch?' inquired Julian, when he returned to the others. 'No? I rather thought so, so I turned down Mrs Stick's kind offer. I vote we go and buy something decent. That shop in the village has good sausage-rolls.'

George was very silent all that day. She was worrying about her mother, the others knew. She was probably thinking about her plan too, they thought, and wondered whatever it could be.

'Shall we go over to Kirrin Island today?' asked Julian, thinking that it would take George's mind off her worries, if they went to her beloved island.

George shook her head.

'No,' she said. 'I don't feel like it. The boat's all ready, I know – but I just don't feel like it. You see, till I know Mother is going to get better, I don't feel I want to be out of reach of the house. If a telephone message came from Father, the Sticks could always send Edgar to look for me – and if I was on the island, he couldn't find me.'

The children messed about that day, doing nothing at all. They went back to tea, and Mrs Stick provided them with bread and butter and jam, but no cake. The milk was sour too, and everyone had to have tea without milk, which they all disliked.

As they ate their tea, the children heard Edgar outside the window. He held a tin bowl in his hand, and put it down on the grass outside.

'Your dog's dinner,' he yelled.

'He looks like a dog's dinner himself,' said Dick, in disgust. 'Messy creature!'

That made everyone laugh. 'Edgar, the Dog's Dinner!' said Anne. 'Any biscuits in that tin on the sideboard, do you think, George?'

George got up to see. Timothy slipped out of doors and went to the dish put down for him. He sniffed at it. George, coming back from the sideboard, looked out of the window as she passed and saw him. At once the thought of poison came back to her mind and she yelled to Timothy, making the others jump out of their skins.

'TIM! TIM! Don't touch it!'

Timothy wagged his tail as if to say he didn't mean to touch it, anyway. George rushed out of doors, and picked up the mess of raw meat. She sniffed at it.

'You haven't touched it, have you, Timothy?' she said, anxiously.

Dick leaned out of the window.

'No, he didn't eat any. I watched him. He sniffed all round and about it, but he wouldn't touch it. I bet it's been dosed with rat-poison or something.'

George was very white. 'Oh Timmy!' she said.

'You're such a sensible dog. You wouldn't touch poisoned stuff, would you?'

'Woof!' said Timmy, decidedly. Stinker heard the bark and put his nose out of the kitchen door.

George called to him in a loud voice:

'Stinker, Stinker, come here! Timmy doesn't want his dinner. You can have it. Come along, Stinker, here it is!'

Edgar came rushing out behind Stinker. 'Don't you give that to him,' he said.

'Why not?' asked George. 'Go on, Edgar – tell me why not.'

'He doesn't eat raw meat,' said Edgar, after a pause. 'He only eats dog biscuits.'

'That's a lie!' said George, flaming up. 'I saw him eating meat yesterday. Here, Stinker – you come and eat this.'

Edgar snatched the bowl from George, almost snarling at her, and ran indoors at top speed. George was about to go after him, but Julian, who had jumped out of the window when Edgar came up, stopped her.

'No good, old thing!' he said. 'You won't get anything out of him. The meat's probably at the back of the kitchen fire by now. From now on, we feed Timothy ourselves with meat bought from the butcher with our own money. Don't be afraid that he'll eat poisoned stuff. He's too wise a dog for that.'

'He might, if he was terribly, awfully hungry, Julian,' said George, looking rather green now. She felt sick inside. 'I wasn't going to let Stinker eat that poisoned stuff, of course, but I guessed that if it *was* poisoned, one of the Sticks would come rushing out and stop Stinker eating it. And Edgar did. So it proves it was poisoned, doesn't it?'

'I rather think it does,' said Julian. 'But don't worry, George. Timmy won't be poisoned.'

'But he might, he might,' said George, putting her hand on the big dog's head. 'Oh, I can't bear the thought of it, Julian. I can't, I really can't.'

'Don't think about it then,' said Julian, taking her indoors again. 'Here, have a biscuit!'

'You don't think the Sticks would poison *us*, do you?' said Anne, looking suddenly scared and gazing at her biscuit as if it might bite her.

'No, idiot. They only want to get Timmy out of the way because he guards us so well,' said Julian. 'Don't look so scared. All this will settle down in a day or two, and we'll have a grand time after all. You'll see!'

But Julian only said this to comfort his little sister. Secretly he was very worried. He wished he could take Anne, Dick and George back to his own home. But he knew George wouldn't come. And how could they leave her to the Sticks? It was quite impossible. Friends must stick together, and somehow they must face things until Aunt Fanny and Uncle Quentin came back.

7 Better news

'Do you think we'd better slip down after the Sticks have gone to bed and get some food out of the larder again?' said Dick, when no supper appeared that evening.

Julian didn't feel inclined to sneak down and confront Mr Stick again. Not that he was afraid of him, but the whole thing was so unpleasant. This was their house, the food was theirs – so why should they have to beg for it, or take it on the sly? It was ridiculous.

'Come here, Timothy!' said Julian. The dog left George's side and went to Julian, looking up at the boy inquiringly. 'You're going to come with me and persuade dear kind Mrs Stick to give us the best things out of the larder!' said Julian, with a grin.

The others laughed, cheering up at once.

'Good idea!' said Dick. 'Can we all come and see the fun.'

'Better not,' said Julian. 'I can manage fine by myself.'

He went down the passage to the kitchen. The radio was going inside, so no one in the kitchen heard Julian till he was actually standing inside the door. Then Edgar looked up and saw Timothy as well as Julian.

Edgar was scared of the big dog, who was now growling fiercely. He went behind the kitchen sofa and stayed there, eyeing Timmy fearfully.

'What do you want?' said Mrs Stick, turning off the radio.

'Supper,' said Julian, pleasantly. 'Supper! The best things out of the larder – bought with my uncle's money, cooked on my aunt's stove with gas she pays for – yes, supper! Open the larder door and let's see what there is in there.'

'Well, of all the nerve!' began Mr Stick, in amazement.

'You can have a loaf of bread and some cheese,' said Mrs Stick, 'and that's my last word.'

'Well, it isn't my last word,' said Julian, and he went to the larder door. 'Timmy, keep to heel! Growl all you like, but don't bite anybody – yet!'

Timmy's growls were really frightful. Even Mr Stick put himself at the other end of the room. As for Stinker, he was nowhere to be seen. He had gone into the scullery at the very first growl, and was now shivering behind the wringer.

Mrs Stick's mouth went into a hard straight line. 'You take the bread and cheese and clear out,' she said.

Julian opened the larder door, whistling softly, which annoyed Mrs Stick more than anything else. 'My word!' said Julian, admiringly. 'You do know how to stock a larder, I must say, Mrs Stick. A roast chicken! I thought I smelt one cooking. I suppose Mr Stick killed one of our chickens today. I thought I heard a lot of squawking. And what fine tomatoes! Best to be got from the village, I've no doubt. And oh, Mrs Stick – what a perfectly *marvellous* treacle tart! I must say you're a good cook, I really must.'

Julian picked up the chicken, the dish of tomatoes, and then balanced the plate with the treacle tart on the top.

Mrs Stick yelled at him.

'You leave those things alone! That's our supper! You leave them there.'

'You've made a little mistake,' said Julian, politely. 'It's *our* supper! We've had very little to eat today, and we could do with a good supper. Thanks awfully!'

'Now look 'ere!' began Mr Stick, angrily, furious at seeing his lovely supper walking away.

'You surely don't want me to look at you *again*,' said Julian, in a tone of amazement. 'What for? Have you shaved yet – or washed? I'm afraid not. So, if you don't mind I think I'd rather *not* look at you.'

Mr Stick was speechless. He was not ready with his tongue at any time, and a boy like Julian took his breath away, and left him with nothing to say except his favourite 'Now, look 'ere!'

'Put those things down,' said Mrs Stick sharply. 'What do you think we're going to have for *our* supper if you walk off with them? You tell me that!'

'Easy!' said Julian. 'Let me offer you *our* supper – bread and cheese, Mrs Stick, bread and cheese!'

Mrs Stick made an angry noise, and started to go after Julian with her hand raised. But Timothy immediately leapt at her, and his teeth snapped together with a loud click.

'Oh!' howled Mrs Stick. 'That dog of yours nearly took my hand off! The brute! I'll do for him one day, you see if I don't.'

'You had a good try today, didn't you?' said Julian, in a quiet voice, fixing his eyes straight on the woman's face. 'That's a matter for the police, isn't it? Be careful, Mrs Stick. I've a good mind to go to the police tomorrow.'

Just as before, the mention of the police seemed to

frighten Mrs Stick. She cast a look at her husband and
took a step backwards. Julian wondered if the man had
done something wrong and was hiding from the
police. He never seemed to put a foot out of doors.

The boy went up the passage triumphantly. Timmy
followed at his heels, disappointed that he hadn't been
able to get a nibble at Stinker. Julian marched into the
sitting-room, and set the dishes carefully down on the
table.

'What ho!' he said. 'Look what *I've* got – the Sticks'
own supper!' Then he told the others all that had
happened, and they laughed loudly.

'How do you think of all those things to say?' said
Anne, admiringly. 'I don't wonder you make them
feel wild, Ju. It's a good thing we've got Timmy to
back us up.'

'Yes, I shouldn't feel nearly so bold without
Timmy,' said Julian.

It was a very good supper. There were knives and
forks in the sideboard, and the children made do with
fruit plates from the sideboard too, rather than go and
get plates from the kitchen. There was bread over
from their tea, so they were able to make a very good
meal. They enjoyed it thoroughly.

'Sorry we can't give you the chicken bones, Tim,'
said George, 'but they might splinter inside you and
injure you. You can have all the scraps. See you don't
leave any for Stinker!'

Timmy didn't. With two or three great gulps he
cleared his plate, and then sat waiting for any scraps of
treacle tart that might descend his way.

The children felt cheerful after such a good meal.
They had completely eaten the chicken. Nothing was
left except a pile of bones. They had eaten all the

tomatoes too, finished the bread, and enjoyed every scrap of the treacle tart.

It was late, Anne yawned, and then George yawned too. 'Let's go to bed,' she said. 'I don't feel like having a game of cards or anything.'

So they went to bed, and as usual Timothy lay heavily on George's feet. He lay there awake for some time, his ears cocked to hear noises from below. He heard the Sticks go up to bed. He heard doors closing. He heard a whine from Stinker. Then all was silence. Timmy dropped his head on to his paws and slept – but he kept one ear cocked for danger. Timothy didn't trust the Sticks any more than the children did!

The children awoke very early in the morning. Julian awoke first. It was a marvellous day. Julian went to the window and looked out. The sky was a very pale blue, and rosy-pink clouds floated about it. The sea was a clear blue too, smooth and calm. Julian remembered what Anne often said – she said that the world in the early morning always looked as if it had come back fresh from the laundry – so clean and new and fresh!

The children all bathed before breakfast, and this time they were back at half-past eight, afraid that George's father might telephone early again. Julian saw Mrs Stick on the stairs and called to her.

'Has my uncle telephoned yet?'

'No,' said the woman, in a surly tone. She had been hoping that the telephone would ring while the children were out, then, as she had done the day before, she could answer it, and get a few words in first.

'We'll have breakfast now, please,' said Julian. 'A *good* breakfast, Mrs Stick. My uncle *might* ask us what we'd had for breakfast, mightn't he? You never know.'

Mrs Stick evidently thought that Julian might tell his uncle if she gave them only bread and butter for breakfast, so very soon the children smelt a delicious smell of bacon frying. Mrs Stick brought in a dish of it garnished with tomatoes. She banged it down on the table with the plates. Edgar arrived with a pot of tea and a tray of cups and saucers.

'Ah, here is dear Edgar!' said Julian, in a tone of amiable surprise. 'Dear old spotty-face!'

'Garn!' said Edgar, and banged down the teapot. Timmy growled, and Edgar fled for his life.

George didn't want any breakfast. Julian put hers back in the warm dish and put a plate over it. He knew that she was waiting for news. If only the telephone would ring – then she would know if her mother was really better or not.

It did ring as they were half-way through the meal. George was there before the bell had stopped pealing. She put the receiver to her ear. 'Father! Yes, it's George. How's Mother?'

There was a pause as George listened. All the children stopped eating and listened in silence, waiting for George to speak. They would know by her next words if the news was good or not.

'Oh – oh, I'm so glad!' they heard George say. 'Did she have the operation yesterday? Oh, you never told me! But it's all right now, is it? Poor Mother! Give her my love. I do want to see her. Oh Father, can't I come?'

Evidently the answer was no. George listened for a while then spoke a few more words and said good-bye.

She ran into the sitting-room. 'You heard, didn't you?' she said, joyfully. 'Mother's better. She'll get all right now, and will be back home soon – in about ten days. Father won't come back till he brings her home. It's good news about Mother – but I'm afraid we can't get rid of the Sticks.'

8 George's plan

Mrs Stick had overheard the conversation on the telephone – at least, she had heard George's side of it. She knew that George's mother was better and that her father would not return till her mother could be brought home. That would be in about ten days! The Sticks could have a fine time till then, no doubt about that!

George suddenly found that her appetite had come back. She ate her bacon hungrily, and scraped the dish round with a piece of bread. She had three cups of tea, and then sat back contentedly.

'I feel better,' she said. Anne slipped her hand in hers. She was very glad that her aunt was going to be all right. If it wasn't for those awful Sticks they could have a lovely time. Then George said something that made Julian cross.

'Well, now that I know Mother is going to be better, I can stand up to the Sticks all right by myself with Timmy. So I want you three to go back home and finish the hols without me. I shall be all right.'

'Shut up, George,' said Julian. 'We've argued this all out before. I've made up my mind – and I don't change it, any more than *you* do, when I've made it up. You make me cross.'

'Well,' said George, 'I told you I'd got a plan – and you don't come into it, I'm afraid – and you'll find you'll have to go back home whether you mean to or not.'

'Don't be so mysterious, George!' said Julian, impatiently. 'What is this strange plan? You'd better tell us, even if we're not in it. Can't you trust us?'

'Yes, of course. But you might try to stop me,' said George, looking sulky.

'Then you'd certainly better tell us,' said Julian feeling uneasy. George could be so reckless once she got ideas into her head. Goodness knows what she might do!

But George wouldn't say another word. Julian gave it up at last, but secretly made up his mind not to let George out of his sight that day. If she was going to carry out some wild plan, then she would have to do it under his, Julian's, eye!

But George didn't seem to be carrying out any wild plan. She bathed again with the others, went out for a walk with them, and went for a row on the sea. She didn't want to go to Kirrin Island, so the others didn't press her, thinking that she didn't want to be out of sight of the beach in case Edgar came with a message from her father.

It was quite a pleasant day. The children bought sausage rolls again, and fruit, and picnicked on the beach. Timmy had a large and juicy bone from the butcher's.

'I've got a bit of shopping to do,' said George, about tea-time. 'You others go and see if Mrs Stick is getting some tea for us, and I'll fly down to the shops and get what I want.'

Julian pricked up his ears at once. Was George sending them off so that she could be alone to carry out this mysterious plan of hers?

'I'll come with you,' said Julian, getting up. 'Dick can tackle Mrs Stick for once, and take Timmy with him.'

'No, you go,' said George. 'I won't be long.'

But Julian was determined not to go. In the end they all went with George, for Dick did not want to face Mrs Stick without Julian or George.

George went into the little general shop and got a new battery for her torch. She bought two boxes of matches, and a bottle of methylated spirit.

'Whatever do you want that for?' said Anne in surprise.

'Oh, it might come in useful,' said George, and said no more.

They all went back to Kirrin Cottage. Tea was actually on the table! True, it was not a thrilling tea, being merely bread and jam and a pot of hot tea – still it was there, and was edible.

It rained that evening. The children sat round the table and played cards. Their hearts were lighter now that they had had good news of George's mother. In the middle of the game Julian got up and rang the bell. The others stared at him in the greatest surprise.

'What are you ringing the bell for?' asked George, her eyes wide with astonishment.

'To tell Mrs Stick to bring some supper,' said Julian, with a grin. But no one answered the bell. So Julian rang again and then again.

The kitchen door opened at last and Mrs Stick came up the passage, evidently in a bad temper. She came into the sitting-room.

'You stop ringing that bell!' she said, angrily. 'I'm not answering any bells rung by you.'

'I rang it to tell you that we wanted some supper,'

said Julian. 'And to say that if you would rather I came and got it myself from the larder – with Timmy – as I did last night, I'll come with pleasure. But if not, you can bring a decent supper to us yourself.'

'If you come stealing things out of my larder again, I'll – I'll . . .' began Mrs Stick.

'You'll call in the police!' Julian finished for her. 'Do. That would please us very much. I can see our local policeman taking down all the details in his note book. I could give him quite a few.'

Mrs Stick muttered something rude under her breath, glared at Julian as if she could kill him, and went off down the passage again. By the sound of the clattering and crashing of crockery in the kitchen it was plain that Mrs Stick was getting some sort of supper for them, and Julian grinned to himself as he dealt out the cards.

Supper was not as good as the night before, but it was not bad. It was a little cold ham, cheese and the remains of a milk pudding. There was also a plate of cooked meat for Timmy.

George looked at it sharply. 'Take that away,' she said. 'I bet you've poisoned it again. Take it away!'

'No. On the contrary, leave it here,' said Julian. 'I'll take it down to the local chemist tomorrow and get him to test it. If, as George thinks, it's poisoned, the chemist might have a lot of interesting things to tell us.'

Mrs Stick took the meat away without a word. 'Horrible woman!' said George, pulling Timothy close to her. 'How I hate her! I feel so afraid for Timmy.'

Somehow that spoilt the evening. As it grew dark the children became sleepy. 'It's ten o'clock,' said

Julian. 'Bed, I think, everyone! Anne ought to have gone long ago. She isn't nearly old enough to stay up as late as this.'

'*Well!*' began Anne, indignantly. 'I'm nearly as old as George, aren't I? I can't help being younger, can I?'

'All right, all right!' said Julian laughing. 'I shan't make you go off to bed by yourself, don't worry. We all keep together in this house while the Sticks are about. Come on! We'll go now, shall we?'

The children were tired. They had swum, walked and rowed that day. Julian tried to keep awake a little while, but he too fell asleep very quickly.

He awoke with a jump, thinking that he had heard a noise. But everything was quiet. What could the noise have been? Was it one of the Sticks creeping about? No – it couldn't be that, or Tim would have barked the house down. Then what was it? *Some*thing must have woken him.

'I suppose it's not old George doing anything about that plan of hers!' thought Julian, suddenly. He sat up. He felt about for his dressing-gown and put it on. Without waking Dick he crept to the girls' room, and switched on his torch to see that they were all right.

Anne was in her bed, sleeping peacefully. But George's bed was empty. George's clothes were gone!

'Blow!' said Julian, under his breath. 'Where has she gone? I bet she's run away to find where her mother is!'

His torch picked out a white envelope pinned to George's pillow. He stepped softly over to it.

It had his name printed on it in bold letters. 'JULIAN.'

Julian ripped it open and read it.

'Dear JULIAN,' said the note,

'Don't be angry with me, please. I daren't stay in Kirrin Cottage any longer in case the Sticks somehow poison Timmy. You know that would break my heart. So I've gone to live by myself on our island till Mother and Father come back. Please leave a note for Father and tell him to ask Jim to sail near Kirrin Island with his little red flag flying from the mast as soon as they are back. Then I'll come home. You and Dick and Anne must go back to your own parents now I've gone. It would be silly to stay at Kirrin Cottage with the Sticks now I'm not there.

Love from
GEORGE.'

Julian read the note through. 'Well, why didn't I *guess* that was her plan!' he said to himself. 'That's why we didn't come into it! She meant to go off by herself with Timmy. I can't let her do that. She can't live all by herself on Kirrin Island for so long. She might fall ill. She might slip on a rock and hurt herself, and no one would ever know!'

The boy was really worried about the determined little girl. He wondered what to do. That noise he heard must have been made by George. So she couldn't have got a very long start really. If he tore down to the beach, George might still be there, and he could stop her.

So, in his dressing-gown, he ran down the front path, out of the gate, and took the road to the beach. The rain had stopped, and the stars were out. But it was not at all a light night.

'How can George expect to get through those rocks

in the dark,' he thought. 'She's mad! She'll strike her boat on a rock, and sink.'

He tore on in the darkness, talking aloud to himself. 'No wonder she wanted a new battery for her torch, and matches – and I suppose the methylated spirit was for her little cooking stove! Why ever couldn't she tell us? It would have been fun to go with her.'

He came to the beach. He saw the light of a torch where George kept her boat. He ran to it, his feet sinking in the soft wet sand.

'George! Idiot! You're not to go off like this all alone, in the dead of night!' called Julian.

George was pushing her boat out into the water. She jumped when she heard Julian's voice. 'You can't stop me!' she said. 'I'm just off!'

But Julian caught hold of the boat, as he waded up to his waist in the water. 'George, listen to me! You can't go like this. You'll strike a rock. Come back!'

'No,' said George, getting cross. 'You can go back to your own home, Julian. I shall be all right. Let go my boat!'

'George, why didn't you tell me your plan?' said Julian, almost swept off his feet by a wave. 'Dash these waves! I shall have to get into the boat.'

He climbed in. He could not see George, but he felt quite certain she was glaring at him. Timmy licked his wet legs.

'You're spoiling everything,' said George, with a break in her voice that meant she was upset.

'I'm not, silly!' said Julian, in a gentle voice. 'Listen! – you come back to Kirrin Cottage with me now, George, and I'll faithfully promise you something. Tomorrow we'll *all* go to the island with you. See? The whole lot of us. Why shouldn't we? Your mother

said we could spend a week there, anyway, didn't she?
We shall be out of the reach of those horrible Sticks.
We shall enjoy ourselves, and have a marvellous time.
So will you come back now, George, and let us go
together tomorrow?'

9 An exciting night

There was a silence, except for the waves splashing round the boat. Then George's voice came out of the darkness, lifted joyfully.

'Oh Julian – do you really mean it? Will you really come with me? I was afraid I'd get into trouble for doing this, because Father said I must stay at Kirrin Cottage till he came back – and you know how he hates disobedience. But I knew if I stayed there, you would too – and I didn't want you to be miserable with those horrid Sticks – so I thought I'd come away. I didn't think you'd come too, because of getting into trouble! I never even thought of asking you.'

'You're a very stupid person sometimes, aren't you, George?' said Julian. 'As if we'd care about getting into trouble, so long as we were all together, sticking by one another! Of course we'll come with you – and I'll take all the responsibility for this escape, and tell your father it's my fault.'

'Oh no you won't,' said George, quickly. 'I shall say it was my idea. If I do wrong, I'm not afraid to own up to it. You know that.'

'Well, we won't argue that now,' said Julian. 'We shall have at least a week or ten days on Kirrin Island to do all the arguing we want to. The thing is – let's get back now, wake up the others for a bit, and have a nice quiet talk in the dead of night about this plan of yours. I must say it's a very, very good idea!'

George was overjoyed. 'I feel as if I could hug you, Julian,' she said. 'Where are the oars? Oh, here they are! The boat's floated quite a long way out.'

She rowed strongly back to the shore. Julian jumped out and pulled the boat up the beach, with George's help. He shone his torch into the boat and gave an exclamation.

'You've quite a nice little store of things here,' he said. 'Bread and ham and butter and stuff. How did you manage to get them without old Mr Stick seeing you tonight? I suppose you slipped down and got them out of the larder?'

'Yes, I did,' said George. 'But there was no one in the kitchen tonight. Perhaps Mr Stick has gone to sleep upstairs. Or maybe he has gone back to his ship. Anyway, there was no one there when I crept down, not even Stinker.'

'We'd better leave them here,' said Julian. 'Stuff them into that locker and shut down the lid. No one will guess there's anything there. We'll have to bring down a lot more stuff if we're all going to live on the island. Golly, this is going to be fun!'

The children made their way back to the house, feeling thrilled and excited. Julian's wet dressing-gown flapped round his legs, and he pulled it up high to be out of the way. Timothy gambolled round, not seeming at all surprised at the night's doings.

When they got back to the house they woke the other two, who listened in astonishment to what had happened that night. Anne was so excited to think that they were all going to live on the island that she raised her voice in joy.

'Oh! That's the loveliest thing that could happen! Oh, I do think . . .'

'Shut up!' said three furious voices in loud whispers. 'You'll wake the Sticks!'

'Sorry!' whispered Anne. 'But oh – it's so terribly, awfully exciting.'

They began to discuss the plans. 'If we go for a week or ten days, we must take plenty of stores,' said Julian.

'The thing is – can we possibly find food enough for so long? Even if we entirely empty the larder I doubt if that would be enough for a week or so. We all seem such hungry people, somehow.'

'Julian,' said George, suddenly remembering something, '*I* know what we'll do! Mother has a store-cupboard in her room. She keeps dozens and dozens of tins of food there, in case we ever get snowed up in the winter, and can't go to the village. That has happened once or twice, you know. And I know where Mother keeps the key! Can't we open the cupboard and get out some tins?'

'Of course!' said Julian, delighted. 'I know Aunt Fanny wouldn't mind. And anyway, we can make a list of what we take and replace them for her, if she does mind. It will be my birthday soon, and I am sure to get money then.'

'Where's the key?' whispered Dick.

'Let's go into Mother's room, and I'll show you where she keeps it,' said George. 'I only hope she hasn't taken it with her.'

But George's mother had felt far too ill when she left home to think of cupboard keys. George fumbled at the back of a drawer in the dressing-table and brought out two or three keys tied together with thin string. She fitted first one and then another into a cupboard set in the wall. The second one opened the door.

Julian shone his torch into the cupboard. It was filled with tins of food of all kinds, neatly arranged on the shelves.

'Golly!' said Dick, his eyes gleaming. 'Soup – tins of meat – tins of fruit – tinned milk – sardines – tinned butter – biscuits – tinned vegetables! There's everything we want here!'

'Yes,' said Julian, pleased. 'It's fine. We'll take all we can carry. Is there a sack or two anywhere about, George, do you know?'

Soon the tins were quietly packed into two sacks. The cupboard door was shut and locked again. The children stole to their own rooms once more.

'Well, that's the biggest problem solved – food,' said Julian. 'We'll raid the larder too, and take what bread there is – and cake. What about water, George? Is there any on the island?'

'Well, I suppose there is some in that old well,' said George, thinking, 'but as there's no bucket or anything, we can't get any. I was taking a big container of fresh water with me – but we'd better fill two or three more now you are all coming! I know where there are some, quite clean and new.'

So they filled some containers with fresh water, and put them with the sacks, ready to take to the boat. It was so exciting doing all these things in the middle of the night! Anne could hardly keep her voice down to a whisper, and it was a wonder that Timothy didn't bark for he sensed the excitement of the others.

There was a tin of cakes in the larder, freshly made, so those were added to the heap that was forming in the front garden. There was a large joint of meat too, and George wrapped it in a cloth and put that with the

heap, telling Timmy in a fierce voice that if he so much
as sniffed at it she would leave him behind!

'I've got my little stove for boiling water on, or
heating up anything,' whispered George. 'It's in the
boat. That's what I bought the methylated spirit for, of
course. You didn't guess, did you? And the matches
for lighting it. I say – what about candles? We can't use
our torches all the time, the batteries would soon run
out.'

They found a packet of candles in the kitchen cupboard, a kettle, a saucepan, some old knives and forks
and spoons, and a good many other things they
thought they might possibly want. They also came
across some small bottles of ginger-beer, evidently
stored for their own use by the Sticks.

'All bought out of my mother's money!' said
George. 'Well, we'll take the ginger-beer too. It will be
nice to drink it on a hot day.'

'Where are we going to sleep at night?' said Julian.
'In that ruined part of the old castle, where there is just
one room with a roof left, and walls?'

'That's where I planned to sleep,' said George. 'I was
going to make my bed of some of the heather that
grows on the island, covered by a rug or two, which
I've got down in the boat.'

'We'll take all the rugs we can find,' said Julian. 'And
some cushions for pillows. I say, isn't this simply
thrilling? I don't know when I've felt so excited. I feel
like a prisoner escaping to freedom! Won't the Sticks
be amazed when they find us gone!'

'Yes – we'll have to decide what to say to them,' said
George, rather soberly. 'We don't want them sending
people after us to the island, making us come back. I
don't think they should know we've gone there.'

'We'll discuss that later,' said Dick. 'The thing is to get everything to the boat while it's dark. It will soon be dawn.'

'How are we going to get all this down to George's boat?' said Anne, looking at the enormous pile of goods by the light of her torch. 'We'll never be able to carry them all!'

Certainly it looked a great pile. Julian had an idea, as usual. 'Are there any barrows in the shed?' he asked George. 'If we could pile the things into a couple of barrows, we could easily take everything in one journey. We could wheel the barrows along on the sandy side of the road so that we don't make any noise.'

'Oh, good idea!' said George, delighted. 'I wish I'd thought of that before. I had to make about five journeys to and from the boat when I took my own things. There are two barrows in the shed. We'll get them. One has a squeaky wheel, but we'll hope no one hears it.'

Stinker heard the squeak, as he lay in a corner of Mrs Stick's room. He pricked up his ears and growled softly. He did not dare to bark, for he was afraid of bringing Timothy up. Mrs Stick did not hear the growl. She slept soundly, not even stirring. She had no idea what was going on downstairs.

The things were all stowed into the boat. The children didn't like leaving them there unguarded. In the end they decided to leave Dick there, sleeping on the rugs. They stood thinking for a moment before they went back without Dick.

'I do hope we've remembered all we shall want,' said George, wrinkling up her forehead. 'Golly – I know! We haven't remembered a tin-opener – nor a thing to take off the tops of the ginger-beer bottles. They've got those little tin lids that have to be forced off by an opener.'

'We'll put those in our pockets when we get back to the house and find them,' said Julian. 'I remember seeing some in the sideboard drawer. Good-bye, Dick. We'll be down very early to row off. We must get some bread at the baker's as soon as he opens, because we've got hardly any, and we'll see if we can pick up a very large bone at the butcher's for Timmy. George has got a bag of biscuits in the boat for him too.'

The three of them set off back to the house with Timmy, leaving Dick curled up comfortably on the rugs. He soon fell asleep again, his face upturned to the stars that would soon fade from the sky.

The others talked about what to tell the Sticks. 'I think we won't tell them anything,' said Julian, at last. 'I don't particularly want to tell them deliberate lies, and I'm certainly not going to tell them the truth. I know what we'll do – there is a train that leaves the station about eight o'clock, which would be the one we'd catch if we were going back to our own home. We'll find a timetable, leave it open on the dining-room table, as if we'd been looking up a train, and then we'll all set off across the moor at the back of the house, as if we were going to the station.'

'Oh yes – then the Sticks will think we've run away, and gone to catch the train back home,' said Anne. 'They will never guess we've gone to the island.'

'That's a good idea,' said George, pleased. 'But how shall we know when Father and Mother get back?'

'Is there anyone you could leave a message with – somebody you could really trust?' asked Julian.

George thought hard. 'There's Alf the fisher-boy,' she said at last. 'He used to look after Tim for me when I wasn't allowed to have him in the house. I know he'd not give us away.'

'We'll call on Alf before we go then,' said Julian. 'Now, let's look for that timetable and lay it open on the table at the right place.'

They hunted for the timetable, found the right page, and underlined the train they hoped that the Sticks would think they were catching. They found the tin and bottle openers and put them into their pockets. Julian found two or three more boxes of matches too. He thought two would not last long enough.

By this time dawn had come and the house was being flooded with early sunshine. 'I wonder if the baker is open,' said Julian. 'We might as well go and see. It's about six o'clock.'

They went to the baker. He was not open, but the new loaves had already been made. The baker was outside, sunning himself. He had baked his bread at night, ready to sell it new-made in the morning. He grinned at the children.

'Up early today,' he said. 'What, you want some of my loaves – how many? Six! Good gracious, whatever for?'

'To eat,' said George, grinning. Julian paid for six enormous loaves, and they went to the butcher's. His shop was not open either, but the butcher himself was sweeping the path outside. 'Could we buy a very big bone for Timmy, please?' asked George. She got an enormous one, and Timmy looked at it longingly. Such a bone would last him for days, he knew!

'Now,' said Julian, as they set off to the boat, 'we'll

pack these things into the boat, then go back to the house, and make a noise so that the Sticks know we're there. Then we'll set off across the moors, and hope the Sticks will think we are making for the train.'

They woke Dick, who was still sleeping peacefully in the boat, and packed in the bread and bone.

'Take the boat into the next cove,' said George. 'Can you do that? We shall be hidden there from anyone on the beach then. The fishermen are all out in their boats, fishing. We shan't be seen, if we set off in about an hour's time. We'll be back by then.'

They went back to the house and made a noise as if they were just getting up. George whistled to Timmy, and Julian sang at the top of his voice. Then, with a great banging of doors, they set out down the path and cut across the moors, in full sight of the kitchen window.

'Hope the Sticks won't notice Dick isn't with us,' said Julian, seeing Edgar staring out of the window. 'I expect they'll think he's gone ahead.'

They kept to the path until they came to a dip, where they were hidden from any watcher at Kirrin Cottage. Then they took another path that led them, unseen, to the cove where Dick had taken the boat. He was there, waiting anxiously for them.

'Ahoy there!' yelled Julian, in excitement. 'The adventure is about to begin.'

10 Kirrin Island once more!

They all clambered into the boat. Timothy leapt in lightly and ran to the prow, where he always stood. His tongue hung out in excitement. He knew quite well that something was up – and he was in it! No wonder he panted and wagged his tail hard.

'Off we go!' said Julian, taking the oars. 'Sit over there a bit, Anne. The luggage is weighing down the boat awfully the other end. Dick, sit by Anne to keep the balance better. That's right. Off we go!'

And off they went in George's boat, rocking up and down on the waves. The sea was fairly calm, but a good breeze blew through their hair. The water splashed round the boat and made a nice gurgly, friendly noise. The children all felt very happy. They were on their own. They were escaping from the horrid Sticks. They were going to stay on Kirrin Island, with the rabbits and gulls and jackdaws.

'Doesn't that new-made bread smell awfully good?' said Dick, feeling very hungry as usual. 'Can we just grab a bit, do you think?'

'Yes, let's,' said George. So they broke off bits of the warm brown crust, handed some to Julian, who was rowing, and chewed the delicious new-made bread. Timmy got a bit too, but his was gone as soon as it went into his mouth.

'Timmy's funny,' said Anne. 'He never eats his food

as we do – he seems to *drink* it – just takes it into his mouth and swallows it, as if it was water!'

The others laughed. 'He doesn't drink his bones,' said George. 'He always eats those all right – chews on them for hours and hours. Don't you, Timothy?'

'Woof!' said Timmy, agreeing. He eyed the place where that enormous bone was, wishing he could have it now. But the children wouldn't let him. They were afraid it might go overboard, and that would be a pity.

'I don't believe anyone has noticed us going,' said Julian. 'Except Alf the fisher-boy, of course. We told him about going to the island, Dick, but nobody else.'

They had called at Alf's house on their way to the cove. Alf was alone in the yard at the back. His mother was away and his father was out fishing. They had told him their secret, and Alf had nodded his tousled head and promised faithfully to tell nobody at all. He was evidently very proud at being trusted.

'If my mother and father come back, you must let us know,' said George. 'Sail as near the island as you dare, and hail us. You can get nearer to it than anyone else.'

'I'll do that,' promised Alf, wishing he could go with them.

'So, you see, Dick,' said Julian, as he rowed out to the island, 'if by any chance Aunt Fanny does return sooner than we expect, we shall know at once and come back. I think we've planned everything very well.'

'Yes, we have,' said Dick. He turned and faced the island, which was coming nearer. 'We shall soon be there. Isn't George going to take the oars and guide the boat in?'

'Yes,' said George. 'We've come to the difficult bit now, where we've got to weave our way in and out of the different rocks that keep sticking up. Give me the oars, Ju.'

She took the oars, and the others watched in admiration as the girl guided the big boat skilfully in and out of the hidden rocks. She certainly was very clever. They felt perfectly safe with her.

The boat slid into the little cove. It was a natural harbour, with the water running up to a stretch of sand. High rocks sheltered it. The children jumped out eagerly, and four pairs of willing hands tugged the boat quickly up the sand.

'Higher up still,' panted George. 'You know what awful storms suddenly blow up in this bay. We want to be sure the boat is quite safe, no matter how high the seas run.'

The boat soon lay on one side, high up the stretch of sand. The children sat down, puffing and blowing. 'Let's have breakfast here,' said Julian. 'I don't feel like unloading all those heavy things at the moment. We'll get what we want for breakfast, and have it here on this warm bit of sand.'

They got a loaf of new bread, some cold ham, a few tomatoes and a pot of jam. Anne found knives and forks and plates. Julian opened two bottles of ginger-beer.

'Funny sort of breakfast,' he said, setting the bottles down on the sand, 'but simply gorgeous when anyone is as hungry as we are.'

They ate everything except about a third of the loaf. Timmy was given his bone and some of his own biscuits. He crunched up the biscuits at once, and then sat down contentedly to gnaw the fine bone.

'How nice to be Timmy – with no plate or knife or fork or cup to bother about,' said Anne, lying on her back in the sun, feeling that she really couldn't eat anything more. 'Oh, if we are always going to have mixed-up meals like this on the island, I shall never want to go back. Who would have thought that ham and jam and ginger-beer would go so well together?'

Timmy was thirsty. He sat with his tongue hanging out wishing that George would give him a drink. He didn't like ginger-beer.

George eyed him lazily.

'Oh Timmy – are you thirsty?' she said. 'Oh dear, I feel as if I really can't get up! You'll have to wait a few minutes, then I'll go to the boat and empty out some water for you.'

But Timothy couldn't wait. He went off to some nearby rocks, which were out of reach of the sea. In a hole in one of them he found some rain-water, and he lapped it up eagerly. The children heard him lapping it, and laughed.

'Isn't Timmy clever?' murmured Anne. 'I should never have thought of that.'

The children had been up half the night, and now they were full of good things, and were very sleepy. One by one they fell asleep on the warm sand. Timothy eyed them in astonishment. It wasn't night-time! Yet here were all the children sleeping tightly. Well, well – a dog could always go to sleep too at any time! So Timothy threw himself down beside George, put his head right on her middle, and closed his eyes.

The sun was high when the little company awoke. Julian awoke first, then Dick, feeling very hot indeed, for the sun was blazing down. They sat up, yawning.

'Goodness!' said Dick, looking at his arms. 'The sun has caught me properly. I shall be terribly sore by tonight. Did we bring any cream, Julian?'

'No. We never thought of it,' said Julian. 'Cheer up! You'll be burnt much more by the time this day ends. The sun's going to be hot – there's not a cloud in the sky!'

They woke up the girls. George pushed Timmy's head off her tummy. 'You give me nightmares when you put your heavy head there,' she complained. 'Oh, I say – we're on the island, aren't we? For a moment I thought I was back in bed at Kirrin Cottage!'

'Isn't it gorgeous? – here we are for ages, all by ourselves, with tons of nice things to eat, able to do just what we like!' said Anne, contentedly.

'I guess the old Sticks are glad we've gone,' said Dick. 'Spotty Face will be able to loll in the sitting-room and read all our books, if he wants to.'

'And Stinker-dog will be able to wander all over the house and lie on anybody's bed without being afraid that Timothy will eat him whole,' said George. 'Well, let him. I don't care about anything now that I've escaped.'

It was fun to lie there and talk about everything. But soon Julian, who could never rest for long, once he was awake, got up and stretched himself.

'Come on!' he said to the others. 'There is work to do, Lazy-Bones! Come along!'

'Work to do? What do you mean?' said George in astonishment.

'Well, we've got to unload the boat and pack everything somewhere where it won't get spoilt if the rain happens to come,' said Julian. 'And we've got to decide exactly where we're going to sleep, and get the heather for our beds and pile the rugs on them. There's plenty to do!'

'Oh, don't let's do it yet,' said Anne, not at all

wanting to get up out of the warm sand. But the others pulled her up, and together they all set to work to unload the boat.

'Let's go and have a look at the castle,' said Julian. 'And find the little room where we'll sleep. It's the only one left whole, so it will have to be that one.'

They went right to the top of the inlet, climbed up on to the rocks and made their way towards the old ruined castle, whose walls rose up from the middle of the little island. They stopped to gaze at it.

'It's a fine old ruin,' said Dick. 'Aren't we lucky to have an island and castle of our own! Fancy, this is all ours!'

They gazed through a big broken-down archway, to old steps beyond. The castle had once had two fine towers, but now one was almost gone. The other rose high in the air, half-ruined. The black jackdaws collected there, talking loudly. 'Chack, chack, chack! Chack, chack, chack!'

'Nice birds,' said Dick. 'I like them. See the grey patch at the back of their heads, Anne? I wonder if they ever stop talking.'

'I don't think so,' said George. 'Oh, look at the rabbits – tamer than ever!'

The courtyard was full of big rabbits, who eyed them as they came near. It really seemed as if it would be possible to pat them, they were so tame – but one by one they edged away as the children approached.

Timothy was in a great state of excitement, and his tail quivered from end to end. Oh those rabbits! Why couldn't he chase them? Why was George so difficult about rabbits? Why couldn't he make them run a bit?

But George had her hand on his collar, and gave him a stern glance. 'Now, Timothy, don't you *dare* to chase even the smallest of these rabbits. They're mine, every one of them.'

'Ours!' corrected Anne at once. She wanted to share in the rabbits, as well as in the castle and the island.

'Ours!' said George. 'Let's go and have a look at the little dark room where we'll spend the nights.'

They made their way to where the castle did not seem to be quite so ruined. They came to a doorway and looked inside.

'Here it is!' said Julian, peeping in. 'I shall have to use my torch. The windows are only slits here, and it's quite dark.'

He turned on his torch – and the children all gazed into the old room where they proposed to store their goods and sleep.

George gave a loud exclamation. 'Golly! We can't use this room! The roof has fallen in since last summer.'

So it had. Julian's torch shone on to a heap of fallen stones, scattered all over the floor. It was quite impossible to use the old room now. In any case it might be dangerous to do so, for it looked as if more stones might fall at any moment.

'Blow!' said Julian. 'What shall we do about this? We shall have to find somewhere else for a storing and sleeping-place!'

11 On the old wreck

It was quite a shock to have their plans spoilt. They knew there was no other room in the ruined castle that was sufficiently whole to shelter them. And they must find some sort of shelter, for although the weather was fine at the moment, it might rain hard any day – or a storm might blow up.

'And storms round about Kirrin are so very violent,' said Julian, remembering one or two. 'Do you remember the storm that tossed your wreck up from the bottom of the sea, George?'

'Oh yes,' said George and Anne, together, and Anne added eagerly: 'Let's go and see the wreck today if we can. I'd love to see if it's still balanced on those rocks, as it was last year, when we explored it.'

'Well, first we must make up our minds where we are going to sleep,' said Julian, firmly. 'I don't know if you realise it, but it's about three o'clock in the afternoon! We slept for hours on the sand – tired out with our exciting night, I suppose. We really must find some safe place and put our things there at once, and make our beds.'

'Well, but where shall we go?' said Dick. 'There's no other place in the old castle.'

'There's the dungeon below,' said Anne, shivering. 'But I don't want to go there. It's so dark and mysterious.'

Nobody wanted to sleep down in the dungeons! Dick frowned and thought hard. 'What about the wreck?' he said. 'Any chance of living there?'

'We might go and see,' said Julian. 'I don't somehow fancy living on a damp old rotting wreck – but if it's still high on the rocks, maybe the sun will have dried it, and it might be possible to have our beds and stores there.'

'Let's go and see now,' said George. So they made their way from the ruined castle to the old wall that ran round it. From there they would be able to see the wreck. It had been cast up the year before, and had settled firmly on some rocks.

They stood on the wall and looked for the wreck, but it was not where they had expected it. 'It's moved,' said Julian, in surprise. 'There it is, look, on those rocks – nearer to the shore than it was before. Poor old wreck! It's been battered about a good bit this last winter, hasn't it? It looks much more of a real wreck than it did last summer.'

'I don't believe we shall be able to sleep there,' said Dick. 'It's dreadfully battered. We might be able to store food there, though. Do you know, I believe we could get to it from those rocks that run out from the island!'

'Yes, I believe we could,' said George. 'We could only reach it safely by boat last summer – but when the tide is down, I think we *could* climb out over the line of rocks, right to the wreck itself.'

'We'll try in about an hour,' said Julian, feeling excited. 'The tide will be off the rocks by then.'

'Let's go and have a look at the old well,' said Dick, and they made their way back to the courtyard of the castle. Here, the summer before, they had found the entrance to the well-shaft that ran deep down through the rock, past the dungeons below, lower than the level of the sea, to fresh water.

The children looked about for the well, and came to the old wooden cover. They drew it back.

'There are the rungs of the old iron ladder I went down last year,' said Dick, peering in. 'Now let's find the entrance to the dungeon. The steps down into it are somewhere near here.'

They found the entrance, but to their surprise some enormous stones had been pulled across it. 'Who did that?' said George, frowning. 'We didn't. Someone has been here!'

'Trippers, I suppose,' said Julian. 'Do you remember that we thought we saw a spire of smoke here the other day? I bet it was trippers. You know, the story of Kirrin Island, and its old castle and dungeons, and the treasure we found in it last year, was all in the newspapers. I expect one of the fishermen has been making money by taking trippers and landing them on *our* island.'

'How dare they?' said George, looking very fierce. 'I shall put up a board that says "Trespassers will be sent to prison". I won't have strangers on our island.'

'Well, don't worry about the stones pulled across the dungeon entrance,' said Julian. 'I don't think any of us want to go down there. Look at poor old Timmy! He's gazing at those rabbits most unhappily. Isn't he funny?'

Timothy was sitting down behind the children, looking most mournfully at the ring of rabbits all round the weed-grown courtyard. He looked at the rabbits and then he looked at George, then he looked back at the rabbits.

'No good, Timmy,' said George, firmly. 'I'm not going to change my mind about rabbits. You're not to chase them on our island.'

'I expect he thinks you're most unfair to him,' said Anne. 'After all, you said he might share your quarter of the island with you – and so he thinks he ought to have his share of your rabbits too!'

Everyone laughed. Timmy wagged his tail and looked hopefully at George. They all walked across the courtyard – and then Julian suddenly came to a stop.

'Look!' he said in surprise, pointing to something on the ground. 'Look! Someone *has* been here! This is where they built a fire!'

Everyone gazed at the ground. There was a heap of wood-ash there, quite evidently left from a fire. Stamped into the ground was a cigarette end, too. There was absolutely no doubt about it – someone had been on the island!

'If trippers come here I'll set Timmy on to them!' cried George, in a fury. 'This is our own place, it doesn't belong to anybody else at all. Timothy, you mustn't chase rabbits here, but you can chase anybody on two legs, except us! See?'

Timmy wagged his tail at once. 'Woof!' he said, quite agreeing. He looked all round as if he hoped to see somebody appearing that he could chase. But there was no one.

'I should think the tide is about off those rocks by now,' said Julian. 'Let's go and see. If it is we'll climb along them and see if we can get to the wreck. Anne had better not come. She might slip and fall, and the sea is raging all round the rocks.'

'Of course I'm coming!' cried Anne, indignantly.

'You're just as likely to fall as I am.'

'Well, I'll see if it looks too dangerous,' said Julian. They made their way over the castle wall, down to the line of rocks that ran out seawards, towards the wreck. Big waves did wash over the rocks occasionally, but it seemed fairly safe.

'If you keep between me and Dick, you can come, Anne,' said Julian. 'But you must let us help you over difficult parts, and not make a fuss. We don't want you to fall in and get washed away.'

They began to make their way along the line of rugged, slippery rocks. The tide went down even farther as they got nearer to the wreck, and soon there was very little danger of being washed off the rocks. It was possible now to get right to the wreck across the rocks – a thing they had not been able to do the summer before.

'Here we are!' said Julian at last, and he put his hand on the side of the old wreck. She was a big ship now that they were near to her. She towered above them, thick with shellfish and seaweed, smelling musty and old. The water washed round the bottom part of her, but the top part was right out of the water, even when the tide was at its highest.

'She's been thrown about a bit last winter,' said George, looking at her. 'There are a lot more new holes in her side, aren't there? And part of her old mast is gone, and some of the deck. How can we get up to her?'

'I've got a rope,' said Julian, and he undid a rope that he had wound round his waist. 'Half a minute – I'll make a loop and see if I can throw it round that post sticking out up there.'

He threw the rope two or three times, but could not

get the loop round the post. George took it from him impatiently. At the first throw she got it round the post. She was very good indeed at things like that – better than a boy in some things, Anne thought admiringly.

She was up the rope like a monkey, and soon stood on the sloping slippery deck. She almost slipped, but caught at a broken piece of deck just in time. Julian helped Anne to go up, and then the two boys followed.

'It's a horrid smell, isn't it?' said Anne, wrinkling up her nose. 'Do all wrecks smell like this? I don't think I'll go and look down in the cabins like we did last time. The smell would be worse there.'

So the others left Anne up on the half-rotten deck while they went to explore a bit. They went down to the smelly, seaweed-hung cabins, and into the captain's old cabin, the biggest of the lot. But it was quite plain that not only could they not sleep there, but they could certainly not hope to store anything there, either. The whole place was damp and rotten. Julian was half afraid his foot would go through the planking at any moment.

'Let's go up to the deck,' he said. 'It's nasty down here – awfully dark too.'

They were just going up, when they heard a shout from Anne. 'I say! Come here, quick! I've found something!'

They hurried up as fast as they could, slipping and sliding on the sloping deck. Anne was standing where they had left her, her eyes shining brightly. She was pointing to something on the opposite side of the ship.

'What is it?' said George. 'What's the matter?'

'Look – that wasn't here when we came here before,

surely!' said Anne, still pointing. The others looked where she pointed. They saw an open locker at the other side of the deck, and stuffed into it was a small black trunk! How extraordinary!

'A little black trunk!' said Julian, in surprise. 'No – that wasn't there before. It's not been there long either – it's quite dry and new! Whoever does it belong to? And why should it be here?'

12 The cave in the cliff

Cautiously the children made their way down the slippery deck towards the locker. The door of this had evidently been shut on the trunk but had come open, so that the trunk was not hidden, as had been intended.

Julian pulled out the little black trunk. All the children were amazed. *Why* should anyone put a trunk there?

'Smugglers, do you think?' said Dick, his eyes gleaming.

'Yes – it might be,' said Julian, thoughtfully, trying to undo the straps of the trunk. 'This would be a very good place for smugglers. Ships that knew the way could put in, cast off a boat with smuggled goods, leave them here, and go on their way, knowing that people could come and collect the goods at their leisure.'

'Do you think there are smuggled goods inside the trunk?' asked Anne, in excitement. 'What would there be? Diamonds? Silks?'

'Anything that has a duty to be paid on it before it can get into the country,' said Julian. 'Blow these straps! I can't undo them.'

'Let *me* try,' said Anne, who had very deft little fingers. She began to work at the buckles, and in a short time had the straps undone. But a further disappointment awaited them. The trunk was well and truly locked! There were two good locks, and no keys!

'Blow!' said George. 'How sickening! How can we get the trunk open now?'

'We can't,' said Julian. 'And we mustn't smash it open, because it would warn whoever it belongs to that the goods had been found. We don't want to warn the smugglers that we have discovered their little game. We want to try and catch them!'

'Ooooh!' said Anne, going red with excitement. 'Catch the smugglers! Oh Julian! Do you really think we could?'

'Why not?' said Julian. 'No one knows we are here. If we hid whenever we saw a ship approaching the island, we might see a boat coming to it, and we could watch and find out what is happening. I should think that the smugglers are using this island as a sort of dropping-place for goods. I wonder who comes and fetches them? Someone from Kirrin Village or the nearby places, I should think.'

'This is going to be awfully exciting,' said Dick. 'We always seem to have adventures when we come to Kirrin. It's absolutely *full* of them. This will be the third one we have had.'

'I think we ought to be getting back over the rocks,' said Julian, suddenly looking over the side of the ship and seeing that the tide had turned. 'Come on – we don't want to be caught by the tide and have to stay here for hours and hours! I'll go down the rope first. Then you come, Anne.'

They were soon climbing over the rocks again, feeling very excited. Just as they reached the last stretch of rocks leading to the rocky cliff of the island itself, Dick stopped.

'What's up?' said George, pushing behind him. 'Do get on!'

'Isn't that a cave, just beyond that big rock there?' said Dick, pointing. 'It looks awfully like one to me. If it was, it would be a simply lovely place to store our things in, and even to sleep in, if it was out of reach of the sea.'

'There aren't any caves on Kirrin,' began George, and then she stopped short. What Dick was pointing at really did look like a cave. It was worthwhile seeing if it was one. After all, George had never explored this line of rocks, and so had never been able to catch sight of the cave that lay just beyond. It could not possibly be seen from the land.

'We'll go and see,' she said. So they changed their direction, and instead of climbing back the way they had come, they cut across the mass of rock and made their way towards a jutting-out part of the cliff, in which the cave seemed to be.

They came to it at last. Steep rocks guarded the entrance, and half hid it. Except from where Dick had seen it, it was really impossible to catch sight of it, it was so well-hidden.

'It *is* a cave!' said Dick, in delight, stepping into it. 'And my, what a fine one!'

It really was a beauty. Its floor was spread with fine white sand, as soft as powder, and perfectly dry, for the cave was clearly higher than the tide reached, except, possibly, in a bad winter storm. Round one side of it ran a stone ledge.

'Exactly like a shelf made for us!' cried Anne, in joy. 'We can put all our things here. How lovely! Let's come and live here and sleep here. And look, Julian – we've even got a skylight in the roof!'

The little girl pointed upwards, and the others saw that the roof of the cave was open in one part, giving on to the cliff-top itself. It was plain that somewhere on the heathery cliff above was a hole that looked down to the cave, making what Anne called a 'skylight'.

'We could drop all our things down through that hole,' said Julian, quickly making plans. 'We would have an awful time bringing them over the rocks. If we can find that hole up there when we are out on the cliff again, we can let down everything on a rope. It's not a very high "skylight", as Anne calls it, for the cliffs are low just here. I believe we could swing ourselves down a rope easily, so that we needn't have the bother of clambering over the rocks to the seaward entrance we have just come in by!'

This was a grand discovery. 'Our island is even more exciting than we thought,' said Anne, happily. 'We've got a beautiful cave to share now!'

The next thing to do, of course, was to go up on the cliff and find the hole that led to the roof of the cave. So out they all went, Timmy too. Timmy was funny on the slippery rocks. His feet slithered about, and two or three times he fell into the water. But he just swam across the pools he fell into, clambered out and went on again with his slithering.

'He's like George!' said Anne, with a laugh. 'He never gives up, whatever happens to him!'

They climbed up to the top of the cliff. It was easy to find the hole once they knew it was there.

'Pretty dangerous, really,' said Julian, when he had found it, and was peering down. 'Any one of us might have run on this cliff and popped down the hole by accident. See, it's all criss-crossed with blackberry brambles.'

They scratched their hands, trying to free the hole from the brambles. Once they had cleared the hole, they could look right down into the cave quite easily.

'It's not very far down,' said Anne. 'It looks almost as if we could jump down, if we let ourselves slide down this hole.'

'Don't you do anything of the sort,' said Julian. 'You'd break your leg. Wait till we get a rope fixed up, hanging down into the cave. Then we can manage to get in and out easily.'

They went back to the boat, and began unloading it. They took everything across to the seaward side of the island, where the cave was. Julian took a strong rope and knotted it thickly at intervals.

'To give our feet a hold as we go down,' he explained. 'If we drop down too quickly, we'll hurt our hands. These knots will stop us slipping and help us to climb up.'

'Let me go down first, and then you can lower all our things to me,' said George. So down she went, hand over hand, her feet easily finding the thick knots, feeling for one after another. It was a good way to go down.

'How shall we get Timmy down?' said Julian. But Timothy, who had been whining anxiously at the edge of the hole, watching George sliding away from him, solved the difficulty himself.

He jumped into the hole and disappeared down it! There came a shriek from below.

'Oh! My goodness, what's this? Oh *Timmy!* Have you hurt yourself?'

The sand was very soft, like a velvet cushion, and Tim had not hurt himself at all. He gave himself a shake and then barked joyfully. He was with George again! He wasn't going to have his mistress disappearing down mysterious holes without following her at once. Not Timmy!

Then followed the business of lowering down all the goods. Anne and Dick tied the things together in rugs, and Julian lowered them carefully. George untied the rope as soon as it reached her, took out the goods, and then back went the rope again to be tied round another bundle.

'Last one!' called Julian, after a long spell of really hard work. 'Then down we come too, and I don't mind telling you that before we make our beds or anything, our next job is to have a jolly good meal! It's hours and hours since we had a meal, and I'm starving.'

Soon they were all sitting on the warm soft floor of the cave. They opened a tin of meat, cut huge slices of bread and made sandwiches. Then they opened a tin of pineapple chunks and ate those, spooning them out of the tin, full of sweetness and juice. After that they still felt hungry, so they opened two tins of sardines and dug them out with biscuits. It made a really grand meal.

'Ginger-pop to finish up with, please,' said Dick. 'My word, why don't people always have meals like this?'

'We'd better hurry up or we shan't be able to get heather for our beds,' said George, sleepily.

'Who wants heather?' said Dick. '*I* don't! This lovely soft sand is all *I* shall want – and a cushion and a rug or two. I shall sleep better here than ever I did in bed!'

So the rugs and cushions were spread out on the sandy floor of the cave. A candle was lit as it grew dark, and the four sleepy children looked at one another. Timmy, as usual, was with George.

'Good-night,' said George. 'I can't keep awake another minute. Good-night, ev . . . ery . . . body . . . good . . . night!'

13   A day on the island

The children hardly knew where they were the next day when they woke up. The sun was pouring into the cave entrance, and fell first of all on George's sleeping face. It awoke her and she lay half-dozing, wondering why her bed felt rather less soft than usual.

'But I'm not in my bed – I'm on Kirrin Island, of course!' she thought suddenly to herself. She sat up and gave Anne a punch. 'Wake up, sleepy-head! We're on the island!'

Soon they were all awake rubbing the sleep from their eyes. 'I think I'm going to get heather today for my bed, after all,' said Anne. 'The sand feels soft at first, but it gets hard after a bit.'

The others agreed that they would all get heather for their beds, set on the sand, with rugs for covering. Then they would have really fine beds.

'It's fun to live in a cave,' said Dick. 'Fancy having a fine cave like this on our island, as well as a castle and dungeons! We are really very lucky.'

'I feel sticky and dirty,' said Julian. 'Let's go and have a bathe before we have breakfast. Then cold ham, bread, pickles and marmalade for me!'

'We shall be cold after our bathe,' said George. 'We'd better light my little stove and put the kettle on to boil while we're bathing. Then we can make some hot cocoa when we come back shivering!'

'Oh yes,' said Anne, who had never boiled anything on such a tiny stove before. 'Do let's. I'll fill the kettle with water from one of the containers. What shall we do for milk?'

'There's a tin of milk somewhere in the pile,' said Julian. 'We can open that. Where's the tin-opener?'

It was not to be found, which was most exasperating. But at last Julian discovered it in his pocket, so all was well.

The little stove was filled with methylated spirit, and lit. The kettle was filled and set on top. Then the children went off to bathe.

'Look! There's a simply marvellous pool in the middle of those rocks over there!' called Julian, pointing. 'We've never spotted it before. Golly, it's like a small swimming-pool, made specially for us!'

'Kirrin Swimming Pool, twenty pence a dip!' said Dick. 'Free to the owners, though! Come on – it looks gorgeous! And see how the waves keep washing over the top of the rocks and splashing into the pool. Couldn't be better!'

It really was a lovely rock-pool, deep, clear and not too cold. The children enjoyed themselves thoroughly, splashing about and swimming and floating. George tried a dive off one of the rocks, and went in beautifully.

'George can do anything in the water,' said Anne, admiringly. 'I wish I could dive and swim like George. But I never shall.'

'We can see the old wreck nicely from here,' said Julian, coming out of the water. 'Blow! We didn't bring any towels.'

'We'll use one of the rugs, turn and turn about,' said Dick. 'I'll go and fetch the thinnest one. I say – do you remember that trunk we saw in the wreck yesterday? Odd, wasn't it?'

'Yes, very odd,' said Julian. 'I don't understand it. We'll have to keep a watch on the wreck and see who comes to collect the trunk.'

'I suppose the smugglers – if they are smugglers – will come slinking round this side of the island and quietly send off a boat to the wreck,' said George, drying herself vigorously. 'Well, we'd better keep a strict look-out, and see if anything appears on the sea out there in the way of a small steamer, boat or ship.'

'Yes. We don't want them to spot us,' said Dick. 'We shan't find out anything if they see us and are warned. They'd at once give up coming to the island. I vote we each of us take turns at keeping a look-out, so that we can spot anything at once and get under cover.'

'Good idea!' said Julian. 'Well, I'm dry, but not very warm. Let's race to the cave, and get that hot drink. And breakfast – golly, I could eat a whole chicken and probably a duck as well, to say nothing of a turkey.'

The others laughed. They all felt the same. They raced off to the cave, running over the sand and climbing over a few rocks, then down to the cave-beach and into the big entrance, still splashed with sunshine.

The kettle was boiling away merrily, sending a cloud of steam up from its tin spout. 'Get the ham out and a loaf of bread, and that jar of pickles we brought,' ordered Julian. 'I'll open the tin of milk. George, you take the tin of cocoa and that jug, and make enough for all of us.'

'I'm so terribly happy,' said Anne, as she sat at the entrance to the cave, eating her breakfast. 'It's a lovely feeling. It's simply gorgeous being on our island like this, all by ourselves, able to do what we like.'

They all felt the same. It was such a lovely day too, and the sky and sea were so blue. They sat eating and drinking, gazing out to sea, watching the waves break into spray over the rocks beyond the old wreck. It certainly was a very rocky coast.

'Let's arrange everything very nicely in the cave,' said Anne, who was the tidiest of the four, and always liked to play at 'houses' if she could. 'This shall be our house, our home. We'll make four proper beds. And we'll each have our own place to sit in. And we'll arrange everything tidily on that big stone shelf there. It might have been made for us!'

'We'll leave Anne to play "houses" by herself,' said George, who was longing to stretch her legs again. 'We'll go and get some heather for beds. And oh! – what about one of us keeping a watch on the old wreck, to see who comes there?'

'Yes – that's important,' said Julian at once. 'I'll take first watch. The best place would be up on the cliff just above this cave. I can find a gorse bush that will hide me all right from anyone out at sea. You others get the heather. We will take two-hourly watches. We can read if we like, so long as we keep on looking up.'

Dick and George went to get the heather. Julian climbed up the knotted rope that still hung down through the hole, tied firmly to the great old root of an enormous gorse bush. He pulled himself out on the cliff and lay on the heather panting.

He could see nothing out to sea at all except for some big steamer miles out on the sky-line. He lay down in the sun, enjoying the warmth that poured in to every inch of his body. This look-out job was going to be very nice!

He could hear Anne singing down in the cave as she tidied up her 'house'. Her voice came up through the cave roof hole, rather muffled. Julian smiled. He knew Anne was enjoying herself thoroughly.

So she was. She had washed the few bits of crockery they had used for breakfast, in a most convenient little rain-pool outside the cave. Timmy used it for drinking-water too, but he didn't seem to mind Anne using it for washing-up water, though she apologised to him for doing so.

'I'm sorry if I spoil your drinking water, Timmy darling,' she said, 'but you are such a sensible dog that I know if it suddenly tastes nasty to you, you will go off and find another rain-pool.'

'Woof!' said Timmy, and ran off to meet George, who was just arriving back with Dick, armed with masses of soft, sweet-smelling heather for beds.

'Put the heather outside the cave, please, George', said Anne. 'I'll make the beds inside when I'm ready.'

'Right!' said George. 'We'll go and get some more. Aren't we having fun?'

'Julian's gone up the rope to the top of the cliff,' said Anne. 'He'll yell if he sees anything unusual. I hope he does, don't you?'

'It would be exciting,' agreed Dick, putting down his heather on top of Timmy, and nearly burying him. 'Oh sorry, Timmy – are you there? Bad luck!'

Anne had a very happy morning. She arranged everything beautifully on the shelf – crockery and knives and forks and spoons in one place – saucepan and kettle in another – tins of meat next, tins of soup together, tins of fruit neatly piled on top of one another. It really was a splendid larder and dresser!

She wrapped all the bread up in an old tablecloth

they had brought, and put it at the back of the cave in the coolest place she could find. The containers of water went there too, and so did all the bottles of drinks.

Then the little girl set to work to make the beds. She decided to make two nice big ones, one on each side of the cave.

'George and I and Tim will have the one this side,' she thought, busy patting down the heather into the shape of a bed. 'And Julian and Dick can have the other side. I shall want lots more heather. Oh, is that you, Dick? You're just in time! I want more heather.'

Soon the beds were made beautifully, and each had an old rug for an under-blanket, and two better rugs for covers. Cushions made pillows.

'What a pity we didn't bring night-things,' thought Anne. 'I could have folded them neatly and put them under the cushions. There! It all looks lovely. We've got a beautiful house.'

Julian came sliding down the rope from the cliff to the cave. He looked round admiringly. 'My word, Anne – the cave does look fine! Everything in order and looking so tidy. You are a good little girl.'

Anne was pleased to hear Julian's praise, though she didn't like him calling her a little girl.

'Yes, it does look nice, doesn't it?' she said. 'But why aren't you watching up on the cliff, Ju?'

'It's Dick's turn now,' said Julian. 'The two hours are up. Did we bring any biscuits? I feel as if I could do with one or two, and I bet the others could too. Let's all go up to the cliff-top and have some. George and Timmy are there with Dick.'

Anne knew exactly where to put her hand on the tin of biscuits. She took out ten and climbed up to the cliff-top. Julian went up the rope. Soon all five were sitting by the big gorse-bush, nibbling at biscuits, Timmy too. At least, he didn't nibble. He just swallowed.

The day passed very pleasantly and rather lazily. They took turns at being look-out, though Anne was severely scolded by Julian in the afternoon for falling asleep during her watch. She was very ashamed of herself and cried.

'You're too little to be a look-out, that's what it is,' said Julian. 'We three and Timmy had better do it.'

'Oh, no, do let me too,' begged poor Anne. 'I never, never will fall asleep again. But the sun was so hot and . . .'

'Don't make excuses,' said Julian. 'It only makes things worse if you do. All right – we'll give you another chance, Anne, and see if you are really big enough to do the things we do.'

But though they all took their turns, and kept a watch on the sea for any strange vessel, none appeared. The children were disappointed. They did so badly want to know who had put that trunk on the wreck and why, and what it contained.

'Better go to bed now,' said Julian, when the sun sank low. 'It's about nine o'clock. Come on! I'm really looking forward to a sleep on those lovely heathery beds that Anne has made so nicely!'

14   Disturbance in the night

It was dark in the cave, not really quite dark enough to light a candle, but the cave looked so nice by candle-light that it was fun to light one. So Anne took down the candle-stick and lit the candle. At once strange shadows jumped all round the cave, and it became a rather exciting place, not at all like the cave they knew by daylight!

'I wish we could have a fire,' said Anne.

'We'd be far too hot,' said Julian. 'And it would smoke us out. You can't have a fire in a cave like this. There's no chimney.'

'Yes, there is,' said Anne, pointing to the hole in the roof. 'If we lit a fire just under that hole, it would act as a chimney, wouldn't it?'

'It might,' said Dick, thoughtfully. 'But I don't think so. We'd simply get the cave full of stifling smoke, and we wouldn't be able to sleep for choking.'

'Well, couldn't we light a fire at the cave entrance then?' said Anne who felt that a real home ought to have a fire somewhere. 'Just to keep away wild beasts, say! That's what the people of old times did. It says so in my history book. They lit fires at the cave entrance at night to keep away any wild animal that might be prowling around.'

'Well, what wild beasts do you think are likely to come and peep into this cave?' asked Julian, lazily, finishing up a cup of cocoa. 'Lions? Tigers? Or perhaps you are afraid of an elephant or two.'

Everyone laughed. 'No – I don't really think animals like that would come,' said Anne. 'Only – it would be nice to have a red, glowing fire to watch when we go to sleep.'

'Perhaps Anne thinks the rabbits might come in and nibble our toes or something,' said Dick.

'Woof!' said Tim, pricking up his ears as he always did at the mention of rabbits.

'I don't think we ought to have a fire,' said Julian, 'because it might be seen out at sea and give a warning to anyone thinking of coming to the island to do a bit of smuggling.'

'Oh no, Julian – the entrance to this cave is so well-hidden that I'm sure no one could see a fire out to sea,' said George, at once. 'There's that line of high rocks in front, which must hide it completely. I think it would be rather fun to have a fire. It would light up the cave so strangely and excitingly.'

'Oh good, George!' said Anne, delighted to find someone agreeing with her.

'Well, we can't possibly trek out and get sticks for it now,' said Dick, who was far too comfortable to move.

'You don't need to,' said Anne, eagerly. 'I got plenty myself today, and stored them at the back of the cave, in case we wanted a fire.'

'Isn't she a good housewife!' said Julian, in great admiration. 'She may go to sleep when she's look-out, but she's wide-awake enough when it comes to making a house for us out of a cave! All right, Anne – we'll make a fire for you!'

They all got up and fetched the sticks from the back

of the cave. Anne had been to the jackdaw tower and had picked up armfuls that the birds had dropped when making their nests in the tower. They built them up to make a nice little fire. Julian got some dried seaweed too, to drop into it.

They lit the fire at the cave entrance, and the dry sticks blazed up at once. The children went back to their heather-beds, and lay down on them, watching the red flames leaping and crackling. The red glow lit up the cave and made it very weird and exciting.

'This is lovely,' said Anne, half-asleep. 'Really lovely. Oh Timmy, move a bit, do. You're so heavy on my feet. Here, George, pull Timothy over to your side. You're used to him lying on you.'

'Good-night,' said Dick, sleepily. 'The fire is dying down, but I can't be bothered to put any more wood on it. I'm sure all the lions and tigers and bears and elephants have been frightened away.'

'Silly!' said Anne. 'You needn't tease me about it – you've enjoyed it as much as I have! Good-night.'

They all fell asleep and dreamed peacefully of many things. Julian awoke with a jump. Some strange noise had awakened him. He lay still, listening.

Timothy was growling deeply, right down in his throat. 'R-r-r-r-r-r-r,' he went. 'Gr-r-r-r-r-r-r-r-r!'

George awoke too, and put out her hand sleepily. 'What's the matter, Tim?' she said.

'He's heard something, George,' said Julian, in a low voice from his bed on the other side of the cave.

George sat up cautiously. Timmy was still growling. 'Sh!' said George and he stopped. He was sitting up straight, his ears well cocked.

'Perhaps it's the smugglers come in the night,' whispered George, and a funny prickly feeling ran down her back. Somehow smugglers in the day time were rather exciting and quite welcome – but at night they seemed different. George didn't at all want to meet any just then!

'I'm going out to see if I can spy anything,' said Julian, getting off his bed quietly, so as not to wake Dick. 'I'll go up the rope to the top of the cliff. I can see better from there.'

'Take my torch,' said George. But Julian didn't want it.

'No, thanks. I can feel the way up that knotted rope quite well, whether I can see or not,' he said.

He went up the rope in the dark, his body twisting round as the rope turned. He climbed up on to the cliff and looked out to sea. It was a very dark night, and he could see no ship at all, not even the wreck. It was far too dark.

'Pity there's no moon,' thought Julian. 'I might be able to see something then.'

He watched for a few minutes, and then George's voice came through the hole in the roof, coming out strangely at his feet.

'Julian! Is there anything to see? Shall I come up?'

'Nothing at all,' said Julian. 'Is Timmy still growling?'

'Yes, when I take my hand off his collar,' said George. 'I can't imagine what's upset him.'

Suddenly Julian caught sight of something. It was a light, a good way beyond the line of rocks. He watched in excitement. That would be just about where the wreck was! Yes – it must be someone on the wreck with a lantern!

'George! Come up!' he said, putting his head inside the hole.

George came up, hand over hand, like a monkey, leaving Timothy growling below. She sat by Julian on the cliff-top. 'See the wreck – look, over there!' said Julian. 'At least, you can't see the wreck itself, it's too dark – but you can see a lantern that someone has put there.'

'Yes – that's someone on our wreck, with a lantern!' said George, feeling excited. 'Oh, I wonder if it's the smugglers – coming to bring more things.'

'Or somebody fetching that trunk,' said Julian. 'Well, we'll know tomorrow, for we'll go and see. Look! – whoever is there is moving off now – the light of the lantern is going lower – they must be getting into a boat by the side of the wreck. And now the light's gone out.'

The children strained their ears to hear if they could discover the splash of oars or the sound of voices over the water. They both thought they could hear voices.

'The boat must have gone off to join a ship or something,' said Julian. 'I believe I can see a faint light right out there – out to sea, look! Maybe the boat is going to it.'

There was nothing more to see or hear, and soon the two of them slid down the knotted rope back to the cave. They didn't wake the others, who were still sleeping peacefully. Timothy leapt up and licked Julian and George, whining joyfully. He did not growl any more.

'You're a good dog, aren't you?' said Julian, patting him. 'Nothing ever escapes *your* sharp ears, does it?'

Timothy settled down on George's feet again. It was plain that whatever it was that had disturbed him had gone. It must have been the presence of the stranger or strangers on the old wreck. Well, they would go there in the morning and see if they could discover what had been taken away or brought there in the night.

Anne and Dick were most indignant the next morning when they heard Julian's tale. 'You *might* have woken us!' said Dick, crossly.

'We would have if there had been anything much to see,' said George. 'But there was only just the light from a lantern, and nothing else except that we thought we heard the sound of voices.'

When the tide was low enough the children and Timothy set off over the rocks to the wreck. They clambered up and stood on the slanting, slippery deck. They looked towards the locker where the little trunk had stood. The door of the locker was shut this time.

Julian slid down towards it and tried to pull it open. Someone had stuffed a piece of wood in to keep the locker from swinging open. Julian pulled it out. Then the door opened easily.

'Anything else in there?' said George, stepping carefully over the slimy deck to Julian.

'Yes,' said Julian. 'Look! Tins of food! And cups and plates and things – just as if someone was going to come and live on the island too! Isn't it funny? The trunk is still here too, locked as before. And here are some candles – and a little lamp – and a bundle of rags. Whatever *are* they here for?'

It really was a puzzle. Julian frowned for a few minutes, trying to think it out.

'It looks as if someone is going to come and stay on the island for a bit – probably to wait there and take in whatever goods are going to be smuggled. Well – we shall be on the look-out for them, day or night!'

They left the wreck, feeling excited. They had a fine hiding-place in their cave – no one could possibly find them there. And, from their hiding-place they could watch anyone coming to and from the wreck, and, from the wreck, to the island.

'What about our cove, where we put our boat?' said George, suddenly. 'They might use that cove, you know – if they came in a boat. 'It's rather dangerous to reach the island from the wreck, if anyone tried to get to the rocky beach nearby.'

'Well – if anyone came to our cove, they'd see our boat,' said Dick, in alarm. 'We'd better hide it, hadn't we?'

'How?' said Anne, thinking that it would be a difficult thing to hide a boat as big as theirs.

'Don't know,' said Julian. 'We'll go and have a look.'

All four and Timmy went off to the cove into which they had rowed their boat. The boat was pulled high up, out of reach of the waves. George explored the cove well, and then had an idea. 'Do you think we could pull the boat round this big rock? It would just about hide it, though anyone going round the rock would see it at once.'

The others thought it would be worthwhile trying, anyway. So, with much panting and puffing, they hauled the boat round the rock, which almost completely hid her.

'Good!' said George, going down into the cove to see if very much of the boat showed. 'A bit of her does show still. Let's drape it with seaweed!'

So they draped the prow of the boat with all the seaweed they could find at hand, and after that, unless anyone went deliberately round the big rock, the boat really was not noticeable at all.

'Good!' said Julian, looking at his watch. 'I say – it's

long past tea-time – and, you know, while we've been doing all this with the boat, we quite forgot to have someone on the look-out post on the cliff-top. What idiots we are!'

'Well, I don't expect anything has happened since we've been away from the cave,' said Dick, putting a fine big bit of seaweed on the prow of the boat, as a last touch. 'I bet the smugglers will only come at night.'

'I dare say you're right,' said Julian. 'I think we'd better keep a look-out at night, too. The look-out could take rugs up to the cliff-top and curl up there.'

'Timmy could be with whoever is keeping watch,' said Anne. 'Then if the look-out goes to sleep by mistake, Timmy would growl and wake them up if he saw anything.'

'You mean, when *you* go to sleep,' said Dick, grinning. 'Come on – let's get back to the cave and have some tea.'

And then Timothy suddenly began to growl again!

15 Who is on the island?

'Sh!' said Julian, at once. 'Get down behind this bush, quick, everyone!'

They had left the cove and were walking towards the castle when Timmy growled. Now they all crouched behind a mass of brambles, their hearts beating fast.

'Don't growl, Timmy,' said George, in Timothy's nearest ear. He stopped at once, but he stood stiff and quivering, on the watch.

Julian peeped through the bush, parting the brambles and scratching his hands. He could just see somebody in the courtyard – one person – two persons – maybe three. He strained his eyes to try and see, but even as he looked, they disappeared.

'I believe they've moved those big stones over the entrance to the dungeons, and have gone down there,' he whispered. 'Stay here, and I'll creep out a bit and see. I won't let anyone spot me.'

He came back and nodded. 'Yes – they've gone down the dungeons. Do you think they can be the smugglers? Do you suppose they are storing their smuggled goods down there? It would be a marvellous place, of course.'

'Let's get back to the cave while they are underground,' said George. 'I'm so afraid Timmy will give the game away by barking. He's just bursting himself trying not to make some sort of noise.'

'Come on, then!' said Julian. 'Don't go across the courtyard – make for the shore and we'll scramble round it till we get to the cave. Then one of us can pop up through the hole and hide behind that big gorse-bush there to see who the smugglers are. They must have come in by boat either from the wreck, or by rowing cleverly through the rocks off-shore.'

They got to the cave at last and went in. But no sooner had Julian shinned up the rope, helped by the others, than Timothy disappeared! He ran out of the cave while the others' backs were turned, and when George turned round there was no Timmy to be seen!

'Timmy!' she called in a low voice. 'Timmy! Where are you?'

But no answer came! Timmy had gone off on his own. If only the smugglers didn't see him! What a bad dog he was to do that!

But Timmy had smelt something exciting – he had smelt a smell he knew – a dog-smell – and he meant to find the owner of it and bite off his ears and tail! 'Gr-r-r-r-r-r!' Timmy was not going to allow dogs on *his* island!

Julian sat close beside the gorse-bush, watching all round. There was nothing to be seen on the wreck, and there was no ship out to sea. Probably the boat that had brought the strangers to the island was hidden down below among the rocks. Julian looked behind him, towards the castle – and even as he looked, he saw an astonishing sight!

A dog was sniffing about the bushes not far away – and creeping up behind him, all his hackles up, was Timothy! Timothy was stalking the dog as if he were a cat stalking a rabbit! The other dog suddenly heard him and leapt round, facing Timothy. Timmy flung himself on the dog with a blood-curdling howl, and the dog howled in fright.

Julian watched in horror, not knowing what to do. The two dogs made a fearful noise, especially the other dog whose howls of terror and yelps of rage resounded everywhere.

'This will bring the smugglers up, and they will see Timmy and know there's someone on the island,' thought Julian. 'Oh, blow you, Timmy! – why didn't you stay with George and keep quiet?'

From the walls of the ruined castle came three figures, running pell-mell to see what was happening to their dog – and Julian stared at them in the very greatest amazement – for the three people were no other than Mr Stick, Mrs Stick and Edgar!

'Golly!' said Julian, crawling round the bush to get to the hole quickly. 'They've come after us! They've guessed we've gone here and they've come to look for us, the beasts, to make us go back! Well, they won't find us! But oh, what a pity Timmy's given the show away!'

There came a shrill whistle from down below him. It was George, who, hearing the row from the dogs, was feeling worried, and had sent out her piercing whistle for Timmy. It was a whistle the dog always obeyed, and he let go his hold on the dog and shot off to the cliff-top at once, just as the three Sticks arrived on the scene, and picked up their bleeding, whining mongrel.

Edgar tore after Timmy, up to the cliff-top. Julian dropped down to the cave when he spotted Edgar appearing. Timmy ran to the hole and dropped bodily down, landing almost on top of Julian. He flung himself on George.

'Shut up, shut up!' said George, in an urgent whisper to the excited dog. 'Do you want to give our hiding-place away, you idiot?'

Edgar, panting and puffing, arrived on the cliff-top, and was completely amazed to see Timothy apparently disappear into the solid earth. He hunted about for a bit, but it was clear that the dog was no longer on the cliff.

Mr and Mrs Stick came up too. 'Where did that dog go?' shouted Mrs Stick. 'What was he like?'

'He looked awfully like that horrible dog of the children's,' said Edgar. His voice could clearly be heard by everyone down in the cave. The children kept as quiet as mice.

'But it *couldn't* be!' came Mrs Stick's voice. 'The children have gone home – we saw them, *and* the dog too, making off towards the railway. It must be some sort of stray dog left here by a tripper.'

'Well, where is he, then?' said Mr Stick's hoarse voice. 'Can't see any dog anywhere about now.'

'He disappeared into the earth,' said Edgar, in a surprised voice.

Mr Stick made a rude and scornful noise. 'You tell lovely tales, you do,' he said. 'Disappeared into the earth! What next? Fell over the cliff, I should think. Well, he got his teeth into poor Tinker good and proper. My word, if I see that dog, I'll shoot him!'

'He might have some hiding-place about this cliff,' said Mrs Stick. 'Let's have a look!'

The children sat as quiet as mice, George with a warning hand on Timmy's collar. They could hear that the Sticks were really very near. Julian expected one of them to fall down the hole at any moment!

But mercifully they didn't happen on the hole that led down to the cave. They stood quite near to it, though, while they were discussing the problem.

'If it's the children's dog, then those tiresome kids must have come to this island, instead of going home,' said Mrs Stick. 'That would upset our plan all right! We shall have to find out. I'll have no peace till I know.'

'We can soon find out,' said Mr Stick. 'No need to worry about that. Their boat will be here somewhere – and they'll all be about, too! It's impossible for four children, a dog and a boat to be hidden on this small island once anyone starts hunting for them! Edgar, you go round that way. Clara, you get along round about the castle. They may be hiding somewhere in the ruins. I'll have a look about here.'

The children crouched together in the cave. How they hoped that their boat would not be found! How they hoped that no one would find any traces of them at all! Timmy growled softly, wishing that he could go and find that Stinker-dog again! It had been lovely to bite his ears hard.

Edgar was half-scared of finding the children, and a good deal more scared of coming up against Timmy somewhere. So he did not make much of a search for either the children or the boat. He went into the cove where the boat had been pulled up, and although he saw traces where the vessel had been hauled up, barely smoothed out by the sea-water at high-tide, he did not notice the seaweedy prow of the boat sticking out round the rock behind which it was hidden.

'Nothing here!' he called to his mother, who was going round and about the ruins, looking into every

likely nook. But she found nothing either, and neither
did Mr Stick.

'Couldn't have been the children's dog,' said Mr
Stick, at last. 'They'd be here if he was, and so would
their boat, but there's no sign of them at all. That dog
must have been some wild stray. Have to look out for
him, no doubt about it. Gone wild, I should think.'

The children relaxed after about an hour, thinking
that the Sticks must have given up looking for them.
They boiled the kettle to make some tea, and Anne
began to cut some sandwiches. Timmy was tied up in
case he wandered out again to look for Stinker.

They ate their tea quietly, not speaking above a
whisper. 'The Sticks haven't come here to look for us,
after all,' said Julian. 'It's quite plain from what they
said that they thought we had gone to catch the train
home, taking George and Timmy with us.'

'Then what are they here for?' demanded George,
fiercely. 'It's *our* island! They've no right here. Let's go
and turn them off! They're scared of Timmy. We'll
take him with us and say we'll set him on to them if
they don't clear out.'

'No, George,' said Julian. 'Do be sensible. We don't
want them rushing off and telling your father we are
here, or he may lose his temper and come flying home
to order us back. And — there's another thing I've
thought of.'

'What?' asked the others, seeing Julian's eyes gleam
in the way they did when he had an idea.

'Well,' said Julian, 'don't you think it's possible that
the Sticks are something to do with the smugglers?
Don't you think they may come here to take off
smuggled goods, or to hide them till they can take
them off in safety? Mr Stick is a sailor, isn't he? He

would know all about smuggling. I bet he's in the pay of the smugglers all right.'

'I believe you're right!' said George, in excitement. 'Well – we'll wait till the Sticks have gone, and then we'll go down into the dungeons and see if they've hidden anything there! We'll find out their little game and stop it! It will be terribly thrilling, won't it?'

16   *The Sticks get a fright*

But the Sticks didn't go! The children peeped out of
the spy-hole at the top of the cave-roof every now and
again, and saw one or other of the Sticks. The evening
went on and it began to be dark. Still the Sticks didn't
go. Julian ran down to the nearby shore and discovered
a small boat there. So the Sticks had managed to find
their way round the island, rowed near the wreck,
maybe landed on it too, and then came to the shore,
cleverly avoiding the rocks they might strike against.

'It looks as if the Sticks have come to stay for the
night,' said Julian, gloomily. 'This is going to spoil our
stay here, isn't it? We rush away here to escape from
the Sticks – and lo and behold! the Sticks are on top of
us again. It's too bad.'

'Let's frighten them,' said George, her eyes shining
by the light of the one candle in the cave.

'What do you mean?' said Dick, cheering up. He
always liked George's ideas, mad as they sometimes
were.

'Well, I suppose they must be living down in one of
the dungeon rooms, mustn't they?' said George.
'There is no place in the ruins to live in proper shelter,
or we'd be there ourselves – and the only other place is
down in the dungeons. I wouldn't care to sleep there
myself, but I don't suppose the Sticks would mind.'

'Well, what about it?' said Dick. 'What's your idea?'

'Couldn't we creep down, and do a bit of shouting, so that the echoes start up all round?' said George. 'You know how frightening we found the echoes when we first went down into the dungeons. We only had to say one or two words, and the echoes began saying them over and over again shouting them back at us.'

'Oh yes, I remember,' said Anne. 'And wasn't Timmy frightened when he barked! The echoes barked back at him, and he thought there were thousands of dogs hiding down there! He was awfully frightened.'

'It's a good idea,' said Julian. 'Serve the Sticks right for coming to our island like this! If we can frighten them away, that would be one up to us! Let's do it.'

'What about Timothy?' said Anne. 'Hadn't we better leave him behind?'

'No. He can come and stand at the dungeon entrance to guard it for us,' said George. 'Then if any of the real smugglers happened to come, Timmy could give us warning. I'm not going to leave him behind.'

'Come on, then, let's go now!' said Julian. 'It would be a fine trick to play. It's quite dark, but I've got my torch, and as soon as we are certain that the Sticks are down in the dungeons, we can start to play our joke.'

There was no sign or sound of the Sticks anywhere about. No light of fire or candle was to be seen, no sound of voices to be heard. Either they had gone, or they were below in the dungeons. The stones had been taken from the entrance, so the children felt sure they were down there.

'Now Timmy, you stay quite still and quiet here,' whispered George to Timmy. 'Bark if anyone comes, but not unless. We're going down into the dungeons.'

'I think perhaps I'll stay up here with Timothy,' said Anne, suddenly. She didn't like the dark look of the dungeon entrance. 'You see, George – Timmy might be frightened or lonely up here by himself.'

The others chuckled. They knew Anne was frightened. Julian squeezed her arm. 'You stay here, then,' he said, kindly. 'You keep old Timmy company.'

Then Julian, George and Dick went down the long flight of steps that led into the deep old dungeons of Kirrin Castle. They had been there the summer before, when they had been seeking for lost treasure; now here they were again!

They crept down the steps and came to the many cellars or dungeons cut out of the rock below the castle. There were scores of those, some big and some small, weird, damp underground rooms in which, maybe, unhappy prisoners had been kept in the olden days.

The children crept down the dark passages. Julian had a piece of white chalk with him, and drew a chalk line here and there on the rocky walls as he went, so that he might easily find the way back.

Suddenly they heard voices and saw a light. They stopped and whispered softly together in each other's ears.

'They're in that room where we found the treasure last year! That's where they're camping out! What noises shall we make?'

'I'll be a cow,' said Dick. 'I can moo awfully like a cow. I'll be a cow.'

'I'll be a sheep,' said Julian. 'George, you be a horse. You can whinny and hrrrumph just like a horse. Dick, you begin!'

So Dick began. Hidden behind a rocky pillar, he opened his mouth and mooed dolefully, like a cow in pain. At once the echoes took up the mooing, magnified it, sent it along all the underground passages, till it seemed as if a thousand cows had wandered there and were mooing together.

'Moo – oo – oo – OOOOOOOO, ooo – oo – MOOOOOOO!'

The Sticks listened in amazement and fright at the sudden awful noise.

'What is it, Ma?' said Edgar, almost in tears. Stinker crouched at the back of the cave, terrified.

'It's cows,' said Mr Stick, amazed. 'I think it's cows. Can't you hear the moos? But how did cows get to be here?'

'Nonsense!' said Mrs Stick, recovering herself a little. 'Cows down these caves! You're mad! You'll be telling me there're sheep next!'

It was funny that she should have said that, for Julian chose that moment to begin baa-ing like a flock of sheep. His one long, bleating 'baa-baa-aa-aa' was taken up by the echoes at once, and it seemed suddenly as if hundreds of poor lost sheep were baa-ing their way down the dungeons!

Mr Stick jumped to his feet, as white as a sheet.

'Well, if it isn't sheep now!' he said. 'What's up? What's in these 'ere dungeons? I never did like them.'

'Baa-baa-baa-aa-AAAAAAAAAA!' went the mournful bleats all round and about. And then George started her whinnying and neighing, just like an impatient horse. The little girl tossed her head in the darkness and hrrrumphed exactly like a horse and then she stamped with her foot, and at once the echoes stamped too, sending her whinnying and neighing and stamping into the Sticks's cave twenty times louder than George had made them.

Poor Stinker began to whine pitifully. He was frightened almost out of his life. He pressed himself against the floor as if he would like to disappear into it. Edgar clutched his mother's arm. 'Let's go up,' he said. 'I can't stay here. There're hundreds of sheep and horses and cows roaming these dungeons, you can hear them. They're not real, but they've got voices and hoofs, and I'm scared of them.'

Mr Stick went to the door of the room they were in, and shouted loudly.

'Get out, you! Clear out! Whoever you are!'

George giggled. Then she shouted out in a very deep, hoarse voice.

'BE-WARE!' And the echoes thundered out all round.

''WARE! 'WARE! 'WARE-ARE-ARE!'

Mr Stick went back quickly into the cave-room, and lit another candle. He shut the big wooden door that led into the room. His hands were shaking.

'Peculiar goings-on,' he said. 'Shan't stay here much longer if we get this kind of thing happening every night.'

Julian, Dick and George were now in such a state of giggles that they could not imitate any more cows, horses or sheep. George did begin to be a pig, and gave such a realistic snort and grunt that Dick nearly died of laughing. The snorts and grunts were echoed everywhere.

'Come out,' gasped Julian, at last. 'I shall burst with trying not to laugh. Come out!'

'Come out!' whispered the echoes. 'Come out, out, out!'

They stumbled out, stuffing hankies into their

mouths as they went, following Julian's chalk marks easily by the light of his torch. It was impossible to take the wrong passage if they followed his guiding lines.

They sat on the dungeon steps with Anne and Timmy, and choked with laughter as they related all they had done. 'We heard old Stick yelling to us to clear out,' said George, 'and he sounded scared stiff. As for Stinker, we never heard even the smallest growl from him. I bet the Sticks will clear off tomorrow after this! It must have given them a most terrible fright.'

'Oh, that was grand!' said Julian. 'It was a pity I began to laugh. I was just feeling I might trumpet like an elephant next. The echoes would like that!'

'Funny the Sticks all staying on the island like this,' said Dick, thoughtfully. 'They've left Kirrin Cottage – but they're not looking for us. They must be in league with the smugglers all right. Perhaps that's why Mrs Stick took the job with your mother, George – to be near the island when the time came – when the smugglers wanted their help.'

'We could really go back to Kirrin Cottage, couldn't we?' said Anne, who, much as she loved the island, was not nearly so keen on it now that the Sticks were there.

'Go back! Leave an adventure just when it's beginning!' said George, scornfully. 'How silly you are, Anne. Go back if you want to – but I'm sure nobody will go with you.'

'Oh, Anne will stay with us all right,' said Julian, knowing that Anne would feel hurt at the suggestion she should leave them. 'It will be the Sticks who have to go, don't worry!'

'Let's go back to the cave,' said Anne, thinking

longingly of its safety and bright little candle. They got up and made their way across the courtyard to the little wall that ran round the castle. They climbed over it and turned their steps to the cliff. Julian switched on his torch when he thought it was safe, for it was impossible to see clearly in the dark, and he did not want any of them to fall down the hole, instead of climbing down properly by the rope.

Julian stood by the hole at last, shining his torch so that the others might climb down the rope in safety, one by one. He glanced up, looking over the dark sea as he stood there, and then stared intently.

There was a light out to sea, and it was signalling. It must have seen his torchlight! Julian watched, wondering if it was a ship that was signalling, and how far out it was, and why it was signalling.

'Perhaps they're going to put more stuff into the old wreck for the Sticks to find,' he thought. 'I wonder if they are. How I'd like to find out – but it would be dangerous to go there in daylight in case the Sticks see us.'

The signalling went on for a long time, as if a message was being flashed. Julian could not for the life of him make out what it was. It simply looked like the flash-flash-flash of a lantern to him. But it must mean a signal or message of some sort to the Sticks.

'Well, they won't get it tonight!' thought Julian, with a chuckle, when at last the signalling stopped. 'I rather think the Stick family will stay where they are tonight, too scared of sheep and cows and horses rushing about in those dungeons!'

Julian was quite right – the Sticks did stay where they were! Nothing would get them out of their underground room till morning.

17   *A shock for Edgar*

The children slept well that night, and as Timothy did
not growl at all, they were sure that nothing important
could have happened. They had a fine breakfast of
tongue, tinned peaches, bread and butter, golden
syrup and ginger-beer.

'That's the end of the ginger-beer, I'm afraid,' said
Julian, regretfully. 'I must say ginger-beer is a
gorgeous drink – seems to go with simply everything.'

'That was the nicest meal I've ever had,' said Anne.
'It really was. We do have lovely meals on Kirrin
Island. I wonder if the Sticks are having nice meals
too.'

'You bet they are!' said Dick. 'I expect they have
ransacked Aunt Fanny's cupboards and taken the best
they can find.'

'Oh, the beasts!' said George, her eyes flashing. 'I
never thought of that – they may have robbed the
house and taken all kinds of things.'

'They probably have,' said Julian, and he frowned.
'I say, I never thought of that, somehow. How awful,
George, if your mother came back, feeling ill and
weak, and found half her belongings gone!'

'Oh dear!' said Anne, dismayed. 'George, wouldn't
that be dreadful?'

'Yes,' said George, looking very angry. 'I would
believe anything of those Sticks! If they have the cheek

to come to our island and live here, they've the cheek
to steal from my mother's house. I wish we could find
out.'

'They could have brought quite a lot of things away
in their boat,' said Julian. 'They must have come here
by boat. If they did bring stolen goods, they must have
put them somewhere – down in the dungeons, I
suppose.'

'We might have a look round and see if we can spy
anything, without the Sticks seeing us,' suggested
Dick.

'Let's have a look round now,' said George, who
always liked doing things at once. 'Anne, you do the
washing-up and tidy our cave-house for us, will
you?'

Anne was torn between wanting to go with the
others, and longing to play 'house' again. She did so
love arranging everything and making the beds and
tidying up the cave. In the end she said she would stay
and the others could go.

So up the rope they went. Timothy stayed with
Anne, because they were afraid he might bark. Anne
tied him up, and he whined a little, but did not make a
terrible noise.

The other three lay flat on the cliff-top, looking
down on the ruined castle. There seemed to be no one
about, but, even as they watched, the three Sticks
appeared, apparently coming up from the dungeons.
They seemed glad to be in the sunshine, and the
children were not surprised, for the dungeons were so
cold and dark.

The Sticks looked all round. Stinker kept close to
Mrs Stick, his tail well down.

'They're looking for the cows and sheep and

horses they heard down in the dungeons last night!'
whispered Dick to Julian.

The Sticks spoke together for a minute or two, and
then went off in the direction of the shore that faced the
wreck. Edgar went to the room in which the children
had first planned to sleep – the one whose roof had
fallen in.

'I'm going to stalk the two Sticks,' whispered Julian
to the others. 'You two see what Edgar is up to.'

Julian disappeared, keeping behind bushes as he
watched where the Sticks went, and followed them.
George and Dick went cautiously and quietly over the
cliff to the castle in the middle of the little island. They
could hear Edgar whistling. Stinker was running
about the courtyard of the castle.

Edgar appeared out of the ruined room, carrying a
pile of cushions, which had evidently been stored
there. George went red with rage and clutched Dick's
arm fiercely.

'Mother's best cushions!' she whispered. 'Oh, the
beasts!'

Dick felt angry too. It was quite plain that the Sticks
had helped themselves to anything handy when they
had left Kirrin Cottage. He picked up a clod of earth,
took careful aim, and flung it into the air. It fell
between Edgar and Stinker, breaking into a shower of
earth.

Edgar dropped the cushions, and looked up into the
air in fright. It was plain that he thought something
had fallen from the sky. George picked up another
clod, took aim, and flung it higher into the air. It fell all
over Stinker, and the dog gave a yelp, and scuttled
down the hole that led into the dungeons.

Edgar looked up into the sky and then all around and

about him, his mouth wide open. What could be happening? Dick waited until he was looking in the opposite direction, and then once more sent a big clod into the air. It fell into bits and scattered itself all over the startled Edgar.

Then Dick gave one of his realistic moos, exactly like a cow in pain, and Edgar stood rooted to the spot, almost frightened out of his skin. Those cows again! Where were they?

Dick mooed again, and Edgar gave a yell, found his feet, and almost fell down the dungeon steps. He disappeared with a dismal howl, leaving behind all the cushions on the ground.

'Quick!' said Dick, jumping to his feet. 'He won't be back for a few minutes, anyhow. He'll be too scared. Let's grab the cushions and bring them here. I don't see why the Sticks should use them down in those awful old dungeons.'

The two children raced to the courtyard, picked up the cushions and raced back to their hiding-place. Dick looked across to the room where Edgar had brought them from.

'What about slipping across there and seeing what else they've stored away?' he said. 'I don't see why they should be allowed to have anything that isn't theirs.'

'I'll go across, and you keep watch by the dungeon entrance,' said George. 'You've only got to moo again if you see Edgar, and he'll run for miles.'

'Right,' said Dick, with a grin, and went swiftly to the flight of steps that led underground to the dungeons. There was no sign of Edgar at all, nor of Stinker.

George went to the ruined room and gazed round in

anger. Yes, the Sticks certainly *had* helped themselves to her mother's things, no doubt about that! There were blankets and silver and all kinds of food. Mrs Stick must have gone into the big cupboard under the stairs and taken out various things stored there for weekly use.

George ran to Dick. 'There are heaps of our things!' she said, in a fierce whisper. 'Come and help me to get them. We'll see if we can take them all before Edgar appears, or the Sticks come back.'

Just as they were whispering together, they heard a low whistle. They looked round, and saw Julian coming along. He joined them.

'The Sticks have rowed off to the wreck,' he said. 'They've got an old boat somewhere down among those rocks. Old Pa Stick must be a good sailor to be able to take the boat in and out of those awful hidden rocks.'

'Oh, then we've got time to do what we want to do,' said Dick, pleased. He hurriedly told Julian of the things George had seen in the ruined room.

'Awful thieves!' said Julian, indignantly. 'They don't mean to go back to Kirrin Cottage, that's plain. They've got some business on with the smugglers here – and when that is done they'll go off with all their stolen goods, join a ship somewhere, and get off scot-free.'

'No, they won't,' said George at once. 'We are going to get everything and take it to the cave! Dick's going to keep watch for Edgar at the cave entrance, and you and I, Julian, can quickly carry the things away. We can drop them down the hole into the cave.'

'Hurry then!' said Julian. 'We must do it before the Sticks return, and I don't expect they'll be long.

They've probably gone to fetch the trunk and anything else in the wreck. You know I saw a light out to sea last night – maybe that's a signal that the smugglers were leaving something in the wreck for the Sticks to fetch.'

George and Julian ran to the ruined room, piled their arms with the goods there, and then ran to hide them on the cliff, ready to take them to the hole when they had time. It looked as if the Sticks had just taken whatever was easiest to lay their hands on. They had even got the kitchen clock!

Edgar did not appear at all, so Dick had nothing to do but sit by the steps of the dungeon and watch the others. After some time Julian and George gave a sigh of relief and beckoned to Dick. He left his place and went to join them.

'We've got everything now,' said Julian. 'I'm just going to the cliff-edge to see if the Sticks are returning yet. If they're not we'll all carry the things to the hole in the roof of the cave.'

He soon returned. 'I can see their boat tied to the wreck,' he said. 'We're safe for some while yet. Come on, let's get the things to safety! This really is a bit of luck.'

They carried the things to the hole and called down it to Anne. 'Anne! We've got tons of things to put down the hole. Stand by to catch!'

Soon all kinds of things came down the hole into the cave! Anne was most astonished. The silver and anything that might be hurt by a fall was first wrapped up in the blankets, and then let down by a rope.

'My goodness!' said Anne. 'This cave will *really* look like a house soon, when I have arranged all these things too!'

Just as they were finishing their job the children heard voices in the distance.

'The Sticks are back!' said Julian, and looked cautiously over the cliff-top. He was right. They had returned to their boat, and were even now on their way back to the castle, carrying the trunk from the wreck.

'Let's follow them, and see what happens when they find everything gone,' grinned Julian. 'Come on, everyone!'

They wriggled over the cliff on their tummies, and came to a clump of bushes behind which they could hide and watch. The Sticks put the trunk down, and looked round for Edgar. But Edgar was nowhere to be seen.

'Where's that boy?' said Mrs Stick, impatiently. 'He's had plenty of time to do everything. Edgar! Edgar! Edgar!'

Mr Stick went to the ruined room and peeped inside. He came back to Mrs Stick.

'He's taken everything down,' he said. 'He must be down in the dungeon. That room's quite empty.'

'I told him to come up and sit in the sun when he'd finished,' said Mrs Stick. 'It isn't healthy down in those dungeons. EDGAR!'

This time Edgar heard, and his head appeared, looking out of the entrance to the dungeon. He looked extremely scared.

'Come on up!' said Mrs Stick. 'You've got all the things down, and you'd better stay up here in the sunshine now.'

'I'm scared,' said Edgar. 'I'm not staying up here alone.'

'Why not?' said Mr Stick, astonished.

'It's those cows again!' said poor Edgar. 'Hundreds of them, Pa, all a-mooing round me, and throwing things at me. They're dangerous animals, they are, and I'm not coming up here alone!'

18   An unexpected prisoner

The Sticks stared at Edgar as if he was mad.

'Cows throwing things?' said Mrs Stick at last. 'What do you mean by that? Cows don't throw anything.'

'These ones did,' said Edgar, and then began to exaggerate in order to make his parents sympathise with him. 'They were dreadful cows, they were – hundreds of them, with horns as long as reindeer, and awful mooing voices. And they threw things at me and Tinker. He was really scared, and so was I. I dropped the cushions I was taking down, and rushed away to hide.'

'Where are the cushions?' said Mr Stick, looking round. 'I can't see any cushions. I suppose you'll tell us the cows ate them.'

'Didn't you take everything down into the dungeons?' demanded Mrs Stick. 'Because that room's empty now. There's not a thing in it.'

'I didn't take anything down at all,' said Edgar, coming cautiously out of the dungeon entrance. 'I dropped the cushions just about where you're standing. What's happened to them?'

'Look 'ere!' said Mr Stick, in amazement. 'Who's been 'ere since we've been gone? Someone's taken the cushions and everything else too. Where have they put them?'

'Pa, it was the cows,' said Edgar, looking all round as if he expected to see cows walking off with cushions and silver and blankets.

'Shut up about the cows,' said Mrs Stick, suddenly losing her temper. 'For one thing there aren't any cows on this island, and that we do know, for we looked all over it this morning. What we heard last night must have been strange sort of echoes rumbling round. No, my boy – there's something funny about all this. Looks as if there *is* somebody on the island!'

A dismal howl came echoing up from below the ground. It was Stinker, terrified at being alone below, and not daring to come up.

'Poor lamb!' said Mrs Stick, who seemed much fonder of Stinker than of anyone else.

'What's up with him?'

Stinker let out an even more doleful howl, and Mrs Stick hurried down the steps to go to him. Mr Stick followed her, and Edgar lost no time in going after them.

'Quick!' said Julian, standing up. 'Come with me, Dick. We may just have time to get that trunk! Run!'

The two boys ran quickly down to the courtyard of the ruined castle. Each took a handle of the small trunk, and lifted it between them. They staggered back to George with it.

'We'll take it to the cave,' whispered Julian. 'You stay here a few minutes and see what happens.'

The boys went over the cliff with the trunk. George flattened herself behind her bush and watched. Mr Stick appeared again in a few minutes, and looked round for the trunk. His mouth fell open in astonishment when he saw that it was gone. He yelled down the entrance to the dungeon.

'Clara! The trunk's gone!'

Mrs Stick was already on her way up, with Stinker close beside her and Edgar just behind. She climbed out and stared round.

'Gone?' she said, in enormous surprise. 'Gone! Where's it gone?'

'That's what *I'd* like to know!' said Mr Stick. 'We leave it here a few minutes – and then it goes. Walks off by itself – just like all the other things!'

'Look here! There's someone on this island,' said Mrs Stick. 'And I'm going to find out who it is. Got your gun, Pa?'

'I have,' said Mr Stick, slapping his belt. 'You get a good stout stick too, and we'll take Tinker. If we don't ferret out whoever's trying to spoil our plans, my name's not Stick!'

George slipped away quietly to warn the others. Before she slid down the rope into the cave, she pulled several bramble sprays across the hole. She dropped down to the floor of the cave, and told the others what had happened.

Julian had been trying to open the trunk, but it was still locked. He looked up as George panted out her tale.

'We'll be all right here so long as no one falls down that hole in the roof!' he said. 'Now keep quiet everyone, and don't you dare to growl, Timmy!'

Nothing was heard for some time, and then Stinker's bark came in the distance. 'Quiet now,' said Julian. 'They are near here.'

The Sticks were up on the cliff once more, searching carefully behind every bush. They came to the great bush behind which the children often hid, and saw the flattened grass there.

'Someone's been here,' said Mr Stick. 'I wonder if they're in the middle of this bush – it's thick enough to hide half an army! I'll try and force my way in, Clara, while you stand by with my gun.'

Edgar wandered off by himself while this was happening, feeling certain that nobody would be foolish enough to live in the middle of such a prickly bush. He walked across the cliff – and then, to his awful horror, he found himself falling! His legs disappeared into a hole, he clutched at some thorny sprays but could not save himself. Down he went and down and down – and down – crash!

Edgar had fallen down the hole in the roof of the cave. He suddenly appeared before the children's startled eyes, and landed in a heap on the soft sand. Timmy at once pounced on him with a fearsome growl, but George pulled him off just in time.

Edgar was half-stunned with fright and his fall. He lay on the floor of the cave, groaning, his eyes shut. The children stared at him and then at one another. For a few moments they were completely taken aback and didn't know what to do or say. Timmy growled ferociously – so ferociously that Edgar opened his eyes in fright. He stared round at the four children and their dog in the utmost surprise and horror.

He opened his mouth to yell for help, but at once found Julian's large hand over it. 'Yell just once and Timmy shall have a bite out of any part of you he likes!' said Julian, in a voice as ferocious as Timothy's growl. 'See? Like to try it? Timmy's waiting to bite.'

'I shan't yell,' said Edgar, speaking in such a low whisper that the others could hardly hear him. 'Keep that dog off. I shan't yell.'

George spoke to Timothy. 'Now you listen,

Timothy – if this boy shouts, you just go for him! Lie
here by him and show him your big teeth. Bite him
wherever you like if he yells.'

'Woof!' said Timmy, looking really pleased. He lay
down by Edgar, and the boy tried to move away. But
Timmy came nearer every time he moved.

Edgar looked round at the children. 'What are you
doing on this island?' he said. 'We thought you'd gone
home.'

'It's *our* island!' said George, in a very fierce voice.
'We've every right to be on it if we want to – but you
have no right at all. None! What are you and your
father and mother here for?'

'Don't know,' said Edgar, looking sulky.

'You'd better tell us,' said Julian. 'We know you're
in league with smugglers.'

Edgar looked startled. 'Smugglers?' he said. 'I didn't
know that. Pa and Ma don't tell me anything. I don't
want anything to do with smugglers.'

'Don't you know *any*-thing?' said Dick. 'Don't you
know why you've come to Kirrin Island?'

'I don't know anything,' said Edgar, in an injured
tone. 'Pa and Ma are mean to me. They never tell me
anything. I do as I'm told, that's all. I don't know
anything about smugglers, I tell you that.'

It was quite plain to the children that Edgar really
did not know anything of the reasons for his parents
coming to the island. 'Well, I'm not surprised they
don't let Spotty-Face into their secrets,' said Julian.
'He'd blab them if he could, I bet. Anyway, we know
it's smuggling they're mixed up in.'

'You let me go,' said Edgar, sullenly. 'You've got
no right to keep me here.'

'We're not going to let you go,' said George at once.

'You're our prisoner now. If we let you go back to your parents, you'd tell them all about us, and we don't want them to know we're here. We're going to spoil their pretty plans, you see.'

Edgar saw. He saw quite a lot of things. He felt rather sick. 'Was it you that took the cushions and things?'

'Oh no, dear Edgar,' said Dick. 'It was the cows, wasn't it? Don't you remember how you told your mother about the hundreds of cows that mooed at you and threw things and stole the cushions you dropped? Surely you haven't forgotten your cows already?'

'Funny, aren't you?' said Edgar, sulkily. 'What you going to do with me? I won't stay here, that's flat.'

'But you will, Spotty-Face,' said Julian. 'You will stay here till we let you go – and that won't be till we've cleared up this little smuggling mystery. And let me warn you that any nonsense on your part will be punished by Timmy.'

'Lot of beasts you are,' said Edgar, seeing that he could do nothing but obey the four children. 'My pa and ma won't half be furious with you.'

His ma and pa were feeling extremely astonished. There had, of course, been nobody hiding in the big thick bush, and when Mr Stick had wriggled out, scratched and bleeding, he had looked round for Edgar. And Edgar was not to be seen.

'Where's that dratted boy?' he said, and shouted for him. 'Edgar! ED-GAR!'

But Edgar did not answer. The Sticks spent a very long time looking for Edgar, both above ground and underground. Mrs Stick was convinced that poor Edgar was lost in the dungeons, and she tried to send Stinker to find him. But Stinker only went as far as the first cave. He remembered the peculiar noises of the night before and was not at all keen on exploring the dungeons.

Julian turned his attention to the little trunk, once Edgar had been dealt with. 'I'm going to open this somehow,' he said. 'I'm sure it's got smuggled goods in, though goodness knows what.'

'You'll have to smash the locks then,' said Dick. Julian got a small rock and tried to smash the two locks. He managed to wrench one open after a while, and then the other gave way too. The children threw back the lid.

On the top was a child's blanket, embroidered with white rabbits. Julian pulled it off, expecting to see the smuggled goods below. But to his astonishment there were a child's clothes!

He pulled them out. There were two blue jerseys, a blue skirt, some vests and knickers and a warm coat. At the bottom of the trunk were some dolls and a teddy bear!

'Golly!' said Julian, in amazement. 'What are all these for? Why did the Sticks bring these to the island – and why did the smugglers hide them in the wreck? It's a puzzler!'

Edgar appeared to be as astonished as the rest. He too had expected valuable goods of some kind. George and Anne pulled out the dolls. They were lovely ones. Anne cuddled them up to her. She loved dolls, though George scorned them.

'Who do they belong to?' she said. 'Oh won't they be sad not to have them! Julian, isn't it funny? *Why* should anyone bring a trunk full of clothes and dolls to Kirrin Island?'

19   A scream in the night

Nobody could even guess the answers to Anne's surprised questions. The children stared into the trunk and puzzled over it. It seemed such a funny thing to smuggle. They remembered the other things in the wreck too – the tins of food. They were peculiar things to smuggle on to the island. There didn't seem any point in it.

'Funny,' said Dick, at last. 'It beats me. There's no doubt that strange things are afoot here, or the Sticks wouldn't be hanging around our island. And we've seen signals from a ship out to sea. Something's going on. We thought if we opened this trunk it might help us – but it's only made the mystery deeper.'

Just then the voices of the two parent Sticks could be heard shouting for Edgar. But Edgar did not dare to shout back. Timmy's nose was poked against his leg. He might be nipped at any time. Timmy growled every now and again to remind Edgar that he was still there.

'Do you know anything about the ship that signals to this island at night?' asked Julian, turning to Edgar.

The boy shook his head. 'Never heard of any signals,' he said. 'I just heard my mother saying that she expected the *Roamer* tonight, but I don't know what she meant.'

'The *Roamer*?' said George, at once. 'What's that – a

man – or a boat – or what?'

'I don't know,' said Edgar. 'I'd only have got a clip on the ear if I'd asked. Find out yourself.'

'We will,' said Julian, grimly. 'We'll watch out for the *Roamer* tonight! Thanks for the information.'

The children spent a quiet and rather boring day in the cave – all but Anne, who had plenty of things to arrange again. Really, the cave looked most home-like when she had finished! She put the blankets on the bed, and used the rugs as carpets. So the cave really looked most imposing!

Edgar was not allowed to go out of the cave, and Timothy didn't leave him for a moment. He slept most of the time, complaining that 'those cows and things' had frightened him so much the night before that he'd not been able to sleep a wink.

The others discussed their plans in low voices. They decided to keep watch on the cliff-top, two and two together, that night. They would wait and see what happened. If the *Roamer* came, they would hurriedly make fresh plans then.

The sun sank. The night came up dark over the sea. Edgar snored softly, after a very good supper of sardines, corned beef sandwiches, tinned apricots and tinned milk. Anne and Dick went up to keep the first watch. It was about half-past ten.

At half-past twelve Julian and George climbed up the knotted rope and joined the other two. They had nothing to report. They went down into the cave, got into their comfortable beds and went to sleep. Edgar was snoring away in his corner, Timmy still on guard.

Julian and George looked out to sea, watching for any sign of a ship. The moon was up that night, and things were not quite so dark. Suddenly they heard

low voices, and saw shadowy figures down by the
rocks below.

'The two Sticks,' whispered Julian. 'Going to row
out to the wreck again, I suppose.'

There was the splash of oars, and the children saw a
boat move out over the water. At the same time
George nudged Julian violently and pointed out to sea.
A light was being shown a good way out, from a ship
that the children could barely see. Then the moon
went behind a cloud, and they could see nothing for
some time.

They watched breathlessly. Was that shadowy ship
a good way out the *Roamer*? Or was the owner of it the
'*Roamer*'? Were the smugglers at work tonight?

'There's another boat coming – look!' said George.
'It must be coming from that ship out to sea. Now the
moon has come out again, you can just see it. It is
going to the old wreck. It must be a meeting-place, I
should think.'

Then, most irritatingly, the moon went behind a
cloud again, and remained there so long that the
children grew impatient. At last it sailed out again and
lit up the water.

'Both boats are leaving the wreck now,' said Julian
excitedly. 'They've had their meeting – and passed
over the smuggled goods, I suppose – and now one
boat is returning to the ship, and the other, the Sticks'
boat, is coming back here with the goods. We'll follow
the Sticks when they get back and see where they put
the goods.'

After a long time the Sticks' boat came to shore
again. The children could not see anything then, but
presently they saw the Sticks going back towards the
castle. Mr Stick carried what looked like a large

bundle, flung over his shoulder. They could not see if Mrs Stick carried anything.

The Sticks went into the courtyard of the castle, and came to the dungeon entrance. 'They're taking the smuggled goods down there,' whispered Julian to George. The children were now watching from behind a nearby wall. 'We'll go back and tell the others, and make some more plans. We must somehow or other get those goods ourselves, and take them back to the mainland and get in touch with the police!'

Just then a scream rang out in the night. It was a high-pitched, terrified scream, and frightened the watching children very much. They had no idea where it came from.

'Quick! It must be Anne!' said Julian, and the two ran as fast as they could to the hole that led down to the cave. They dropped down the rope and Julian looked round the quiet cave anxiously. What had happened to Anne to make her scream like that?

But Anne was peacefully asleep on her bed, and so was Dick. Edgar still snored and Timmy watched, his eyes gleaming green.

'Funny,' said Julian, still startled. 'Awfully funny. Who screamed like that? It couldn't possibly have been Anne – because if she had screamed in her sleep like that, she would have woken the others.'

'Well, who screamed, then?' said George, feeling rather scared. 'Wasn't it weird, Julian? I didn't like it. It was somebody who was awfully frightened. But who could it be?'

They woke Dick and Anne and told them about the strange scream. Anne was very startled. Dick was interested to hear that two boats had met at the wreck, and that the Sticks had brought back smuggled goods of some sort, and taken them down in the dungeons.

'We'll get those tomorrow, somehow!' he said, cheerfully. 'We'll have good fun.'

'Why did you think it was me screaming?' asked Anne. 'Did you think it was a girl screaming?'

'Yes. It sounded like the scream you give when one of us jumps out at you suddenly,' said Julian.

'It's funny,' said Anne. She cuddled down into her bed again, and George got in beside her.

'Oh Anne!' said George, in disgust. 'You've got our bed simply *full* of those dolls – and that teddy bear is here too! You really are a baby!'

'No, I'm not,' said Anne. 'The dolls and the bear are babies – they are frightened and lonely because they're not with the little girl they belong to. So I had them in bed with me instead! I'm sure the little girl would be glad.'

'The little girl!' said Julian, slowly. 'We thought we heard a little girl scream tonight – we found a small trunk full of a little girl's clothes, and a little girl's dolls. What does it all mean?'

There was a silence – and then Anne spoke excitedly. 'I know! The smuggled goods are a little girl! They've stolen a little girl away – and these are her dolls, and those over there are her clothes that were stolen at the same time, for her to dress in and play with. The little girl's here, on this island now – you heard her scream tonight when those horrid Sticks carried her down into the dungeons!'

'Well – I do believe Anne has hit on the right idea,' said Julian. 'Clever girl, Anne! I think you're right. It isn't smugglers who are using this island – it's kidnappers!'

'What are kidnappers?' said Anne.

'People who steal away children or grown-ups and hide them somewhere till a large sum of money is paid out for them,' explained Julian. 'It's called a ransom. Till the ransom is paid, the prisoner is held by the captors.'

'Well, that's what's happened here then!' said George.

'I bet it has! Some poor little rich girl has been stolen away – and brought to the wreck by boat from some ship – and taken over by those horrible Sticks. Wicked creatures!'

'And we heard the poor little thing scream just as she was taken down underground,' said George. 'Julian, we've got to rescue her.'

'Yes, of course,' said Julian. 'We will, never fear! We'll rescue her tomorrow.'

Edgar woke up and joined in the conversation suddenly. 'What you talking about?' he said. 'Rescue who?'

'Never you mind,' said Julian.

George nudged him and whispered.

'All I hope is that Mrs Stick is feeling as upset about losing her dear Edgar as the mother of the little girl,' she said.

'Tomorrow we find the little girl somehow, and take her away,' said Julian. 'I expect the Sticks will be on guard, but we'll find a way.'

'I'm tired now,' said George, lying down. 'Let's go to sleep. We'll wake up nice and fresh. Oh Anne, do put these dolls your side. I'm lying on at least three.'

Anne took the dolls and the bear and arranged them on her side of the bed. 'Don't feel lonely,' George heard her say. 'I'll look after you all right till you go back to your own mistress. Sleep tight!'

Soon they all slept – all but Timothy, who lay with one eye open all night long. There was no need to put anyone on guard while Timmy was there. He was the best guardian they could have.

20   A rescue – and a new prisoner!

The next day Julian was awake early and went up the rope to the cliff-top to see if the Sticks were about. He saw them coming up the steps that led from the dungeons. Mrs Stick looked pale and worried.

'We've got to find our Edgar,' she kept saying to Mr Stick. 'I tell you we've got to find our Edgar. He's not down in the dungeons. That I do know. We've yelled ourselves hoarse down there.'

'And he's not on the island,' said Mr Stick. 'We hunted all over it yesterday. I think whoever was here then, took our goods, caught Edgar, and made off with him and everything else in their boat. That's what I think.'

'Well, they've taken him to the mainland then,' said Mrs Stick. 'We'd better take our boat and go back there and ask a few questions. What I'd like to know is – who is it messing about here and interfering with our plans? It makes me scared. Just when things are going nicely too!'

'Is it all right to leave here just now?' said Mr Stick, doubtfully. 'Suppose whoever was here yesterday is still here – they might pop down into the dungeons when we're gone.'

'Well, they're not here,' said Mrs Stick, firmly. 'Use your common sense, if you've got any – wouldn't our Edgar yell the place down if he was being kept prisoner

on this little island – and wouldn't we hear him? I tell
you he must have been taken off in a boat, together
with all the other things that are gone. And I don't like
it.'

'All right, all right!' said Mr Stick, in a grumbling
tone. 'That boy's always a nuisance – always in silly
trouble of some sort.'

'How can you talk of poor Edgar like that?' cried
Mrs Stick. 'Do you think the poor child *likes* being
captured! Goodness knows what he's going through –
feeling frightened and lonely without me.'

Julian felt disgusted. Here was Mrs Stick talking like
that about old Spotty-Face – and yet she had a little girl
down in the dungeons – a child much younger than
Edgar! What a beast she was.

'What about Tinker?' said Mr Stick, in a sulky tone.
'Better leave him here, hadn't we, to guard the entrance to the dungeons? Not that there will be anyone
here, if what you say is right.'

'Oh, we'll leave Tinker,' said Mrs Stick, setting off
to the boat. Julian saw them embark, leaving the dog
behind. Tinker watched them rowing away, his tail
well down between his legs. Then he turned and ran
back to the courtyard, and lay down dolefully in the
sun. He was very uneasy. His ears were cocked and he
kept looking this way and that. He didn't like this
strange island and its unexpected noises.

Julian tore back to the cave and dropped down the
rope, startling Edgar very much. 'Come outside
the cave and I'll tell you my plans,' said Julian to the
others. He didn't want Edgar to hear them. They all
went outside. Anne had got breakfast ready while
Julian had been gone, and the kettle was boiling away
merrily on the little stove.

'Listen!' said Julian. 'The Sticks have gone off in their boat back to the mainland to see if they can find their precious little darling Edgar. Mrs Stick is all hot and bothered because she thinks someone's gone off with him and she's afraid the poor boy will be feeling frightened and lonely!'

'*Well*!' said George. 'Doesn't she think that the little kidnapped girl must be feeling much worse? What a horrid woman she is!'

'You're right,' said Julian. 'Well, what I propose to do is this – we'll go down into the dungeons now and rescue the little girl – and bring her here to our cave for breakfast. Then we'll take her off in our boat, go to the police, find out where her parents are, and telephone to them that she is safe.'

'What shall we do with Edgar?' said Anne.

'*I* know!' said George at once. 'We'll put Edgar into the dungeon instead of the little girl! Think how astonished the Sticks will be to find the little girl gone – and their dear Edgar shut up in the dungeon instead!'

'Oooh! – that *is* a good idea,' said Anne, and all the others laughed and agreed.

'You stay here, Anne, and cut some more bread and butter for the little girl,' said Julian. He knew that Anne hated going down into the dungeons.

Anne nodded, pleased.

'All right, I will. I'll just take the kettle off for a bit too, or else the water will boil away.'

They all went back into the cave. 'Come with us, Edgar,' said Julian. 'You come too, Timmy.'

'Where're you going to take me?' said Edgar, suspiciously.

'A nice cosy, comfortable place, where cows can't get at you,' said Julian. 'Come on! Buck up.'

'Gr-r-r-r-r-r,' said Timmy, his nose against Edgar's leg. Edgar got up in a hurry.

They all went up the rope, one after another, though Edgar was terribly scared, and was sure he couldn't. But with Timmy snapping at his ankles below, he climbed up the rope remarkably quickly, and was hauled out at the top by Julian.

'Now, quick march!' said Julian, who wanted to get everything over before the Sticks thought of returning. And quick march it was, over the cliffs, over the low wall of the castle, and down into the courtyard.

'I'm not going down into those dungeons with you,' said Edgar, in alarm.

'You are, Spotty-Face,' said Julian, amiably.

'Where's my Pa and Ma?' said Edgar, looking anxiously all round.

'Those cows have got them, I expect,' said George. 'The ones that came and mooed at you and threw things, you know.'

Everyone giggled, except Edgar, who looked worried and pale. He did not like this kind of adventure at all. The children came to the dungeon entrance, and found that the Sticks had not only closed down the stone that opened the way to the dungeons, but had also dragged heavy rocks across it.

'Blow your parents!' said Julian, to Edgar. 'Making a lot of trouble for everybody. Come on, stir yourself – all hands to these stones. Edgar, pull when we pull. Go on! You'll get into trouble if you don't.'

Edgar pulled with the rest, and one by one the rocks were moved away. Then the heavy trapdoor stone was hauled up too, and the flight of steps was exposed leading down into darkness.

'There's Tinker!' suddenly cried Edgar, pointing to

a bush some distance away. Tinker was there, hiding, quite terrified at seeing Timothy again.

'Fat lot of good Stinker is,' said Julian. 'No, Timmy – you're not to eat him. Stay here! He wouldn't taste nice if you did eat him!'

Timothy was sorry not to be able to chase Stinker round and round the island. If he couldn't chase rabbits, he might at least be allowed to chase Stinker!

They all went down into the dungeons. Julian's white chalk-marks were still on the rocky walls, so it was easy to find the way to the cave-like room where the children, last summer, had found piles of golden ingots. They felt sure that the little kidnapped girl had been put there, for this cave had a big wooden door that could be bolted on the outside.

They came to the door. It was well and truly bolted. There was no sound from inside. Everyone halted outside and Timmy scratched at the door, whining gently. He knew there was someone inside.

'Hallo, there!' shouted Julian, in a loud and cheerful voice. 'Are you all right? We've come to rescue you.'

There was a scrambling noise, as if someone had got up from a stool. Then a small voice sounded from the cave.

'Hallo! Who are you? Oh, do please rescue me! I'm so lonely and frightened!'

'Just undoing the door!' called back Julian, cheerfully. 'We're all children out here, so don't be afraid. You'll soon be safe.'

He shot back the bolts, and flung open the door. Inside the cave, which was lit by a lantern, stood a small girl, with a scared little white face, and large dark eyes. Dark red hair tumbled round her cheeks, and she had evidently been crying bitterly, for her face was dirty and tear-stained.

Dick went to her and put his arm round her. 'Everything's all right now,' he said. 'You're safe. We'll take you back to your mother.'

'I do want her, I do, I do,' said the little girl, and tears ran down her cheeks again. 'Why am I here? I don't like being here.'

'Oh, it's just an adventure you've had,' said Julian. 'It's over now – at least, nearly over. There's still a bit of it left – a nice bit, though. We want you to come and have breakfast with us in our cave. We've a lovely cave.'

'Oh, have you?' said the little girl, rubbing her eyes. 'I want to go with you, I like you, but I didn't like those other people.'

'Of course you didn't,' said George. 'Look! This is Timothy, our dog. He wants to be friends with you.'

'What a simply lovely dog!' said the little girl, and flung her arms around Timmy's neck. He licked her in delight. George was pleased. She put her arm round the little girl.

'What's your name?' she said.

'Jennifer Mary Armstrong,' said the little girl. 'What's yours?'

'George,' said George, and the little girl nodded, thinking that George was a boy, not a girl, for she was dressed in jeans just like Julian and Dick, and her hair was short, too, though very curly.

The others told her their names – and then she looked at Edgar, who had said nothing.

'This is Spotty-Face,' said Julian. 'He isn't a friend of ours. It was his father and mother who put you here, Jennifer. Now we are going to leave him here in your place. It will be such a pleasant surprise for them, won't it?'

Edgar gave a yell of dismay and tried to back away – but Julian gave him a strong shove that sent him flying into the cave.

'There's only one way to teach people like you and your parents that wickedness doesn't pay!' said the boy, grimly. 'And that is to punish you hard. People like you don't understand kindness. You think it's just being soft and silly. All right – you can have a taste of what Jennifer has had. It will do you good, and do your parents a lot of good too! Good-bye!'

Edgar began to howl dismally as Julian bolted the big wooden door top and bottom. 'I shall starve!' he wailed.

'Oh no, you won't,' said Julian. 'There's plenty of food and water in there, so help yourself. It would do you good to go hungry for a while, all the same.'

'Mind the cows don't get you!' called Dick, and he gave a realistic moo that startled Jennifer very much, for the echoes came mooing round too.

'It's all right – only the echoes,' said George, smiling at her in the torch-light. Edgar howled away in the cave, sobbing like a baby.

'Little coward, isn't he?' said Julian. 'Come on – let's get back. I'm awfully hungry for my breakfast.'

'So am I,' said Jennifer, slipping her small hand into Julian's. 'I wasn't hungry at all in that cave – but now I am. Thank you for rescuing me.'

'Don't mention it,' said Julian, grinning at her. 'It's a real pleasure – and an even greater one to put old Spotty-Face there instead of you. Nice to give the Sticks a dose of their own medicine.'

Jennifer didn't know what he meant, but the others

did, and they chuckled. They made their way back through the dark, musty passages of the dungeons, passing many caves, big and small, on the way. They came at last to the flight of steps and went up them into the dazzling sunlight.

'Oh!' said Jennifer, breathing in great gulps of the fresh, sea-smelling air. 'Oh! This is lovely! Where am I?'

'On our island,' said George. 'And this is our ruined castle. You were brought here last night in a boat. We heard you scream, and that's how we guessed you were being made a prisoner.'

They walked to the cliff, and Jennifer was amazed at the way they disappeared down the knotted rope. She was eager to try too, and soon slid down into the cave.

'Nice kid, isn't she?' said Julian to George. 'My word, she's had even more of an adventure than we have!'

21 A visit to the police station

Anne liked Jennifer very much, and gave her a hug and a kiss. Jennifer looked round the well-furnished cave in amazement and wonder – and then she gave a scream of surprise and joy. She pointed to Anne's neatly-made bed, on which sat a number of beautiful dolls, and a large teddy-bear.

'My dolls!' she said. 'Oh, and Teddy, too! Oh, oh, where did you get them? I've missed them so! Oh Josephine and Angela and Rosebud and Marigold, have you missed me?'

She flung herself on the dolls. Anne was very interested to hear their names. 'I've looked after them well,' she told Jennifer. 'They're quite all right.'

'Oh, thank you,' said the little girl, happily. 'I do think you're all nice. Oh, I say – what a lovely breakfast!'

It was. Anne had opened a tin of salmon, two tins of peaches, a tin of milk, cut some bread and butter, and made a big jug of cocoa. Jennifer sat down and began to eat. She was very hungry, and as she ate, she began to lose her paleness and look rosy and happy.

The children talked busily as they ate. Jennifer told them about herself.

'I was playing in the garden with my nanny,' she said, 'and suddenly, when nanny had gone indoors to fetch something, a man climbed over the wall, threw a shawl round my head, and took me away. We live by the sea, you know, and I soon heard the sound of the waves splashing on the shore, and I knew I was being put into a boat. I was taken to a big ship, and locked down in a cabin for two days. Then I suppose I was brought here one night. I was so frightened that I screamed.'

'That was the scream we heard,' said George. 'It was lucky we heard it. We had thought there was smuggling going on here, in our island – we didn't guess it was a case of kidnapping, till we heard you scream – though we had found your trunk with your clothes and toys.'

'I don't know how the man got those,' said Jennifer. 'Maybe one of our maids helped him. There was one I didn't like at all. She was called Sarah Stick.'

'Ah!' said Julian, at once. 'That's the one, then! It was Mr and Mrs Stick who brought you here. Sarah Stick, your maid, must be some relation of theirs. They must have been in the pay of someone else, I should think – someone who had a ship, and could bring you here to hide you.'

'Jolly good hiding-place, too,' said George. 'No one but us would ever have found it out.'

They ate all their breakfast, made some more cocoa, and discussed their future plans.

'We'll take our boat and go to the mainland this morning,' said Julian. 'We'll go straight to the police-station with Jennifer. I expect the newspapers are full of her disappearance, and the police will recognise her at once.'

'I hope they catch the Sticks,' said George. 'I hope they won't disappear into thin air as soon as they hear that Jennifer is found.'

'Yes – we must warn the police of that,' said Julian, thoughtfully. 'Better not spread the news abroad till the Sticks are caught. I wonder where they are?'

'Let's get the boat now,' said Dick. 'There's no point in waiting about. Jennifer's parents will be thrilled to know she is safe.'

'I don't really want to leave this lovely cave,' said Jennifer, who was thoroughly enjoying herself now. I wish I lived here, too. Are you going to come back to the island and live here, Julian?'

'Well, we shall come back for a few days more, I expect,' said Julian. 'You see, our aunt's home is empty at the moment because she is away ill and our uncle is with her. So we might as well stay on our island till they come back.'

'Oh, *could* I come back with you?' begged Jennifer, her small round face alight with joy at the thought of living in a cave on an island with these nice children and their lovely dog. 'Oh, do let me! I would so like it. And I do so love Timmy.'

'I don't expect your parents would let you, especially after you've just been kidnapped,' said Julian. 'But you can ask them, if you like.'

They all went to the boat and got in. Julian pushed off. George steered the boat in and out of the rocks. They saw the wreck, which interested Jenny very much indeed. She badly wanted to stop, but the others thought they ought to get to land as quickly as possible.

Soon they were near the beach. Alf, the fisher-boy was there. He saw them and waved. He ran to help them to pull in their boat.

'I was coming out in my boat this morning,' he said. 'Your father's back, Master George. But not your mother. She's getting better, they say, and will be back in a week's time.'

'Well, what's my father come back for?' demanded George, in surprise.

'He got worried because nobody answered the telephone,' explained Alf. 'He came down and asked me where you all were. I didn't tell him, of course. I kept your secret. But I was just coming out to warn you this morning. He got back last night – and wasn't he wild? No one there to give him any food – all the house upside down and half the things gone! He's at the police station now.'

'Golly!' said George. 'That's just where *we* are going too! We shall meet him there. Oh dear, I do hope he won't be in an awful temper. You just can't do anything with my father when he's cross.'

'Come on!' said Julian. 'It's a good thing, in a way, that your father is here, George – we can explain everything to him and to the police at the same time.'

They left Alf, who looked very surprised to see Jennifer with the others. He couldn't make out where she had come from. Certainly she had not started out to the island with them – but she had come back in their boat. How was that? It seemed very mysterious to Alf.

The children arrived at the police station and marched in, much to the surprise of the policeman there.

'Hallo!' he said. 'What's the matter? Been doing a burglary, or something, and come to own up?'

'Listen!' said George, suddenly, hearing a loud voice in the room next to theirs. 'That's Father's voice!'

She darted to the door. The policeman called to her, shocked. 'Now don't you go in there. The Inspector's

in there. Come over here special, he has, and mustn't
be interrupted.'

But George had flung open the door and gone
inside. Her father turned and saw her. He rose to his
feet. 'George! Where have you been? How dare you go
away like this and leave the house and everything! It's
been robbed right and left! I've just been telling the
Inspector about all the things that have been stolen.'

'Don't worry, Father,' said George. 'Really don't
worry. We've found them all. How's Mother?'

'Better, much better,' said her father, still looking
amazed and angry. 'Thank goodness I can go back and
tell her where you are. She kept asking me about you
all, and I had to keep saying you were all right, so as
not to worry her – but I hadn't any idea what was
happening to you or where you had gone. I feel very
displeased with you. Where were you?'

'On the island,' said George, looking rather sulky,
as she often did when her father was angry with her.
'Julian will tell you all about it.'

Julian came in, followed by Dick, Anne, Jennifer
and Timothy. The Inspector, a big, clever-looking
man with dark eyes under shaggy eyebrows, looked
at them all closely. When he saw Jennifer, he stared
hard – and then suddenly rose to his feet.

'What's your name, little girl?' he said.

'Jennifer Mary Armstrong,' said Jenny, in a surprised voice.

'Bless us all!' said the Inspector, in a startled voice.
'Here's the child the whole country is looking for – and
she walks in here as cool as a cucumber! Lands sakes,
where did she come from?'

'What do you mean?' said George's father, looking
surprised. 'What child is the whole country looking

for? I haven't read the papers for some days.'

'Then you don't know about little Jenny Armstrong being kidnapped?' said the Inspector, sitting down and pulling Jenny near him. 'She's the daughter of Harry Armstrong, the millionaire, you know. Well, somebody kidnapped her and wants a hundred thousand pounds ransom for her. My word, we've combed the country for her – and here she is, as merry as you please. Well, I'm blessed – this is the strangest thing I ever knew. Where have you been, little Missy?'

'On the island,' said Jenny. 'Julian – you tell it all.'

So Julian told the whole story from beginning to end. The policeman from outside came in, and took notes down as he spoke. Everyone listened in amazement. As for George's father, his eyes nearly fell out of his head. What adventures these children did have to be sure, and how well they managed everything!

'And do you happen to know who was the owner of the ship that brought little Miss Jenny along – the one that sent a boat off to the wreck and put her there for the Sticks to take?' asked the Inspector.

'No,' said Julian. 'All we heard was that the *Roamer* was coming that night.'

'A-HA!' said the Inspector, with great satisfaction in his voice. 'Aha and oho! We know the *Roamer* all right – a ship we've been watching for some time – owned by somebody we're very, very suspicious of – we think he's dabbling in a whole lot of shady deals. Now this is very good news indeed. The thing is – where are the Sticks – and how can we catch them red-handed, now you've got Miss Jenny out of their clutches? They'll probably deny everything.'

'I know how we could catch them,' said Julian, quickly. 'We've left their nasty son, Edgar, locked in the same dungeon where they put Jenny. If only one of us could pass the word to the Sticks, that that is where Edgar is, they'd go back to the island all right, and go right into the dungeons – so if you found them there, it wouldn't be much good them denying that they don't know anything about the island, and have never been there.'

'That would certainly make things a lot easier,' said the Inspector. He pressed a bell and another policeman came into the room. The Inspector gave him a full description of Mr and Mrs Stick, and told him to watch the countryside round about, and report when they were found.

'Then, Julian, you might like to go and have a little conversation with them about their son, Edgar,' said the Inspector, smiling. 'If they do go back to the island, we shall follow them, and get all the evidence we want. Thank you for your very great help. Now we must telephone to Jenny's parents and tell them she is safe.'

'She can come back to Kirrin Cottage with us,' said George's father, still looking rather dazed at all that had happened. 'I've got Joanna, our old cook, to come back for a while to put things straight, so there will be someone there to see to the children. They must all come back.'

'Well, Father,' said George, firmly, 'we will come back just for today, but we plan to spend another week on Kirrin Island till Mother comes back. She said we could, and we are having such a fine time there. Let Joanna stay at Kirrin Cottage and keep it in order and get it ready for Mother when she comes home – she won't want the bother of looking after us too. We can look after ourselves on the island.'

'I certainly think these children deserve a reward for the good work they have done,' remarked the Inspector, and that settled the matter.

'Very well,' said George's father, 'you can all go off to the island again – but you must be back when your mother returns, George.'

'Of course I will,' said George. 'I badly want to see Mother. But home isn't nice without her. I would rather be on our island.'

'And I want to be there, too,' said Jenny, unexpectedly. 'Ask my parents to come to Kirrin, please – so that I can ask them if I can go with the other children.'

'I'll do my best,' said the Inspector, grinning at the five children. They liked him very much. George's father stood up.

'Come along!' he said. 'I want my lunch. All this has made me feel hungry. We'll go and see if Joanna has got anything for us.'

Off they all went, talking nineteen to the dozen, making George's poor father feel quite bewildered. He always seemed to get into the middle of some adventure when these children were about!

22   Back to Kirrin Island!

Soon everyone was at Kirrin Cottage. Joanna, the old cook they had had before, gave them a good welcome, and listened to their adventures in astonishment, getting the lunch ready all the while.

It was while they were having lunch that Julian, looking out of the window, suddenly caught sight of a figure he knew very well – someone skulking along behind the hedge.

'Old Pa Stick!' he said, and jumped up. 'I'll go after him. Stay here, everyone.'

He went out of the house, ran round a corner and came face to face with Mr Stick.

'Do you want to know where Edgar is?' said Julian mysteriously.

Mr Stick looked startled. He stared at Julian not knowing what to say.

'He's down in the dungeons, locked in that cave,' said Julian, even more mysteriously.

'You don't know anything about Edgar,' said Mr Stick. 'Where have you been? Didn't you go home?'

'Never you mind,' said Julian. 'But if you want to find Edgar – look in that cave!'

Mr Stick gave the boy a glare and left him. Julian hurried indoors and rang up the police station. He felt sure that Mr Stick would tell Mrs Stick what he had said, and that Mrs Stick would insist on going back to the island to see if what he had said was true. So all that needed to be done was for the police to keep a watch on the boats along the shore and see when the Sticks left.

The children finished their dinner, and Uncle Quentin announced that he must return to his wife, who would want to know his news. 'I'll tell her you are having a fine time on the island,' he said, 'and we can tell her all the extraordinary details when she returns home, better.'

He left in a car, and the children wondered whether they might now return to their island or not. But they decided to wait a little, for they did not know what to do with Jennifer.

Very soon a large car drove up and stopped outside the gate of Kirrin Cottage. Out jumped a tall man with dark red hair, and a pretty woman. 'They must be your father and mother, Jenny,' said Julian.

They were – and Jennifer got so many hugs and kisses that she quite lost her breath. She had to tell her story again and again, and her father could not thank Julian and the others enough for all they had done.

'Ask me for any reward you like,' he said, 'and you can have it. I shall never, never be able to tell you how grateful I am to you for rescuing our little Jenny.'

'Oh – we don't want anything, thank you,' said Julian, politely. 'We enjoyed it all very much. We like adventures.'

'Ah, but you *must* tell me something you want!' said Jenny's father.

Julian glanced round at the others. He knew that none of them wanted a reward. Jenny nudged him hard and nodded her head vigorously. Julian laughed.

'Well,' he said, 'there *is* one thing we'd all like very much.'

'It's granted before you ask it!' said Jenny's father.

'Will you let Jenny come and spend a week with us on our island?' said Julian. Jenny gave a squeal and pressed Julian's arm very hard between her two small hands.

Jenny's parents looked rather taken-aback. 'Well,' said her father, 'well – she's just been kidnapped, you know – and we don't feel inclined to let her out of our sight at the moment – and . . .'

'You promised Julian you'd grant what he asked, you promised, Daddy,' said Jenny, urgently. 'Oh please do let me. I've always wanted to live on an island. And this one has got a perfectly marvellous cave, and a wonderful ruined castle, and the dungeons where I was kept, and –'

'And we take Timothy, our dog, with us,' said Julian. 'See what a big powerful fellow he is – nobody could come to much harm with Timmy about – could they, Tim?'

'Woof!' said Timothy, in his deepest voice.

'Well, you can go, Jenny, on one condition,' said the little girl's father at last, 'and that is that your mother and I come over tomorrow and spend the day on the island, to see that everything is all right for you.'

'Oh, thank you, thank you, Daddy!' cried Jenny, and danced round the room in delight. A whole week on the island with these new friends of hers, and Timmy the dog! What could be lovelier?

'Jenny can stay here the night, can't she?' said George. 'You'll be staying at the hotel, I suppose?'

Soon Jenny's parents left and went to the police station to get all the details of the kidnapping. The children went to see if Joanna was going to make cakes for tea.

Just about tea-time there came a knocking at the door. A large policeman stood outside.

'Is Julian here?' he said. 'Oh, you're the boy we want. The Sticks have just left for the island in their boat, and we've got ours on the beach to follow. But we don't think we know the way in and out of those hidden rocks that lie all round Kirrin Island. Could you or Miss Georgina guide us, do you think?'

'I'm Master George, not Miss Georgina,' said George in a cold voice.

'Sorry,' said the policeman, with a grin. 'Well, could you come too?'

'We'll all come!' said Dick, jumping up. 'I want to go back to the dear old island and sleep in our cave again tonight. Why should we miss a single night? We can fetch Jenny's people tomorrow in our own boat. We'll all come.'

The policeman was a little doubtful about the arrangement, but the children insisted, and as there was no time to waste, they all ended in crowding into the two boats, with three big policemen, George and Julian leading the way in their own boat. Timmy lay down at George's feet as usual.

George guided the boat as cleverly as ever, and soon they landed in the usual little sandy cove. The Sticks had evidently gone round by the wreck as usual, and landed on the rockier part.

'Now, no noise,' said Julian, warningly. They all went quietly towards the ruin, and came into the courtyard. There was no sign of the Sticks.

'We'll go down underground,' said Julian. 'I've got my torch. I expect the Sticks are down there already, letting out dear Edgar.'

They went down the steps into the dark dungeons.

Anne went too, this time, holding on to the hand of one of the big policemen. They moved quietly through the long, dark, winding passages.

They came at last to the door of the cave in which they had imprisoned Edgar. It was still bolted at the top and bottom!

'Look!' said Julian, in a whisper, shining his torch on to the door. 'The Sticks haven't been down here yet.'

'Sh!' said George, as Timmy growled softly. 'There's someone coming. Hide! It's the Sticks, I expect.'

They all hid behind the wall that ran nearby. They could hear footsteps coming nearer, and then the voice of Mrs Stick raised in anger.

'If my Edgar's locked in there, I'll have something to say about it! Locking up a poor innocent boy like that. I don't understand it. If he's there, where's the girl? You answer me that. Where's the girl? It's my belief that the boss has done some double-crossing to do us out of our share of the money. Didn't he say that he'd give us two thousand pounds if we kept Jenny Armstrong for a week? Now I think he must have sent someone to this island, played tricks on us, taken the girl himself and locked up our Edgar.'

'You may be right, Clara,' said Mr Stick, his voice coming nearer and nearer. 'But how did this boy Julian know where Edgar was? There's a lot I don't understand about all this.'

Now the Sticks were right at the door of the cave, with Stinker at their heels. Stinker smelt the others in hiding and whined in fear. Mr Stick kicked him.

'Stop it! It's enough to hear our own voices echoing away all round without your whines too!'

Mrs Stick was calling out loudly: 'Edgar! Are you there? Edgar!'

'Ma! Yes, I'm here!' yelled Edgar. 'Let me out, quick! I'm scared. Let me out!'

Mrs Stick undid the bolts at once and flung open the door. By the light of the lantern in the cave she saw Edgar. He ran to her, half-crying.

'Who put you here?' demanded Mrs Stick. 'You tell your Pa and he'll knock their heads off, won't you, Pa? Putting a poor frightened child into a dark cave like this. It's a wicked thing to do!'

Suddenly the Stick family had the fright of their lives – for a large policeman stepped out of the shadows, torch in one hand and notebook in the other!

'Ah!' said the policeman, in a deep voice. 'You're right, Clara Stick. To shut up a poor frightened child in that cave *is* a wicked thing to do – and that's what you did, isn't it? You put Jenny Armstrong there! She's only a little girl. This boy of yours knew he wasn't coming to any harm – but that little girl was scared to death!'

Mrs Stick stood there, opening and shutting her mouth like a goldfish, not finding a word to say. Mr Stick squealed like a rat caught in a corner.

'We're copped! It's a trap, that's it. We're copped!'

Edgar began to cry, sobbing like a four-year-old. The other children felt disgusted with him. The Sticks suddenly caught sight of all the children when Julian switched on his torch.

'Snakes alive, there's all the children – and there's Jenny Armstrong too!' said Mr Stick, in a tone of the greatest amazement. 'What's all this? What's happening? Who shut up Edgar?'

'We'll tell you the answers when we get to the

police-station,' said the big policeman. 'Now, are you coming quietly?'

The Sticks went quietly, Edgar sobbing away to himself. He imagined his mother and father in prison, and he himself sent to a hard and difficult school, not allowed to see his mother for years. Not that that would matter, for the Sticks, both mother and father, were no good to Edgar, and had taught him nothing but bad things. There might be a chance for the wretched boy if he were kept away from them, and set a good example instead of a bad one.

'We shan't be coming back with you,' said Julian, politely, to the policeman. 'We're staying here the night. You could go back in the Sticks's boat. They know the way all right. Take their dog with you. There he is – Stinker, we call him.' Then he added, 'I guess your colleagues could follow in the police boat!'

The Sticks's boat was found and the policeman, the two grown-up Sticks and Edgar got in. Stinker jumped in too, glad to get away from the glare of Timothy's green eyes.

Julian pushed the boat out. 'Good-bye!' he called, and the other children waved good-bye, too. 'Good-bye, Mr Stick, don't go kidnapping any more children. Good-bye, Mrs Stick, look after Edgar better, in case *he* gets kidnapped again! Good-bye, Spotty-Face, try and be a better boy! Good-bye, Stinker, do get a bath as soon as possible. Good-bye!'

The policemen grinned and waved. The Sticks said not a word, nor did they wave. They sat sullen and angry, trying to work out in their minds what had happened to make things end up like this.

The boats rounded a high rock and were soon out of sight. 'Hurrah!' said Dick. 'They've gone – gone for ever! We've got our island to ourselves at last. Come on, Jenny, we'll show you all over it! What a lovely time we're going to have.'

They raced away, happy and carefree, five children and a dog, alone on an island they loved. And we will leave them there to enjoy their week's happiness. They really do deserve it!

FIVE GO TO SMUGGLER'S TOP

ENID BLYTON

FIVE GO TO SMUGGLER'S TOP

KNIGHT BOOKS
Hodder and Stoughton

Printed and bound in Great Britain
for Hodder and Stoughton Chil-
dren's Books, a division of Hodder
and Stoughton Ltd., Mill Road,
Dunton Green, Sevenoaks, Kent
TN13 2YA. (Editorial Office: 47
Bedford Square, London WC1B
3DP) by Cox & Wyman Ltd.,
Reading, Berks. Photoset by
Rowland Phototypesetting Ltd.,
Bury St Edmunds, Suffolk.

British Library C.IP.

Blyton, Enid
Five Go To Smuggler's Top.–
(Blyton, Enid. Famous Five).
I. Title
823'.9'1J PZ7.B629

Contents

1 Back to Kirrin Cottage

One fine day, right at the beginning of the Easter holidays, four children and a dog travelled by train together.

'Soon be there now,' said Julian, a tall strong boy, with a determined face.

'Woof,' said Timothy the dog, getting excited, and trying to look out of the window too.

'Get down, Tim,' said Julian. 'Let Anne have a look.'

Anne was his younger sister. She put her head out of the window. 'We're coming into Kirrin Station!' she said. 'I do hope Aunt Fanny will be there to meet us.'

'Of course she will!' said Georgina, her cousin. She looked more like a boy than a girl, for she wore her hair very short, and it curled close about her head. She too had a determined face, like Julian. She pushed Anne away and looked out of the window.

'It's nice to be going home,' she said. 'I love school — but it will be fun to be at Kirrin Cottage and perhaps sail out to Kirrin Island and visit the castle there. We haven't been since last summer.'

'Dick's turn to look out now,' said Julian, turning to his younger brother, a boy with a pleasant face, sitting reading in a corner. 'We're just coming into sight of Kirrin, Dick. Can't you stop reading for a second?'

'It's such an exciting book,' said Dick, and shut it

with a clap. 'The most exciting adventure story I've ever read!'

'Pooh! I bet it's not as exciting as some of the adventures *we've* had!' said Anne, at once.

It was quite true that the five of them, counting in Timmy the dog, who always shared everything with them, had had the most amazing adventures together. But now it looked as if they were going to have nice quiet holidays, going for long walks over the cliffs, and perhaps sailing out in George's boat to their island of Kirrin.

'I've worked jolly hard at school this term,' said Julian. 'I could do with a holiday!'

'You've gone thin,' said Georgina. Nobody called her that. They all called her George. She would never answer to any other name. Julian grinned.

'Well, I'll soon get fat at Kirrin Cottage, don't you worry! Aunt Fanny will see to that. She's a great one for trying to fatten people up. It will be nice to see your mother again, George. She's an awfully good sort.'

'Yes. I hope Father will be in a good temper these hols,' said George. 'He ought to be because he has just finished some new experiments, Mother says, which have been quite successful.'

George's father was a scientist, always working out new ideas. He liked to be quiet, and sometimes he flew into a temper when he could not get the peace he needed or things did not go exactly as he wanted them to. The children often thought that hot-tempered Georgina was very like her father! She too could fly into fierce tempers when things did not go right for her.

Aunt Fanny was there to meet them. The four children jumped out on the platform and rushed to hug her. George got there first. She was very fond of her gentle mother, who had so often tried to shield her when her father got angry with her. Timmy pranced round, barking in delight. He adored George's mother.

She patted him, and he tried to stand up and lick her face. 'Timmy's bigger than ever!' she said, laughing. 'Down, old boy! You'll knock me over.'

Timmy was certainly a big dog. All the children loved him, for he was loyal, loving and faithful. His brown eyes looked from one to the other, enjoying the children's excitement. Timmy shared in it, as he shared in everything.

But the person he loved most, of course, was his mistress, George. She had had him since he was a small puppy. She took him to school with her each term, for she and Anne went to a boarding-school that allowed pets. Otherwise George would most certainly have refused to go!

They set off to Kirrin in the pony-trap. It was very windy and cold, and the children shivered and pulled their coats tightly round them.

'It's awfully cold,' said Anne, her teeth beginning to chatter. 'Colder than in the winter!'

'It's the wind,' said her aunt, and tucked a rug round her. 'It's been getting very strong the last day or two. The fishermen have pulled their boats high up the beach for fear of a big storm.'

The children saw the boats pulled right up as they passed the beach where they had bathed so often. They did not feel like bathing now. It made them shiver even to think of it.

The wind howled over the sea. Great scudding clouds raced overhead. The waves pounded on the beach and made a terrific noise. It excited Timmy, who began to bark.

'Be quiet, Tim,' said George, patting him. 'You will have to learn to be a good quiet dog now we are home again, or Father will be cross with you. Is Father very busy, Mother?'

'Very,' said her mother. 'But he's going to do very little work now you are coming home. He thought he would like to go for walks with you, or go out in the boat, if the weather calms down.'

The children looked at one another. Uncle Quentin was not the best of companions. He had no sense of humour, and when the children went off into fits of laughter, as they did twenty times a day or more, he could not see the joke at all.

'It looks as if these hols won't be quite so jolly if Uncle Quentin parks himself on us most of the time,' said Dick in a low voice to Julian.

'Sh,' said Julian, afraid that his aunt would hear, and be hurt. George frowned.

'Oh Mother! Father will be bored stiff if he comes with us – and we'll be bored too.'

George was very outspoken, and could never learn to keep a guard on her tongue. Her mother sighed. 'Don't talk like that, dear. I daresay your father will get tired of going with you after a bit. But it does him good to have a bit of young life about him.'

'Here we are!' said Julian, as the trap stopped outside an old house. 'Kirrin Cottage! My word, how the wind is howling round it, Aunt Fanny!'

'Yes. It made a terrible noise last night,' said his aunt. 'You take the trap round to the back, Julian, when we've got the things out. Oh, here's your uncle to help!'

Uncle Quentin came out, a tall, clever-looking man, with rather frowning eyebrows. He smiled at the children and kissed George and Anne.

'Welcome to Kirrin Cottage!' he said. 'I'm quite glad your mother and father are away, Anne, because now we shall have you all here once again!'

Soon they were sitting round the table eating a big tea. Aunt Fanny always got ready a fine meal for their first one, for she knew they were very hungry after their long journey in the train.

Even George was satisfied at last, and leaned back in her chair, wishing she could manage just one more of her mother's delicious new-made buns.

Timmy sat close to her. He was not supposed to be fed at meal-times but it was really surprising how many titbits found their way to him under the table!

The wind howled round the house. The windows rattled, the doors shook, and the mats lifted themselves up and down as the draught got under them.

'They look as if they've got snakes wriggling underneath them,' said Anne. Timmy watched them and growled. He was a clever dog, but he did not know why the mats wriggled in such a strange way.

'I hope the wind will die down tonight,' said Aunt Fanny. 'It kept me awake last night. Julian dear, you look rather thin. Have you been working hard? I must fatten you up.'

The children laughed. 'Just what we thought you'd say, Mother!' said George. 'Goodness, what's that?'

They all sat still, startled. There was a loud bumping noise on the roof, and Timmy put up his ears and growled fiercely.

'A tile off the roof,' said Uncle Quentin. 'How tiresome! We shall have to get the loose tiles seen to, Fanny, when the storm is over, or the rain will come in.'

The children rather hoped that their uncle would

retire to his study after tea, as he usually did, but this time he didn't. They wanted to play a game, but it wasn't much good with Uncle Quentin there. He really wasn't any good at all, not even at such a simple game as snap.

'Do you know a boy called Pierre Lenoir?' suddenly asked Uncle Quentin, taking a letter from his pocket. 'I believe he goes to your school and Dick's, Julian.'

'Pierre Lenoir – oh you mean old Sooty,' said Julian. 'Yes – he's in Dick's form. Mad as a hatter.'

'Sooty! Now why do you call him that?' said Uncle Quentin. 'It seems a silly name for a boy.'

'If you saw him you wouldn't think so,' said Dick, with a laugh. 'He's awfully dark! Hair as black as soot, eyes like bits of coal, eyebrows that look as if they've been put in with charcoal. And his name means "The black one", doesn't it? Le-noir – that's French for black.'

'Yes. Quite true. But what a name to give anyone – *Sooty!*' said Uncle Quentin. 'Well, I've been having quite a lot of correspondence with this boy's father. He and I are interested in the same scientific matters. In fact, I've asked him whether he wouldn't like to come and stay with me a few days – and bring his boy, Pierre.'

'Oh really!' said Dick, looking quite pleased. 'Well it wouldn't be bad sport to have old Sooty here, Uncle. But he's quite mad. He never does as he's told, he climbs like a monkey, and he can be awfully cheeky. I don't know if you'd like him much.'

Uncle Quentin looked sorry he had asked Sooty after he had heard what Dick had to say. He didn't like cheeky boys. Nor did he like mad ones.

'Hm,' he said, putting the letter away. 'I wish I'd asked you about the boy first, before suggesting to his father that he might bring him with him. But perhaps I can prevent him coming.'

'No, don't, Father,' said George, who rather liked the sound of Sooty Lenoir. 'Let's have him. He could come out with us and liven things up!'

'We'll see,' said her father, who had already made up his mind on no account to have the boy at Kirrin Cottage, if he was mad, climbed everywhere, and was cheeky. George was enough of a handful without a devil of a boy egging her on!

Much to the children's relief Uncle Quentin retired to read by himself about eight o'clock. Aunt Fanny looked at the clock.

'Time for Anne to go to bed,' she said. 'And you too, George.'

'Just one good game of Slap-Down Patience, all of us playing it together, Mother!' said George. 'Come on – you play it too. It's our first evening at home. Anyway, I shan't sleep for ages, with this gale howling round! Come on, Mother – one good game, then we'll go to bed. Julian's been yawning like anything already!'

2 A shock in the night

It was nice to climb up the steep stairs to their familiar bedrooms that night. All the children were yawning widely. Their long train journey had tired them.

'If only this awful wind would stop!' said Anne, pulling the curtain aside and looking out into the night. 'There's a little moon, George. It keeps bobbing out between the scurrying clouds.'

'Let it bob!' said George, scrambling into bed. 'I'm jolly cold. Hurry, Anne, or you'll catch a chill at that window.'

'Don't the waves make a noise?' said Anne, still at the window. 'And the gale in the old ash-tree is making a whistling, howling sound, and bending it right over.'

'Timmy, hurry up and get on my bed,' commanded George, screwing up her cold toes. 'That's one good thing about being at home, Anne. I can have Timmy on my bed! He's far better than a hot water bottle.'

'You're not supposed to have him on your bed at home, any more than you're supposed to at school,' said Anne, curling up in bed. 'Aunt Fanny thinks he sleeps in his basket over there.'

'Well, I can't stop him coming on my bed at night, can I, if he doesn't want to sleep in his basket?' said George. 'That's right, Timmy darling. Make my feet warm. Where's your nose? Let me pat it. Good-night, Tim. Good-night, Anne.'

'Good-night,' said Anne, sleepily. 'I hope that Sooty boy comes, don't you? He does sound fun.'

'Yes. And anyway Father would stay in with Mr Lenoir, the boy's father, and not come out with us,' said George. 'Father doesn't mean to, but he does spoil things somehow.'

'He's not very good at laughing,' said Anne. 'He's too serious.'

A loud bang made both girls jump. 'That's the bathroom door!' said George, with a groan. 'One of the boys must have left it open. That's the sort of noise that drives Father mad! There it goes again!'

'Well, let Julian or Dick shut it,' said Anne, who was now beginning to feel nice and warm. But Julian and Dick were thinking that George or Anne might shut it, so nobody got out of bed to see to the banging door.

Very soon Uncle Quentin's voice roared up the stairs, louder than the gale.

'Shut that door, one of you! How can I work with that noise going on?'

All four children jumped out of bed like a shot. Timmy leapt off George's bed. Everyone fell over him as they rushed to the bathroom door. There was a lot of giggling and scuffling. Then Uncle Quentin's footsteps were heard on the stairs and the five fled silently to their rooms.

The gale still roared. Uncle Quentin and Aunt Fanny came up to bed. The bedroom door flew out of Uncle Quentin's hand and slammed itself shut so violently that a vase leapt off a nearby shelf.

Uncle Quentin leapt too, startled. 'This wretched gale!' he said, fiercely. 'Never known one like it all the time we've been here. If it gets much worse the fishermen's boats will be smashed up, even though they've pulled them as high up the beach as possible.'

'It will blow itself out soon, dear,' said Aunt Fanny, soothingly. 'Probably by the time morning comes it will be quite calm.'

But she was wrong. The gale did not blow itself out that night. Instead it raged round the house even more fiercely, shrieking and howling like a live thing. No-body could sleep. Timmy kept up a continuous low growling, for he did not like the shakes and rattles and howls.

Towards dawn the wind seemed in a fury. Anne thought it sounded as if it was in a horrible temper, out to do all the harm it could. She lay and trembled, half-frightened.

Suddenly there was a strange noise. It was a loud and woeful groaning and creaking, like someone in great pain. The two girls sat up, terrified. What could it be?

The boys heard it too. Julian leapt out of bed and ran to the window. Outside stood the old ash tree, tall and black in the fitful moonlight. It was gradually bending over!

'It's the ash! It's falling!' yelled Julian, almost startling Dick out of his wits. 'It's falling, I tell you. It'll crash on the house! Quick, warn the girls!'

Shouting at the top of his voice, Julian raced out of his door on to the landing. 'Uncle! Aunt! George and Anne! Come downstairs quickly. The ash tree is falling!'

George jumped out of bed, snatched at her dressing-gown, and raced to the door, yelling to Anne. The little girl was soon with her. Timmy ran in front. At the door of Aunt Fanny's bedroom Uncle Quentin appeared, tall and amazed, wrapping his dressing-gown round him.

'What's all this noise? Julian, what's – ?'

'Aunt Fanny! Come downstairs – the ash tree is falling! Listen to its terrible groans and creaks!' yelled Julian, almost beside himself with impatience. 'It'll smash in the room and the bedrooms! Listen, here it comes!'

Everyone fled downstairs, as with an appalling wail, the great ash tree hauled up its roots and fell heavily on to Kirrin Cottage. There was a terrible crash, and the sound of tiles slipping to the ground everywhere.

'Oh dear!' said poor Aunt Fanny, covering her eyes. 'I knew something would happen! Quentin, we ought to have had that ash tree topped. I knew it would fall in a great gale like this. What has it done to the roof?'

After the great crash there had come other smaller noises, sounds of things falling, thuds and little smashing noises. The children could not imagine what was happening. Timmy was thoroughly angry, and barked loudly. Uncle Quentin slapped his hand angrily on the table, and made everyone jump.

'Stop that dog barking! I'll turn him out!' But nothing would stop Timmy barking or growling that night, and George at last pushed him into the warm kitchen, and shut the door on him.

'I feel like barking or growling myself,' said Anne, who knew exactly what Timmy felt like. 'Julian, has the tree broken in the roof?'

Uncle Quentin took a powerful torch and went carefully up the stairs to the landing to see what damage had been done. He came down looking rather pale.

'The tree has crashed through the attic, smashed the roof in, and wrecked the girls' bedroom,' he said. 'A big branch has penetrated the boys' room too, but not badly. But the girls' room is ruined! They would have been killed if they had been in their beds.'

Everyone was silent. It was an awful thought that George and Anne had had such a narrow escape.

'Good thing I yelled my head off to warn them, then,' said Julian, cheerfully, seeing how white Anne had gone. 'Cheer up, Anne – think what a tale you'll have to tell at school next term.'

'I think some hot cocoa would do us all good,' said Aunt Fanny, pulling herself together, though she felt very shaken. 'I'll go and make some. Quentin, see if the fire is still alight in your study. We want a little warmth!'

The fire was still alight. Everyone crowded round it. They welcomed Aunt Fanny when she came in with some steaming milk-cocoa.

Anne looked curiously round the room as she sat sipping her drink. This was where her uncle did his work, his very clever work. He wrote his difficult books here, books which Anne could not understand at all. He drew his weird diagrams here, and made many strange experiments.

But just at the moment Uncle Quentin did not look very clever. He looked rather ashamed, somehow. Anne soon knew why.

'Quentin, it is a mercy none of us was hurt or killed,' said Aunt Fanny, looking at him rather sternly. 'I told you a dozen times you should get that ash tree topped. I knew it was too big and heavy to withstand a great gale. I was always afraid it would blow down on the house.'

'Yes, I know, my dear,' said Uncle Quentin, stirring his cup of cocoa very vigorously. 'But I was so busy these last months.'

'You always make that an excuse for not doing urgent things,' said Aunt Fanny, with a sigh. 'I shall have to manage things myself in the future. I can't risk our lives like this!'

'Well, a thing like this would only happen once in a blue moon!' cried Uncle Quentin, getting angry. Then he calmed down, seeing that Aunt Fanny was really shocked and upset, very near to tears. He put down his cocoa and slipped his arm round her.

'You've had a terrible shock,' he said. 'Don't you worry about things. Maybe they won't be so bad when morning comes.'

'Oh, Quentin – they'll be much worse!' said his wife. 'Where shall we sleep tonight, all of us, and what shall we do till the roof and upstairs rooms are repaired? The children have only just come home. The house will be full of workmen for weeks! I don't know how I'm going to manage.'

'Leave it all to me!' said Uncle Quentin. 'I'll settle everything. Don't worry. I'm sorry about this, very sorry, particularly as it's my fault. But I'll straighten things out for everyone, you just see!'

Aunt Fanny didn't really believe him, but she was grateful for his comforting. The children listened in silence, drinking their hot cocoa. Uncle Quentin was so very clever, and knew so many things – but it was so like him to neglect something urgent like cutting off the top of the old ash tree. Sometimes he didn't seem to live in this world at all!

It was no use going up to bed! The rooms upstairs were either completely ruined, or so messed up with bits and pieces, and clouds of dust, that it was impossible to sleep there. Aunt Fanny began to pile rugs on sofas. There was one in the study, a big one in the sitting-room and a smaller one in the dining-room. She found a camp bed in a cupboard and, with Julian's help, put that up too.

'We'll just have to do the best we can,' she said.
'There isn't much left of the night, but we'll get a little
sleep if we can! The gale is not nearly so wild now.'

'No – it's done all the damage it can, so it's satisfied,'
said Uncle Quentin, grimly. 'Well, we'll talk things
over in the morning.'

The children found it very difficult to go to sleep
after such an excitement, tired though they were.
Anne felt worried. How could they all stay at Kirrin
Cottage now? It wouldn't be fair on Aunt Fanny. But
they couldn't go home because her father and mother
were both away and the house was shut up for a
month.

'I hope we shan't be sent back to school,' thought
Anne, trying to get comfortable on the sofa. 'It would
be too awful, after having left there, and starting off so
cheerfully for the holidays.'

George was afraid of that, too. She felt sure that they
would all be packed back to their schools the next
morning. That would mean that she and Anne
wouldn't see Julian and Dick any more these holidays,
for the boys, of course, went to a different school.

Timmy was the only one who didn't worry about
things. He lay on George's feet, snoring a little, quite
happy. So long as he was with George he didn't really
mind *where* he went!

3   Uncle Quentin has an idea

Next morning the wind was still high, but the fury of the gale was gone. The fishermen on the beach were relieved to find that their boats had suffered very little damage. But word soon went round about the accident to Kirrin Cottage, and a few sightseers came up to marvel at the sight of the great, uprooted tree, lying heavily on the little house.

The children rather enjoyed the importance of relating how nearly they had escaped with their lives. In the light of day it was surprising what damage the big tree had done. It had cracked the roof of the house like an eggshell, and the rooms upstairs were in a terrible mess.

The woman who came up from the village to help Aunt Fanny during the day exclaimed at the sight: 'Why, it'll take weeks to set that right!' she said. 'Have you got on to the builders? I'd get them up here right away and let them see what's to be done.'

'*I'm* seeing to things, Mrs Daly,' said Uncle Quentin. 'My wife has had a great shock. She is not fit to see to things herself. The first thing to do is to decide what is to happen to the children. They can't remain here while there are no usable bedrooms.'

'They had better go back to school, poor things,' said Aunt Fanny.

'No. I've a better idea than that,' said Uncle Quentin, fishing a letter out of his pocket. 'Much better. I've had a letter from that fellow Lenoir this morning – you know, the one who's interested in the same kind of experiments as I am. He says – er, wait a minute, I'll read you the bit. Yes here it is.'

Uncle Quentin read it out: 'It is most kind of you to suggest my coming to stay with you and bringing my boy Pierre. Allow me to extend hospitality to you and your children also. I do not know how many you have, but all are welcome here in this big house. My Pierre will be glad of company, and so will his sister, Marybelle.'

Uncle Quentin looked up triumphantly at his wife. 'There you are! I call that a most generous invitation! It couldn't have come at a better time. We'll pack the whole of the children off to this fellow's house.'

'But Quentin – you can't possibly do that! Why, we don't know anything about him or his family!' said Aunt Fanny.

'His boy goes to the same school as Julian and Dick, and I know Lenoir is a remarkable, clever fellow,' said Uncle Quentin, as if that was all that really mattered. 'I'll telephone him now. What's his number?'

Aunt Fanny felt helpless in the face of her husband's sudden determination to settle everything himself. He was ashamed because it was his forgetfulness that had brought on the accident to the house. Now he was going to show that he *could* see to things if he liked. She heard him telephoning, and frowned. How could they possibly send off the children to a strange place like that?

Uncle Quentin put down the receiver, and went to find his wife, looking jubilant and very pleased with himself.

'It's all settled,' he said. 'Lenoir is delighted, most delighted. Says he loves children about the place, and so does his wife, and his two will be thrilled to have them. If we can hire a car today, they can go at once.'

'But Quentin – we *can't* let them go off like that to strange people! They'll hate it! I shouldn't be surprised if George refuses to go,' said his wife.

'Oh – that reminds me. She's not to take Timothy,' said Uncle Quentin. 'Apparently Lenoir doesn't like dogs.'

'Well, then, you know George won't go!' said his wife. 'That's foolish, Quentin. George won't go anywhere without Timmy.'

'She'll have to, this time,' said Uncle Quentin, quite determined that George should not upset all his marvellous plans. 'Here are the children. I'll ask them what *they* feel about going, and see what they say!'

He called them into his study. They came in, feeling sure that they were to hear bad news – probably they were all to return to school!

'You remember that boy I spoke to you about last night?' began Uncle Quentin. 'Pierre Lenoir. You had some absurd name for him.'

'Sooty,' said Dick and Julian together.

'Ah yes, Sooty. Well, his father has kindly invited you all to go and stay with him at Smuggler's Top,' said Uncle Quentin.

The children were astonished.

'*Smuggler's Top!*' said Dick, his fancy caught by the peculiar name. 'What's Smuggler's Top?'

'The name of his house,' said Uncle Quentin. 'It's very old, built on the top of a strange hill surrounded by marshes over which the sea once flowed. The hill was once an island, but now it's just a tall hill rising up from the marsh. Smuggling went on there in the old days. It's a very peculiar place, so I've heard.'

All this made the children feel excited. Also Julian

and Dick had always liked Sooty Lenoir. He was quite mad, but awfully good fun. They might have a first-rate time with him.

'Well – would you like to go? Or would you rather go back to school for the holidays?' asked Uncle Quentin impatiently.

'Oh *no* – not back to school!' said everyone at once.

'I'd *love* to go to Smuggler's Top,' said Dick. 'It sounds a thrilling place. And I always liked old Sooty, especially since he sawed half-way through one of the legs of our form-master's chair. It gave way at once when Mr Toms sat down!'

'Hm. I don't see that a trick like that is any reason for liking someone,' said Uncle Quentin, beginning to feel a little doubtful about Master Lenoir. 'Perhaps, on the whole, school would be best for you.'

'Oh no, no!' cried everyone. 'Let's go to Smuggler's Top! Do, do let's!'

'Very well,' said Uncle Quentin, pleased at their eagerness to follow his plan. 'As a matter of fact, I have already settled it. I telephoned a few minutes ago. Mr Lenoir was very kind about it all.'

'Can I take Timmy?' asked George, suddenly.

'No,' said her father. 'I'm afraid not. Mr Lenoir doesn't like dogs.'

'Then I shan't like *him*,' said George, sulkily. 'I won't go without Timmy.'

'You'll have to go back to school, then,' said her father, sharply. 'And take off that sulky expression, George. You know how I dislike it.'

But George wouldn't. She turned away. The others looked at her in dismay. Surely old George wasn't going to get into one of her moods, and spoil everything! It would be fun to go to Smuggler's Top. But, of course, it certainly wouldn't be so much fun without Timmy. Still – they couldn't all go back to school just because George wouldn't go anywhere without her dog.

They all went into the sitting-room. Anne put her arm through George's. George shook it off.

'George! You simply *must* come with us,' said Anne. 'I can't bear to go without you – it would be awful to see you going back to school all alone.'

'I shouldn't be all alone,' said George. 'I should have Timmy.'

The others pressed her to change her mind, but she shook them off. 'Leave me alone,' she said. 'I want to think. How are we supposed to get to Smuggler's Top, and where is it? Which road do we take?'

'We're going by car, and it's right up the coast somewhere, so I expect we'll take the coast-road,' said Julian. 'Why, George?'

'Don't ask questions,' said George. She went out with Timmy. The others didn't follow her. George was not very nice when she was cross.

Aunt Fanny began to pack for them, though it was impossible to get some of the things from the girls' room. After a time George came back, but Timmy was not with her. She looked more cheerful.

'Where's Tim?' asked Anne, at once.

'Out somewhere,' said George.

'Are you coming with us, George?' asked Julian, looking at her.

'Yes. I've made up my mind to,' said George, but for some reason she wouldn't look Julian in the eyes. He wondered why.

Aunt Fanny gave them all an early lunch, and then a big car came for them. They packed themselves inside. Uncle Quentin gave them all sorts of messages for Mr Lenoir, and Aunt Fanny kissed them good-bye. 'I do hope you have a nice time at Smuggler's Top,' she said. 'Mind you write at once and tell me all about it.'

'Aren't we going to say good-bye to Timmy?' said Anne, her eyes opening wide in amazement at George, forgetting. 'George, surely you're not going without saying good-bye to old Timmy!'

'Can't stop now,' said Uncle Quentin, afraid that George might suddenly become awkward again. 'Right, driver! You can go off now. Don't drive too fast, please.'

Waving and shouting the children drove away from Kirrin Cottage, sad when they looked back and saw the smashed roof under the fallen tree. Never mind – they had not been sent back to school. That was the main thing. Their spirits rose as they thought of Sooty and his oddly-named home, Smuggler's Top.

'Smuggler's Top! It sounds too exciting for words!' said Anne. 'I can picture it, an old house right on the top of a hill. Fancy being an island once. I wonder why the sea went back and left marshes instead.'

George said nothing for a while, and the car sped on. The others glanced at her once or twice, but came to the conclusion that she was grieving about Timmy. Still she didn't look very sad!

The car went over a hill and sped down to the bottom. When they got there George leaned forward and touched the driver's arm.

'Would you stop a moment, please? We have to pick somebody up here.'

Julian, Dick and Anne stared at George in surprise. The driver, also rather surprised, drew the car to a standstill. George opened the car door and gave a loud whistle.

Something shot out of the hedge and hurled itself joyfully into the car. It was Timmy! He licked everyone, trod on everyone's toes, and gave the little short barks that showed he was excited and happy.

'Well,' said the driver, doubtfully, 'I don't know if you're supposed to take that dog in. Your father didn't say anything about him.'

'It's all right,' said George, her face red with joy. 'Quite all right. You needn't worry. Start the car again, please.'

'You *are* a monkey!' said Julian, half-annoyed with George, and half-pleased because Timmy was with them after all. 'Mr Lenoir may send him back, you know.'

'Well, he'll have to send *me* back too,' said George, defiantly. 'Anyhow, the main thing is, we've got Timmy after all, and I am coming with you.'

'Yes – that's fine,' said Anne, and gave first George and then Timmy a hug. '*I* didn't like going without Tim either.'

'On to Smuggler's Top!' said Dick, as the car started off again. 'On to Smuggler's Top. I wonder if we shall have any adventures there!'

4 Smuggler's Top

The car sped on, mostly along the coast, though it sometimes went inland for a few miles. But sooner or later it was in sight of the sea again. The children enjoyed the long drive. They were to stop somewhere for lunch, and the driver told them he knew of a good inn.

At half past twelve he drew up outside an old inn, and they all trooped in. Julian took charge, and ordered lunch. It was a very good one, and all the children enjoyed it. So did Timmy. The innkeeper liked dogs, and put down such a piled-up plate for Timmy that the dog hardly liked to begin on his meal in case it was not for him!

He looked up at George and she nodded to him. 'It's your dinner, Timmy. Eat it up.'

So he ate it, hoping that if they were going to stay anywhere they might be staying at the inn. Meals like this did not arrive every day for a hungry dog!

But after lunch the children got up. They went to find the driver, who was having his lunch in the kitchen with the innkeeper and his wife. They were old friends of his.

'Well, I hear you're going to Castaway,' said the innkeeper, getting up. 'You be careful there!'

'Castaway!' said Julian. 'Is that what the hill is called, where Smuggler's Top is?'

'That's its name,' said the innkeeper.

'Why is it called that?' said Anne. 'What a funny name! Were people cast away on it once, when it was an island?'

'Oh no. The old story goes that the hill was once joined to the mainland,' said the innkeeper. 'But it was the haunt of bad people, and one of the saints became angry with the place, and cast it away into the sea, where it became an island.'

'And so it was called Castaway,' said Dick. 'But perhaps it has got good again, because the sea has gone away from it, and you can walk from the mainland to the hill, can't you?'

'Yes. There's one good road you can take,' said the innkeeper. 'But you be careful of wandering away from it, if you go walking on it! The marsh will suck you down in no time if you set foot on it!'

'It does sound a most exciting place,' said George. 'Smuggler's Top on Castaway Hill! Only one road to it!'

'Time to get on,' said the driver, looking at the clock. 'You've got to be there before tea, your uncle said.'

They got into the car again, Timmy clambering over legs and feet to a comfortable place on George's lap. He was far too big and heavy to lie there but just occasionally he seemed to want to, and George never had the heart to refuse him.

They drove off once more. Anne fell asleep, and the others felt drowsy too. The car purred on and on. It began to rain, and the countryside looked rather dreary.

The driver turned round after a while and spoke to Julian. 'We're coming near to Castaway Hill. We'll soon be leaving the mainland, and taking the road across the marsh.'

Julian woke Anne. They all sat up expectantly. But it was very disappointing after all! The marshes were full of mist! The children could not pierce through it with their eyes, and could only see the flat road they were on, raised a little higher than the surrounding flat marsh. When the mist shifted a little now and again the children saw a dreary space of flat marsh on either side.

'Stop a minute,' said Julian. 'I'd like to see what the marsh is like.'

'Well, don't step off the road,' warned the driver, stopping the car. 'And don't you let that dog out. Once he runs off the road and gets into the marsh he'll be gone for good.'

'What do you mean – gone for good?' said Anne, her eyes wide.

'He means the marsh will suck down Timmy at once,' said Julian. 'Shut him in the car, George.'

So Timmy, much to his disgust, was shut safely in the car. He pawed at the door, and tried to look out of the window. The driver turned and spoke to him. 'It's all right. They'll be back soon old fellow!'

But Timmy whined all the time the others were out of the car. He saw them go to the edge of the road. He saw Julian jump down the couple of feet that raised the road above the marsh.

There was a line of raised stones running in the marsh alongside the road. Julian stood on one of these peering at the flat marsh.

'It's mud,' he said. 'Loose, squelchy mud! Look, when I touch it with my foot it moves! It would soon suck me down if I trod heavily on it.'

Anne didn't like it. She called to Julian. 'Come up on the road again. I'm afraid you'll fall in.'

Mists were wreathing and swirling over the salty marshes. It was a weird place, cold and damp. None of the children liked it. Timmy began to bark in the car.

'Tim will scratch the car to bits if we don't get back,' said George. So they all went back, rather silent. Julian wondered how many travellers had been lost in that strange sea-marsh.

'Oh, there're many that've never been heard of again,' said the driver, when they asked him. 'They say there're one or two winding paths that go to the hill from the mainland, that were used before the road was built. But unless you know every inch of them you're off them in a second, and find your feet sinking in the mud.'

'It's horrid to think about,' said Anne. 'Don't let's talk about it any more. Can we see Castaway Hill yet?'

'Yes. There it is, looming up in the mist,' said the driver. 'The top of it is out of the mist, see? Strange place, isn't it?'

The children looked in silence. Out of the slowly moving mists rose a tall, steep hill, whose rocky sides were as steep as cliffs. The hill seemed to swim in the mists, and to have no roots in the earth. It was covered with buildings which even at that distance looked old and quaint. Some of them had towers.

'That must be Smuggler's Top, right at the summit,' said Julian, pointing. 'It's like an old building of centuries ago – probably is! Look at the tower it has. What a wonderful view you'd get from it.'

The children gazed at the place where they were to stay. It looked exciting and picturesque, certainly – but it also looked rather forbidding.

'It's sort of – sort of *secret*, somehow,' said Anne, putting into words what the others were thinking. 'I mean – it looks as if it had kept all kinds of strange

secrets down the centuries. I guess it could tell plenty
of tales!'

The car drove on again, quite slowly, because the
mists came down thickly. The road had a line of
sparkling round buttons set all along the middle, and
when the driver switched on his fog-lamp, they shone
brightly and guided him well. Then as they neared
Castaway Hill the road began to slope upwards.

'We go through a big archway soon,' said the
driver. 'That used to be where the city gate once was.
The whole town is surrounded by wall still, just as it
used to be in olden times. It's wide enough to walk on,
and if you start at a certain place, and walk long
enough, you'll come round to the place you started
at!'

All the children made up their minds to do this
without fail. What a view they would have all round
the hill, if they chose a fine day!

The road became steeper, and the driver put the
engine into a lower gear. It groaned up the hill. Then it
came to an archway, from which old gates were
fastened back. It passed through, and the children
were in Castaway.

'It's almost as if we've gone back through the centuries, and come to somewhere that existed ages ago!'
said Julian, peering at the old houses and shops, with
their cobbled streets, their diamond-paned windows,
and stout old doors.

They went up the winding high street, and came at
last to a big gateway, set with wrought-iron gates.
The driver hooted and they opened. They swept into a
steep drive, and at last stopped before Smuggler's
Top.

They got out, feeling suddenly shy. The big old
house seemed to frown down at them. It was built of

brick and timber, and its front door was as massive as
that of a castle.

Weird gables jutted here and there over the
diamond-paned windows. The house's one tower
stood sturdily at the east side of the house, with
windows all round. It was not a square tower, but a
rounded one, and ended in a point.

'Smuggler's Top!' said Julian. 'It's a good name for
it somehow. I suppose lots of smuggling went on here
in the old days.'

Dick rang the bell. To do this he had to pull down an
iron handle, and a jangling at once made itself heard in
the house.

There was the sound of running feet, and the door
was opened. It opened slowly, for it was heavy.

Beyond it stood two children, one a girl of about
Anne's age, and the other a boy of Dick's age.

'Here you are at last!' cried the boy, his dark eyes
dancing. 'I thought you were never coming!'

'This is Sooty,' said Dick to the girls, who had not
met him before. They stared at him.

He was certainly very, very dark. Black hair, black
eyes, black eyebrows, and a brown face. In contrast to
him the girl beside him looked pale and delicate. She
had golden hair, blue eyes and her eyebrows were so
faint they could hardly be seen.

'This is Marybelle, my sister,' said Sooty. 'I always
think we look like Beauty and the Beast!'

Sooty was nice. Everyone liked him at once. George
found herself twinkling at him in a way quite strange
to her, for usually she was shy of strangers, and would
not make friends for some time. But who could help
liking Sooty with his dancing black eyes and his really
wicked grin?

'Come in,' said Sooty. 'Driver, you can take the car

round to the next door, and Block will take in the luggage for you and give you tea.'

Suddenly Sooty's face lost its smile and grew very solemn. He had seen Timmy!

'I say! I say – that's not your dog, is it?' he said.

'He's mine,' said George, and she laid a protecting hand on Timmy's head. 'I had to bring him. I can't go anywhere without him.'

'Yes, but – no dog's allowed at Smuggler's Top,' said Sooty, still looking very worried, and glancing behind him as if he was afraid someone might come along and see Timmy. 'My stepfather won't allow any dogs here. Once I brought in a stray one and he licked me till I couldn't sit down – my stepfather licked me, I mean, not the dog.'

Anne gave a frightened little smile at the poor joke. George looked stubborn and sulky.

'I thought – I thought maybe we could hide him somewhere while we were here,' she said. 'But if that's how you feel, I'll go back home with the car. Good-bye.'

She turned and went after the car, which was backing away. Timmy went with her. Sooty stared, and then he yelled after her. 'Come back, stupid! We'll think of *some*thing!'

5 Sooty Lenoir

Sooty ran down the steps that led to the front door, and tore after George. The others followed. Marybelle went too, shutting the big front door behind her carefully.

There was a small door in the wall just where George was. Sooty caught hold of her and pushed her roughly through the door, holding it open for the others.

'Don't shove me like that,' began George, angrily. 'Timmy will bite you if you push me about.'

'No, he won't,' said Sooty, with a cheerful grin. 'Dogs like me. Even if I boxed your ears your dog would only wag his tail at me.'

The children found themselves in a dark passage. There was a door at the farther end. 'Wait here a minute and I'll see if the coast is clear,' said Sooty. 'I know my stepfather is in, and I tell you, if he sees that dog he'll pack you all into the car again, and send you back! And I don't want him to do that because I can't tell you how I've looked forward to having you all!'

He grinned at them, and their hearts warmed towards him again, even George's, though she still felt angry at being so roughly pushed. She kept Timmy close beside her.

All the same everyone felt a bit scared of Mr Lenoir. He sounded rather a fierce sort of person!

Sooty tiptoed to the door at the end of the passage

and opened it. He peeped into the room there, and then came back to the others.

'All clear,' he said. 'We'll take the secret passage to my bedroom. No one will see us then, and once we're there we can make plans to hide the dog. Ready?'

A secret passage sounded thrilling. Feeling rather as if they were in an adventure story, the children went quietly to the door and into the room beyond. It was a dark, oak-panelled room, evidently a study of some sort, for there was a big desk there, and the walls were lined with books. There was no one there.

Sooty went to one of the oak panels in the wall, felt along it deftly, and pressed in a certain place. The panel slid softly aside. Sooty put in his hand and pulled at something. A much larger panel below slid into the wall, and left an opening big enough for the children to pass through.

'Come on,' said Sooty in a low voice. 'Don't make a noise.'

Feeling excited, the children all passed through the opening. Sooty came last, and did something that shut the opening and slid the first panel back into its place again.

He switched on a small torch, for it was pitch dark where the children were standing.

They were in a narrow stone passage, so narrow that two people could not possibly have passed one another unless both were as thin as rakes. Sooty passed his torch along to Julian, who was in front.

'Keep straight on till you come to stone steps,' he said. 'Go up them, turn to the right at the top, and keep straight on till you come to a blank wall, then I'll tell you what to do.'

Julian led the way, holding up the torch for the others. The narrow passage ran straight, and came to some stone steps. It was not only very narrow but rather low, so that Anne and Marybelle were the only ones who did not have to bend their heads.

Anne didn't like it very much. She never liked being in a very narrow enclosed space. It reminded her of dreams she sometimes had of being somewhere she couldn't get away from. She was glad when Julian spoke. 'The steps are here. Up we go, everyone.'

'Don't make a noise,' said Sooty, in a low voice. 'We're passing the dining-room now. There's a way into this passage from there too.'

Everyone fell silent, and tried to walk on tiptoe, though this was unexpectedly difficult when heads had to be bent and shoulders stooped.

They climbed up fourteen steps, which were quite steep, and curved round half-way. Julian turned to the right at the top. The passage ran upwards then, and was as narrow as before. Julian felt certain that a very fat person could not possibly get along it.

He went on until, with a start, he almost bumped into a blank stone wall! He flashed his torch up and down it. A low voice came from the back of the line of children.

'You've got to the blank wall, Julian. Shine your torch up to where the roof of the passage meets the wall. You will see an iron handle there. Press down on it hard.'

Julian flashed his torch up and saw the handle. He put his torch into his left hand, and grasped the thick iron handle with his right. He pressed down as hard as he could.

And, quite silently, the great stone in the middle of the wall slid forward and sideways, leaving a gaping hole.

Julian was astonished. He let go of the iron handle and

flashed his torch into the hole. There was nothing but darkness there!

'It's all right. It leads into a big cupboard in my bedroom!' called Sooty from the back. 'Get through, Julian, and we'll follow. There won't be anyone in my room.'

Julian crawled through the hole and found himself in a spacious cupboard, hung with Sooty's clothes. He groped his way through them and bumped against a door. He opened it and at once daylight flooded into the cupboard, lighting up the way from the passage into the room.

One by one the others clambered through the hole, lost themselves in clothes for a moment and then went thankfully into the room through the cupboard door.

Timmy, puzzled and silent, followed close beside George. He had not liked the dark, narrow passage very much. He was glad to be in daylight again!

Sooty, coming last, carefully closed the opening into the passage by pressing the stone back. It worked easily, though Julian could not imagine how. There must be some sort of pivot, he thought.

Sooty joined the others in his bedroom, grinning. George had her hand on Timmy's collar. 'It's all right, George,' said Sooty. 'We're quite safe here. My room and Marybelle's are separate from the rest of the house. We're in a wing on our own, reached by a long passage!'

He opened the door and showed the others what he meant. There was a room next to his, which was Marybelle's. Beyond stretched a stone-floored, stone-walled passage, laid with mats. At the end of it a big window let in light. There was a door there, a great oak one, which was shut.

'See? We're quite safe here, all by ourselves,' said

Sooty. 'Timmy could bark if he liked, and no one would know.'

'But doesn't anyone ever come?' said Anne surprised. 'Who keeps your rooms tidy, and cleans them?'

'Oh, Sarah comes and does that every morning,' said Sooty. 'But usually no one else comes. And anyway, I've got a way of knowing when anyone opens that door!'

He pointed to the door at the end of the passage. The others stared at him.

'How *do* you know?' said Dick.

'I've rigged up something that makes a buzzing noise here, in my room, as soon as that door is opened,' said Sooty, proudly. 'Look, I'll go along and open it, while you stay here and listen.'

He sped along the passage and opened the heavy door at the end. Immediately a low buzzing noise sounded somewhere in his room, and made everyone jump. Timmy was startled too, pricked up his ears, and growled fiercely.

Sooty shut the door and ran back. 'Did you hear the noise? It's a good idea, isn't it? I'm always thinking of things like that.'

The others thought they had come to rather a strange place! They stared round Sooty's bedroom, which was quite ordinary in its furnishings, and in its general untidiness. There was a big diamond-paned window, and Anne went to look out of it.

She gave a gasp. She had not expected to look down such a precipice! Smuggler's Top was built at the summit of the hill, and, on the side where Sooty's bedroom was, the hill fell away steeply, down and down to the marsh below!

'Oh look!' she said. 'Look how steep it is! It really gives me a very funny feeling to look down there!'

The others crowded round and looked in silence, for it certainly was strange to gaze down such a long way.

The sun was shining up on the hill-summit, but all around, as far as they could see, mists hid the marsh and the far-off sea. The only bit of the marsh that could be seen was far down below, at the bottom of the steep hill.

'When the mists are away, you can see over the flat marshes to where the sea begins,' said Sooty. 'That's quite a fine sight. You can hardly tell where the marsh ends and sea begins except when the sea is very blue. Fancy, once upon a time, the sea came right up and around this hill, and it was an island.'

'Yes. The innkeeper told us that,' said George. 'Why did the sea go back and leave it?'

'I don't know,' said Sooty. 'People say it's going back farther and farther. There's a big scheme afoot to drain the marsh, and turn it into fields, but I don't know if that will ever happen.'

'I don't like that marsh,' said Anne, with a shiver. 'It looks wicked, somehow.'

Timmy whined. George remembered that they must hide him, and make plans for him. She turned to Sooty.

'Did you mean what you said about hiding Tim?' she asked. 'Where shall we put him? And can he be fed? And how can we exercise him? He's a big dog, you know.'

'We'll plan it all,' said Sooty. 'Don't you worry. I love dogs, and I shall be thrilled to have Timmy here. But I do warn you that if my stepfather ever finds out we shall probably all get a jolly good telling off, and you'll be sent home in disgrace.'

'But why doesn't your father like dogs?' said Anne, puzzled. 'Is he afraid of them?'

'No, I don't think so. It's just that he won't have them here in the house,' said Sooty. 'I think he must have a reason for it, but I don't know what it is. He's an odd sort of man, my stepfather!'

'How is he odd?' asked Dick.

'Well – he seems full of secrets,' said Sooty. 'Strange people come here, and they come secretly without anyone knowing. I've seen lights shining in our tower on certain nights, but I don't know who puts them there or why. I've tried to find out, but I can't.'

'Do you think – do you think your father is a smuggler?' said Anne, suddenly.

'I don't think so,' said Sooty. 'We've got one smuggler here, and everyone knows him! See that house over there to the right, lower down the hill? Well, that's where he lives. He's as rich as can be. His name is Barling. Even the police know his goings-on, but they can't stop him! He is very rich and very powerful, so he does what he likes – and he won't let anyone play the same game as he plays! No one else would dare to do any smuggling in Castaway, while *he* does it!'

'This seems rather an exciting place,' said Julian. 'I have a kind of feeling there might be an adventure somewhere about!'

'Oh no,' said Sooty. 'Nothing happens, really. It's only just a feeling you get here, because the place is so old, so full of secret ways and pits and passages. Why, the whole hill is mined with passages in the rock, used by the smugglers of olden times!'

'Well,' began Julian, and stopped very suddenly. Everyone stared at Sooty. His secret buzzer had suddenly barked from its hidden corner! Someone had opened the door at the end of the passage!

6 Sooty's stepfather and mother

'Someone's coming!' said George, in a panic. 'What shall we do with Tim? Quick!'

Sooty took Timmy by the collar and shoved him into the old cupboard, and shut the door on him. 'Keep quiet!' he commanded, and Timmy stood still in the darkness, the hairs at the back of his neck standing up, his ears cocked.

'Well,' began Sooty, in a bright voice, 'perhaps I'd better show you where your bedrooms are now!'

The door opened and a man came in. He was dressed in black trousers and a white linen coat. He had a peculiar face. 'It's a shut face,' thought Anne to herself. 'You can't tell a bit what he's like inside, because his face is all shut and secret.'

'Oh hallo, Block,' said Sooty, airily. He turned to the others. 'This is Block, my stepfather's man,' he said. 'He's deaf, so you can say what you like, but it's better not to, because though he doesn't hear he seems to sense what we say.'

'Anyway, I think it would be beastly to say things we wouldn't say in front of him if he wasn't deaf,' said George, who had very strict ideas about things of that sort.

Block spoke in a curiously monotonous voice. 'Your stepfather and your mother want to know why you have not brought your friends to see them,' he said. 'Why did you rush up here like this?'

Block looked all round as he spoke – almost as if he knew there was a dog, and wondered where he had gone to, George thought, in alarm. She did hope the car-driver had not mentioned Timmy.

'Oh – I was so pleased to see them I took them straight up here!' said Sooty. 'All right, Block. We'll be down in a minute.'

The man went, his face quite impassive. Not a smile, not a frown! 'I don't like him,' said Anne. 'Has he been with you long?'

'No – only about a year,' said Sooty. 'He suddenly appeared one day. Even Mother didn't know he was coming! He just came, and, without a word, changed into that white linen coat, and went to do some work in my stepfather's room. I suppose my stepfather was expecting him – but he didn't say anything to my mother, I'm sure of that. She seemed so surprised.'

'Is she your real mother, or a stepmother, too?' asked Anne.

'You don't have a stepmother *and* a stepfather!' said Sooty, scornfully. 'You only have one or the other. My mother is my real mother, and she's Marybelle's mother, too. But Marybelle and I are only half-brother and sister, because my stepfather is her *real* father.'

'It's rather muddled,' said Anne, trying to sort it out.

'Come on – we'd better go down,' said Sooty, remembering. 'By the way, my stepfather is always being very affable, always smiling and joking – but it isn't real, somehow. He's quite likely to fly into a furious temper at any moment.'

'I hope we shan't see very much of him,' said Anne, uncomfortably. 'What's your mother like, Sooty?'

'Like a frightened mouse!' said Sooty. 'You'll like her, all right. She's a darling. But she doesn't like living here; she doesn't like this house, and she's terrified of my stepfather. She wouldn't say so herself, of course, but I know she is.'

Marybelle, who was too shy to have joined in any talking until then, nodded her head.

'I don't like living here, either,' she said. 'I shall be glad when I go to boarding-school, like Sooty. Except that I shall leave Mother all alone then.'

'Come on,' said Sooty, and led the way. 'We'd better leave Timmy in the cupboard till we come back, just in case Block does a bit of snooping. I'll lock the cupboard door and take the key.'

Feeling rather unhappy at leaving Timmy locked up in the cupboard, the children followed Sooty and Marybelle down the stone passage to the oak door. They went through, and found themselves at the top of a great flight of stairs, wide and shallow. They went down into a big hall.

At the right was a door, and Sooty opened it. He went in and spoke to someone.

'Here they all are,' he said. 'Sorry I rushed them off to my bedroom like that, Father, but I was so excited to see them all!'

'Your manners still need a little polishing, Pierre,' said Mr Lenoir, in a deep voice. The children looked at him. He sat in a big oak chair, a neat, clever-looking man, with fair hair brushed upwards, and eyes as blue as Marybelle's. He smiled all the time, but with his mouth, not his eyes.

'What cold eyes!' thought Anne, when she went forward to shake hands with him. His hand was cold, too. He smiled at her, and patted her on the shoulder.

'What a nice little girl!' he said. 'You will be a good

companion for Marybelle. Three boys for Sooty, and one girl for Marybelle. Ha ha!'

He evidently thought George was a boy, and she did look rather like one – she was wearing jeans and jersey as usual, and her curly hair was very short.

Nobody said that George wasn't a boy. Certainly George was not going to! She, Dick and Julian shook hands with Mr Lenoir. They had not even noticed Sooty's mother!

She was there, though, sitting lost in an armchair, a tiny woman like a doll, with mouse-coloured hair and grey eyes. Anne turned to her.

'Oh, how small you are!' she said, before she could stop herself.

Mr Lenoir laughed. He laughed no matter what anyone said. Mrs Lenoir got up and smiled. She was only as tall as Anne, and had the smallest hands and feet that Anne had ever seen on a grown-up. Anne liked her. She shook hands, and said, 'It's so nice of you to have us all here like this. You know, I expect, that a tree fell on the roof of our house and smashed it.'

Mr Lenoir's laugh came again. He made some kind of joke, and everyone smiled politely.

'Well, I hope you'll have a good time here,' he said. 'Pierre and Marybelle will show you the old town, and, if you promise to be careful, you can walk along the road to the mainland to go to the cinema there.'

'Thank you,' said everyone, and Mr Lenoir laughed his curious laugh again.

'Your father is a very clever man,' he said, suddenly turning to Julian, who guessed that he had mistaken him for George. 'I am hoping he will come here to fetch you home again when you go, and then I shall have the pleasure of talking with him. He and I have been doing the same kind of experiments, but he has got further than I have.'

'Oh!' said Julian, politely. Then the doll-like Mrs Lenoir spoke in her soft voice.

'Block will give you all your meals in Marybelle's schoolroom, then you will not disturb my husband. He does not like talk at meal-times, and that would be rather hard on six children.'

Mr Lenoir laughed again. His cold blue eyes looked intently at all the children. 'By the way, Pierre,' he said suddenly, 'I forbid you to wander about the catacombs in this hill, as I have forbidden you before, and I also forbid you to do any of your dare-devil climbing, nor will I have you acting about on the city wall now that you have others here. I will not have them taking risks. Will you promise me this?'

'I don't act about on the city wall,' protested Sooty. 'I don't take risks, either.'

'You play the fools always,' said Mr Lenoir, and the tip of his nose turned quite white. Anne looked at it with interest. She did not know that it always did this when Mr Lenoir got angry.

'Oh, sir – I was top of my form last term,' said Sooty, in a most injured tone. The others felt certain that he was trying to lead Mr Lenoir away from his request – he was not going to promise him what he had asked!

Mrs Lenoir now joined in. 'He really did do well last term,' she said. 'You must remember –'

'Enough!' snapped Mr Lenoir, and the smiles and laughs he had so freely lavished on everyone vanished, entirely. 'Get out, all of you!'

Rather scared, Julian, Dick, Anne and George huried from the room, followed by Marybelle and Sooty. Sooty was grinning as he shut the door.

'I didn't promise!' he said. 'He wanted to take all our fun away. This place isn't any fun if you don't explore it. I can show you heaps of strange places.'

'What are catacombs?' asked Anne, with a vague picture of cats and combs in her head.

'Winding, secret tunnels in the hill,' said Sooty. 'Nobody knows them all. You can get lost in them easily, and never get out again. Lots of people have.'

'Why are there so many secret ways and things here?' wondered George.

'Easy!' said Julian. 'It was a haunt of smugglers, and there must have been many a time when they had to hide not only their goods, but themselves! And, according to old Sooty, there still *is* a smuggler here! What did you say his name was – Barling, wasn't it?'

'Yes,' said Sooty. 'Come on upstairs and I'll show you your rooms. You've got a good view over the town.'

He took them to two rooms set side by side, on the opposite side of the big staircase from his bedroom and Marybelle's. They were small but well-furnished, and had, as Sooty said, a marvellous view over the quaint roofs and towers of Castaway Hill. They also had a remarkably good view of Mr Barling's house.

George and Anne were to sleep in one room, and Julian and Dick in the other. Evidently Mrs Lenoir had taken the trouble to remember that there were two girls and two boys, not one girl and three boys, as Mr Lenoir imagined!

'Nice cosy rooms,' said Anne. 'I like these dark oak panels. Are there any secret passages in our rooms, Sooty?'

'You wait and see!' grinned Sooty. 'Look, there are your things, all unpacked from your suitcases. I expect

Sarah did that. You'll like Sarah. She's a good sort, fat and round and jolly – not a bit like Block!'

Sooty seemed to have forgotten all about Tim. George reminded him.

'What about Timmy? He'll have to be near me, you know. And we must arrange to feed him and exercise him. Oh, I do hope he'll be all right, Sooty, I'd rather leave straight away than have Timmy unhappy.'

'He'll be all right!' said Sooty. 'I'll give him the free run of that narrow passage we came up to my bed-room by, and we'll smuggle him out by a secret tunnel that opens half-way down the town, and give him plenty of exercise each morning. Oh, we'll have a grand time with Timmy!'

George wasn't so sure. 'Can he sleep with me at night?' she asked. 'He'll howl the place down if he can't.'

'Well – we'll try and manage it,' said Sooty, rather doubtfully. 'You've got to be jolly careful, you know. We don't want to land in serious trouble. You don't know what my stepfather can be like!'

They could guess, though. Julian looked curiously at Sooty. 'Was your own father's name Lenoir, too?' he asked.

Sooty nodded. 'Yes. He was my stepfather's cousin, and was as dark as all the Lenoirs usually are. My stepfather is an exception – he's fair. People say the fair Lenoirs are no good – but don't tell my stepfather that!'

'As if we should!' said George. 'Gracious, he'd cut off our heads or something! Come on – let's go back to Tim.'

7   *The hidden pit*

The children were all very glad to think that they were
going to have meals by themselves in the old schoolroom. Nobody wanted to have much to do with Mr
Lenoir! They felt sorry for Marybelle because she had
such a peculiar father.

They soon settled down at Smuggler's Top. Once
George was satisfied that Timmy was safe and happy,
though rather puzzled about everything, she settled
down too. The only difficulty was getting Timmy to
her room at night. This had to be done in darkness.
Block had a most tiresome way of appearing silently
and suddenly, and George was terrified of him catching a glimpse of the big dog.

Timmy had a strange sort of life the next few days!
While the children were indoors, he had to stay in the
narrow secret passage, where he wandered about,
puzzled and lonely, pricking his ears for a sound of the
whistle that meant he was to come to the cupboard and
be let out.

He was fed very well, for Sooty raided the larder
every night. Sarah, the cook, was amazed at the way
things like soup-bones disappeared. She could not
understand it. But Timmy devoured everything that
was given to him.

Each morning he was given good exercise by the
children. The first morning this had been really very
exciting!

George had reminded Sooty of his promise to take
Timmy for walks each day. 'He simply must have
exercise, or he'll be terribly miserable!' she said. 'But
how can we manage it? We can't possibly take him
through the house and out of the front door! We'd be
certain to walk into your father!'

'I told you I knew a way that came out half-way
down the hill, silly,' said Sooty. 'I'll show you. We
shall be quite safe once we are down there, because
even if we met Block or anyone else that knew us, they
wouldn't know it was our dog. They would think it
was just a stray we had picked up.'

'Well – show us the way,' said George, impatiently.
They were all in Sooty's bedroom, and Timmy was
lying on the mat beside George. They felt really safe in
Sooty's room because of the buzzer that warned them
when anyone opened the door at the end of the long
passage.

'We'll have to go into Marybelle's room,' said
Sooty. 'You'll get a shock when you see the way that
leads down the hill, I can tell you!'

He looked out of the door. The door at the end of
the passage was shut. 'Marybelle, slip along and peep
through the passage door,' said Sooty. 'Warn us if
anyone is coming up the stairs. If not, we'll all slip
quickly into your room.'

Marybelle ran to the door at the end of the passage.
She opened it, and at once the warning buzzer sounded
in Sooty's room, making Timmy growl fiercely. Marybelle looked through the doorway to the stair. Then
she signalled to the others that no one was coming.

They all rushed out of Sooty's room into Marybelle's, and Marybelle came to join them. She was a
funny little mouse of a girl, shy and timid. Anne liked
her, and once or twice teased her for being so shy.

But Marybelle did not like being teased. Her eyes filled with tears at once, and she turned away. 'She'll be better when she goes to school,' Sooty said. 'She can't help being shy, shut up all the year round in this strange house. She hardly ever sees anyone of her own age.'

They crowded into the little girl's bedroom and shut the door. Sooty turned the key in the lock. 'Just in case friend Block comes snooping,' he said with a grin.

Sooty began to move the furniture in the room to the sides, near the walls. The others watched in surprise and then helped. 'What's the idea of the furniture removal?' asked Dick, struggling with a heavy chest.

'Got to get this heavy carpet up,' panted Sooty. 'It's put there to hide the trap-door below. At least, that's what I've always thought.'

Once the furniture stood by the walls, it was easy to drag up the heavy carpet. There was a felt lining under it too, and that had to be pulled aside as well. Then the children saw a trap-door, let flat into the floor, with a ring-handle to pull it up.

They felt excited. Another secret way! This house seemed full of them. Sooty pulled at the ring and the heavy door came up quite easily. The children peered down, but they could see nothing. It was pitch-dark.

'Are there steps down?' asked Julian, holding Anne back in case she fell.

'No,' said Sooty, reaching out for a big torch he had brought in with him. 'Look!'

He switched on his torch, and the children gave a gasp. The trap-door led down to a pit, far, far below!

'Why! It's miles below the foundations of the house, surely!' said Julian, surprised. 'It's just a hole down to a big pit. What's it for?'

'Oh, it was probably used to hide people – or to get

rid of them!' said Sooty. 'Nice little place, isn't it? If you fell down there you'd land with an awful bump!'

'But – how in the world could we get Timmy down there – or get down ourselves?' said George. '*I'm* not going to fall down it, that's certain!'

Sooty laughed. 'You won't have to,' he said. 'Look here.' He opened a cupboard and reached up to a wide shelf. He pulled something down, and the children saw that it was a rope-ladder, fine but very strong.

'There you are! We can all get down by that,' he said.

'Timmy can't,' said George at once. 'He couldn't possibly climb up or down a ladder.'

'Oh, couldn't he?' said Sooty. 'He seems such a clever dog – I should have thought he could easily have done a thing like that.'

'Well, he can't,' said George, decidedly. 'That's a silly idea.'

'I know,' said Marybelle, suddenly, going red at her boldness in breaking in on the conversation. 'I think I know! We could get the laundry basket and shut Timmy in it. And we would tie it with ropes, and let him down – and pull him up the same way!'

The others stared at her. 'Now that really *is* a brainwave!' said Julian, warmly. 'Good for you, Marybelle. Timmy would be quite safe in a basket. But it would have to be a big one.'

'There's a very big one in the kitchen,' said Marybelle. 'It's never used except when we have lots of people to stay, like now. We could borrow it.'

'Oh *yes*!' said Sooty. 'Of course we could. I'll go and get it now.'

'But what excuse will you give?' shouted Julian after

him. Sooty had already unlocked the door and shot out! He was a most impatient person, and could never put off anything for a single minute.

Sooty didn't answer. He sped down the passage. Julian locked the door after him. He didn't want anyone coming in and seeing the carpet up and the yawning hole!

Sooty was back in two minutes, carrying a very heavy wicker laundry basket on his head. He banged on the door, and Julian unlocked it.

'Good!' said Julian. 'How did you get it? Did anyone mind?'

'Didn't ask them,' grinned Sooty. 'Nobody there to ask. Block's with Father, and Sarah has gone out shopping. I can always put it back if any awkward questions are asked.'

The rope-ladder was shaken out down the hole. It slipped like an uncoiling snake, down and down, and reached the pit at the bottom. Then Timmy was fetched from Sooty's room. He came in wagging his tail overjoyed at being with everyone again. George hugged him.

'Darling Timmy! I hate you being hidden away like this. But never mind, we're all going out together this morning!'

'I'll go down first,' said Sooty. 'Then you'd better let Timmy down. I'll tie his basket round with this rope. It's nice and strong, and there's plenty to let down. Better tie the other end to the end of the bed, then when we come up again we can easily pull him up.'

Timmy was made to get inside the big basket and lie down. He was surprised and barked a little. But George put her hand over his mouth.

'Sh! You mustn't say a word, Timmy,' she said. 'I

know all this is very astonishing. But never mind, you'll have a marvellous walk at the end of it.'

Timmy heard the word 'Walk' and was glad. That was what he wanted – a really nice long walk in the open air and sunshine!

He didn't at all like having the lid shut down on him, but as George seemed to think he must put up with all these strange happenings, Timmy did so, with a very good grace.

'He's really a marvellous dog,' said Marybelle. 'Sooty, get down the hole now, and be ready for when we let him down.'

Sooty disappeared down the dark hole, holding his torch between his teeth. Down and down he went, down and down. At last he stood safely at the bottom, and flashed his torch upwards. His voice came to them, sounding rather strange and far away.

'Come on! Lower Timmy down!'

The laundry basket, feeling extraordinarily heavy now, was pushed to the edge of the hole. Then down it went, knocking against the sides here and there. Timmy growled. He didn't like this game!

Dick and Julian had hold of the rope between them. They lowered Timmy as smoothly as they could. He reached the bottom with a slight bump, and Sooty undid the basket. Out leapt Timmy, barking! But his bark sounded very small and distant to the watchers at the top.

'Now come on down, one by one!' shouted up Sooty waving his torch. 'Is the door locked, Julian?'

'Yes,' said Julian. 'Look out for Anne. She's coming now.'

Anne climbed down, a little frightened at first, but, as her feet grew used to searching for and finding the rungs of the rope-ladder, she went down quite quickly.

Then the others followed, and soon they were all standing together at the bottom of the hole, in the enormous pit. They looked round curiously. It had a musty smell, and its walls were damp and greenish. Sooty swung his torch round, and the children saw various passages leading off here and there.

'Where do they all lead to?' asked Julian, in amazement.

'Well, I told you this hill was full of tunnels,' said Sooty. 'This pit is down in the hill and these tunnels lead into the catacombs. There are miles and miles of them. No one explores them now, because so many people have been lost in them and never heard of again. There used to be an old map of them, but it's lost.'

'It's weird!' said Anne, and shivered. 'I wouldn't like to be down here alone.'

'What a place to hide smuggled goods in,' said Dick. 'No one would ever find them here.'

'I guess the old-time smugglers knew every inch of these passages,' said Sooty. 'Come on! We'll take the one that leads out of the hillside. We'll have to do a bit of climbing when we get there. I hope you don't mind.'

'Not a bit,' said Julian. 'We're all good climbers. But I say, Sooty – you're sure you know the way? We don't want to be lost for ever down here!'

''Course I know the way! Come on!' said Sooty, and, flashing his torch in front of him, he led the way into the dark and narrow tunnel.

8   An exciting walk

The tunnel ran slightly downwards, and smelt nasty in places. Sometimes it opened out into pits like the one they themselves had come from. Sooty flashed his torch up them.

'That one goes into Barling's house somewhere,' he said. 'Most of the old houses hereabouts have openings into pits, like ours. Jolly well hidden some of them are, too!'

'There's daylight or something in front!' said Anne, suddenly. 'Oh good! I hate this tunnel.'

Sure enough, it was daylight, creeping in through a kind of cave-entrance in the hillside. The children crowded there, and looked out.

They were outside the hill, and outside the town, somewhere on the steep cliff-side that ran down to the marsh. Sooty climbed out on to a ledge. He put his torch into his pocket.

'We've got to get to that path down there,' he said, pointing. 'That will lead us to a place where the city wall is fairly low, and we can climb over it. Is Timmy sure-footed? We don't want him tumbling into the marsh down there!'

The marsh lay a good way below, looking ugly and flat. George sincerely hoped Timmy would never fall into it. Still, he was very sure-footed, and she didn't think he would slip. The path was steep and rocky, but quite passable.

They all went down it, clambering over rocks now and again. The path led them to the city wall, which, as Sooty had said, was fairly low just there. He climbed up to the top. He was like a cat for climbing!

'No wonder he's got such a name for climbing about everywhere at school!' said Dick to Julian. 'He's had good practice here. Do you remember how he climbed up to the roof of the school the term before last? Everyone was scared he'd slip and fall, but he didn't. He tied the Union Jack to one of the chimney-pots!'

'Come on!' called Sooty. 'The coast is clear. This is a lonely bit of the town, and no one will see us climbing up.'

Soon they were all over the wall, Timmy too. They set off for a good walk, swinging down the hill, enjoying themselves. The mist began to clear after a while, and the sun felt nice and warm.

The town was very old. Some of the houses seemed almost tumble-down, but there were people living in them, for smoke came from the chimneys. The shops were quaint, with their long narrow windows, and overhanging eaves. The children stopped to look into them.

'Look out – here's Block!' said Sooty suddenly in a low voice. 'Don't take any notice of Timmy at all. If he comes around licking us or jumping up, pretend to try and drive him off as if he was a stray.'

They all pretended not to see Block, but gazed earnestly into the window of a shop. Timmy, feeling rather out of it, ran up to George and pawed at her, trying to make her take notice of him.

'Go away, dog!' said Sooty, and flapped at the surprised Timmy. 'Go away! Following us about like this! Go home, can't you?'

Timmy thought this was some sort of a game. He barked happily, and ran round Sooty and George, giving them an occasional lick.

'Home, dog, home!' yelled Sooty, flapping hard again.

Then Block came up to them, no expression on his face at all. 'The dog bothers you?' he said. 'I will throw a stone at him and make him go.'

'Don't you dare!' said George, immediately. 'You go home yourself! I don't mind the dog following us. He's quite a nice one.'

'Block's deaf, silly,' said Sooty. 'It's no good talking to him.' To George's horror Block picked up a big stone, meaning to throw it at Timmy. George flew at him, punched him hard on the arm, and made him drop the stone.

'How dare you throw stones at a dog!' yelled the little girl in a fury. 'I'll – I'll tell the police.'

'Now, now,' said a voice nearby. 'What's all this about? Pierre, what's the trouble?'

The children turned and saw a tall man standing near them, wearing his hair rather long. He had long, narrow eyes, a long nose and a long chin. 'He's long everywhere!' thought Anne, looking at his long thin legs and long narrow feet.

'Oh, Mr Barling! I didn't see you,' said Sooty, politely. 'Nothing's the matter, thanks. It's only that this dog is following us, and Block said he'd make it go away by chucking a stone at it. And George here is fond of dogs and got angry about that.'

'I see. And who are all these children?' said Mr Barling, looking at each one of them out of his long, narrow eyes.

'They've come to stay with us because their uncle's

house had an accident to it,' explained Sooty.
'George's father's house, I mean. At Kirrin.'

'Ah – at Kirrin?' said Mr Barling, and seemed to
prick up his long ears. 'Surely that is where that very
clever scientist friend of Mr Lenoir's lives?'

'Yes. He's my father,' said George. 'Why, do you
know him?'

'I have heard of him – and of his very interesting
experiments,' said Mr Barling. 'Mr Lenoir knows him
well, I believe?'

'Not awfully well,' said George, puzzled. 'They just
write to one another, I think. My father telephoned to
Mr Lenoir to ask him if he could have us to stay while
our own house is being mended.'

'And Mr Lenoir, of course, was only too delighted
to have the whole company of you! said Mr Barling.
'*Such* a good, generous fellow, your father, Pierre!'

The children stared at Mr Barling, thinking that it
was strange of him to say nice things in such a nasty
voice. They felt uncomfortable. It was plain that Mr
Barling did not like Mr Lenoir at all. Well, neither
did they, but they didn't like Mr Barling any
better!

Timmy saw another dog and darted happily after
him. Block had now disappeared, going up the steep
high street with his basket. The children said good-
bye to Mr Barling, not wanting to talk to him any
more.

They went after Timmy, talking eagerly as soon as
they had left Mr Barling behind.

'Goodness – that was a narrow escape from Block!'
said Julian. 'Old beast – going to throw that enormous
stone at Timmy. No wonder you flew at him, George!
But you very nearly gave the game away, though.'

'I don't care,' said George. 'I wasn't going to have

Timmy's leg broken. It was a bit of bad luck meeting Block our very first morning out.'

'We'll probably never meet him again when we take Timmy out,' said Sooty, comfortingly. 'And if we do we'll simply say the dog always joins us when it meets us. Which is perfectly true.'

They enjoyed their walk. They went into a quaint old coffee shop and had steaming cups of delicious creamy coffee and jammy buns. Timmy had two of the buns and gobbled them greedily. George went off to buy some meat for him at the butcher's, choosing a shop that Sooty said Mrs Lenoir did not go to. She did not want any butcher telling Mrs Lenoir that the children had been buying dog-meat!

They went back the same way as they had come. They made their way up the steep cliff-path, and in at the tunnel-entrance, back through the winding tunnel to the pit, and there was the rope-ladder waiting for them. Julian and Dick went up first, while George packed the surprised Timmy into the basket again and tied the rope firmly round it. Then up went the whining Timmy, bumping against the sides of the hole, until the two panting boys pulled the basket in Marybelle's room and undid it.

It was ten minutes before the dinner-hour. 'Just time to shut the trap-door, pull back the carpet and wash our hands,' said Sooty. 'And I'll put old Timmy back into the secret passage behind the cupboard in my room, George. Where is that meat you bought? I'll put that in the passage too. He can eat it when he likes.'

'Did you put him a nice warm rug there, and a dish of fresh water?' asked George, anxiously, for the third or fourth time.

'You know I did. I keep telling you,' said Sooty. 'Look, we won't put back all the furniture except the chairs. We can say we want it left back because we like to play a game on the carpet. It'll be an awful bore if we have to move chests and things every time we exercise Tim.'

They were just in time for their dinner. Block was there to serve it, and so was Sarah. The children sat down hungrily, in spite of having had coffee and buns. Block and Sarah ladled out hot soup on to their plates.

'I hope you got rid of the unpleasant dog,' said Block in his monotonous voice. He gave George a rather nasty look. Evidently he had not forgotten how she had flown at him.

Sooty nodded. It was no good speaking an answer, for Block would not hear. Sarah bustled round, taking away the soup-plates and preparing to give them their second course.

The food was very good at Smuggler's Top. There was plenty of it, and the hungry visitors and Sooty ate everything put before them. Marybelle hadn't much appetite, but she was the only one. George tried to secrete tit-bits and bones whenever she could, for Timmy.

Two or three days went by, and the children fell into their new life quite happily. Timmy was taken out each morning for a long walk. The children soon got used to slipping down the rope-ladder, and making their way with Timmy to the cliff-side.

In the afternoons they went to either Sooty's room or Marybelle's, and played games or read. They could have Timmy there, because the buzzer always warned them if anyone was coming.

At night it was always an excitement to get Timmy to George's room without being seen. This was usually done when Mr and Mrs Lenoir were sitting at their dinner, and Block and Sarah were serving them.

The children had a light supper first, and Mr and Mrs Lenoir had their dinner an hour later. It was quite the best time to smuggle Timmy along to George's room.

Timmy seemed to enjoy the smuggling. He ran silently beside George and Sooty, stopped at every corner, and scampered gladly into George's room as soon as he got there. He lay quietly under the bed till George was in bed herself, and then he came out to lie on her feet.

George always locked their door at night. She didn't want Sarah or Mrs Lenoir coming in and finding Timmy there! But nobody came, and as night after night went by, George grew more easy about Timmy.

Taking him back to Sooty's room in the morning was a bit of a nuisance, because it had to be done early, before anyone was up. But George could always wake herself at any time she chose, and each morning about half past six the little girl slipped through the house with Timmy. She went in at Sooty's door, and he jumped out of bed to deal with Timmy. He was always awakened by the buzzer that sounded when George opened the door at the end of the passage.

'I hope you are all enjoying yourselves,' Mr Lenoir said to the children, whenever they met him in the hall or on the stairs. And they always replied politely. 'Oh yes, Mr Lenoir, thank you.'

'It's quite a peaceful holiday after all,' said Julian. 'Nothing happens at all!'

And then things *did* begin to happen and once they had begun they never stopped!

9 Who is in the tower?

One night Julian was awakened by someone opening his door. He sat up at once. 'Who is it?' he said. 'Me, Sooty,' said Sooty's voice, very low. 'I say, I want you to come and see something.'

Julian woke Dick, and the two of them put on their dressing-gowns. Sooty led them quietly out of the room and took them to a peculiar little room, tucked away in an odd wing of the house. All kinds of things were kept here, trunks and boxes, old toys, chests of old clothes, broken vases that had never been mended, and many other worthless things.

'Look,' said Sooty, taking them to the window. They saw that the little room had a view of the tower belonging to the house. It was the only room in the house that did, for it was built at a strange angle.

The boys looked – and Julian gave an exclamation. Someone was signalling from the tower! A light there flashed every now and again. In and out – pause – flash, flash, in and out – pause. The light went regularly on and off in a certain rhythm.

'Now – who's doing that?' whispered Sooty.

'Your father?' wondered Julian.

'Don't think so,' said Sooty. 'I think I heard him snoring away in his room. We could go and find out though – see if he really is in his bedroom.'

'Well – for goodness' sake don't let's get caught,'

said Julian, not at all liking the idea of prying about in his host's house.

They made their way to where Mr Lenoir had his room. It was quite plain he was there, for a regular low snoring came from behind the closed door.

'It may be Block up in the tower,' said Dick. 'He looks full of secrets. I wouldn't trust him an inch. I bet it's Block.'

'Well – shall we go to his room and see if it's empty?' whispered Sooty. 'Come on. If it's Block signalling, he's doing it without Father knowing.'

'Oh, your father might have told him to,' said Julian, who felt that he wouldn't trust Mr Lenoir much further than he would trust Block.

They went up the back-stairs to the wing where the staff slept. Sarah slept in a room there with Harriet the kitchen-maid. Block slept alone.

Sooty pushed open Block's door very softly and slowly. When he had enough room to put in his head, he did so. The room was full of moonlight. By the window was Block's bed. And Block was there! Sooty could see the humpy shape of his body, and the black round patch that was his head.

He listened, but he could not catch Block's breathing. He must sleep very quietly.

He withdrew his head, and pushed the other two boys quietly down the back-stairs.

'Was he there?' whispered Julian.

'Yes. So it can't be him, signalling up in our tower,' said Sooty. 'Well – who can it be then? I don't like it. It couldn't possibly be Mother or Sarah or Harriet. Is there a stranger in our house, someone we don't know, living here in secret?'

'Can't be!' said Julian, a little shiver running down his back. 'Look here – what about us going up to the tower and trying to peep through the door or some-thing? We'd soon find out who it was then. Perhaps we ought to tell your father.'

'No. Not yet. I want to find out a whole lot more before I say anything to anyone,' said Sooty, sounding obstinate. 'Let's creep up to the tower. We shall have to be jolly careful though. You get to it by a spiral staircase, rather narrow. There's nowhere much to hide if anyone suddenly came down out of the tower.

'What's in the tower?' whispered Dick, as they made their way through the dark and silent house, thin streaks of moonlight coming in here and there between the crack of the closed curtains.

'Nothing much. Just a table and a chair or two, and a bookcase of books,' said Sooty. 'We use it on hot summer days when the breeze gets in strongly through the windows there, and we can see a long way all round us.'

They came to a little landing. From this a winding, narrow stairway of stone went up to the rounded tower. The boys looked up. Moonlight fell on the stairway from a slit-like window in the wall.

'We'd better not all go up,' said Sooty. 'We should find it so difficult to hurry down, three of us, if the person in the tower suddenly came out. I'll go. You stay down here and wait. I'll see if I can spy anything through the crack in the door or the key-hole.'

He crept softly up the stairway, soon lost to view as he rounded the first spiral. Julian and Dick waited in the shadows at the bottom. There was a thick curtain over one of the windows there, and they got behind it, wrapping its folds round them for warmth.

Sooty crept up to the top. The tower-room had a stout oak door, studded and barred. It was shut! It was no use trying to look through the crack, because there wasn't one. He bent down to peer through the key-hole.

But that was stuffed up with something, so he could not see through that either. He pressed his ear to it and listened.

He heard a series of little clicks. Click – click – click – click – click. Nothing else at all.

'That's the click of the light they're using,' thought Sooty. 'Still signalling like mad! What for? Who to? And who is in our tower-room, using it as a signalling-station? How I wish I knew!'

Suddenly the clicking stopped. There was the sound of someone walking across the stone floor of the tower. And almost at once the door opened!

Sooty had no time to hurry down the stairs. All he could do was to squeeze into a niche, and hope that the person would not see him or touch him as he went by. The moon went behind a cloud at that moment, and Sooty was thankful to know he was hidden in black shadow. Someone came down the stairs and actually brushed against Sooty's arm.

Sooty jumped almost out of his skin, expecting to be hauled out of his niche. But the person did not seem to notice, and went on down the spiral stairway, walking softly.

Sooty did not dare to go down after him, for he was afraid the moon would come out, and cast his shadow down for the signaller to see.

So he stayed squeezed in his niche, hoping that Julian and Dick were well-hidden, and would not think it was he, Sooty, who was walking down the stairs!

Julian and Dick heard the soft footsteps coming, and thought at first it was Sooty. Then, not hearing his whisper, they stiffened behind the curtains, guessing that it was the signaller himself who was walking by!

'We'd better follow him!' whispered Julian to Dick. 'Come on. Quiet, now!'

But Julian got muddled up with the great curtains, and could not seem to find his way out. Dick, however, slipped out easily enough, and padded after the disappearing person. The moon was now out again, and Dick could catch glimpses of the signaller as he went past the moonlight streaks. Keeping well in the shadows himself, he darted quietly after him. Where was he going?

He followed him across the landing to a passage. Then across another landing and up the back-stairs! But those led to the staff bedrooms. Surely the man was not going there?

Dick, to his enormous surprise, saw the person disappear silently into Block's bedroom. He crept to the door, which had been left a little ajar. There was no light in the room except that of the moon. There was no sound of talking. Nothing at all except a creak which might have come from the bed.

Dick peeped in, full of the most intense curiosity. Would he see the man waking up Block? Would he see him climbing out of the window?

He stared round the room. There was no one there at all, except Block lying in bed. The moonlight lit up the corners, and Dick could quite plainly see that the room was empty. Only Block lay there, and, as Dick watched, he heard him give a sigh and roll over in bed.

'Well! That's the strangest thing I ever saw,' thought Dick, puzzled. 'A man goes into a room and completely disappears, without a single sound! Where can he have gone?'

He went back to find the others. Sooty by this time had crept down the spiral staircase and had found

Julian, who had explained that Dick had gone to follow the peculiar signaller.

They went to find Dick, and suddenly bumped into him, creeping along quietly in the darkness. They all jumped violently, and Julian almost cried out, but stifled his voice just in time.

'Golly! You gave me a scare, Dick!' he whispered. 'Well, did you see who it was and where he went?'

Dick told them of his strange experience. 'He simply went into Block's room and vanished,' he said. 'Is there any secret passage leading out of Block's room, Sooty?'

'No, none,' said Sooty. 'That wing is much newer than the rest of the house, and hasn't any secrets in at all. I simply can't imagine what happened to the man. How very odd! Who is he, and why does he come, and where on earth does he go?'

'We really must find out,' said Julian. 'It's such a mystery! Sooty, how did you know there was signalling going on from the tower?'

'Well, some time ago I found it out, quite by accident,' said Sooty. 'I couldn't sleep, and I went along to that funny little box-room place, and ferreted about for an old book I thought I'd seen there. And suddenly I looked up at the tower, and saw a light flashing there.'

'Funny,' said Dick.

'Well, I went along there at night a good many times after that, to see if I could see the signals again,' said Sooty, 'and at last I did. The first time I had seen them there was a good moon, and the second time there was, too. So, I thought, next time there's a moon, I'll creep along to that old box-room and see if the signaller is at work again. And sure enough he was!'

'Where does that window look out on, that we saw

the light flashing from?' asked Julian, thoughtfully. 'The seaward side – or the landward?'

'Seaward,' said Sooty at once. 'There's something or someone out at sea that receives those signals. Goodness knows who.'

'Some kind of smugglers, I suppose,' said Dick. 'But it can't be anything to do with your father, Sooty. I say – let's go up into the tower, shall we? We might find something there – or see something.'

They went back to the spiral staircase and climbed up to the tower-room. It was dark, for the moon was behind a cloud. But it came out after a while, and the boys looked out of the seaward window.

There was no mist at all that night. They could see the flat marshes stretching away to the sea. They gazed down in silence. Then the moon went in and darkness covered the marsh.

Suddenly Julian clutched the others, making them jump. 'I can see something!' he whispered. 'Look beyond there. What is it?'

They all looked. It seemed like a tiny line of very small dots of light. They were so far away that it was difficult to see if they stayed still or moved. Then the moon came out again, flooding everywhere with silvery light, and the boys could not see anything except the moonshine.

But when the moon went in again, there was the line of tiny, pricking lights again! 'A bit nearer, surely!' whispered Sooty. 'Smugglers – coming over a secret path from the sea to Castaway Hill! Smugglers!'

10   *Timmy makes a noise*

The three girls were very excited the next day when
the boys told them their adventure of the night before.

'Gracious!' said Anne, her eyes wide with surprise.
'Who can it be signalling like that? And wherever did
he go to? Fancy him going into Block's room, with
Block there in bed!'

'It's very peculiar,' said George. 'I wish you had
come and told me and Anne.'

'There wasn't time – and anyway, we couldn't have
Timmy about at night. He might have flown at the
signaller,' said Dick.

'The man must have been signalling to the smugglers,' said Julian, thoughtfully. 'Let me see – probably
they came over from France in a ship – came as near to
the marsh as they could – waited for a signal to tell
them that the coast was clear – probably the signal
from the tower – and then waded across a path they
knew through the marsh. Each man must have carried
a torch to prevent himself from leaving the path and
falling into the marsh. No doubt there was someone
waiting to receive the goods they brought – someone
at the edge of the marsh below the hill.'

'But who?' said Dick. 'It can't have been Mr
Barling, who, Sooty says, is known to be a smuggler.
Because the signal lights came from *our* house, not his.
It's all very puzzling.'

'Well, we'll do our best to solve the mystery,' said

George. 'There's some peculiar game going on in this very house, without your father's knowledge, Sooty. We'll keep a jolly good lookout and see if we can find out what it is.'

They were at breakfast alone, when they discussed the night's adventure. Block came in to see if they had finished at that moment. Anne did not notice him.

'What does Mr Barling smuggle?' she asked Sooty. Immediately she got a hard kick on her ankle, and stared in pain and surprise. 'Why did you . . . ?' she began, and got another kick, harder still. Then she saw Block.

'But he's deaf,' she said. 'He can't hear anything we say.'

Block began to clear away, his face as usual showing no expression. Sooty glared at Anne. She was upset and cross, but said no more. She rubbed her bruised ankle hard. As soon as Block went out of the room she turned on Sooty.

'You mean thing! You hurt my ankle like anything! Why shouldn't I say things in front of Block? He's quite deaf!' said Anne, her face very red.

'I know he's supposed to be,' said Sooty. 'And I think he is. But I saw a funny look come over his face when you asked me what Mr Barling smuggled – almost as if he had heard what you said, and was surprised.'

'You imagined it!' said Anne, crossly, still rubbing her ankle. 'Anyway, don't kick me so hard again. A gentle push with your toe would have been enough. I won't talk in front of Block if you don't want me to, but it's quite plain he's as deaf as a post!'

'Yes, he's deaf all right,' said Dick. 'I dropped a plate off the table yesterday, by accident, just behind him, and it smashed to bits, if you remember. Well, he didn't jump or turn a hair, as he would have done if he could have heard.'

'All the same – I never trust Block, deaf or not,' said Sooty. 'I always feel he might read our lips or something. Deaf people can often do that, you know.'

They went off to take Timmy for his usual morning walk. Timmy was quite used to being shut in the laundry basket by now, and lowered into the pit. In fact, he always jumped straight into the basket as soon as the lid was opened, and lay down.

That morning they again met Block, who stared with great interest at the dog. He plainly recognised it as the same dog as before.

'There's Block,' said Julian, in a low voice. 'Don't drive Timmy off this time. We'll pretend he's a stray who always meets us each morning.'

So they let Timmy run round them, and when Block came up, they nodded to him, and made as if to go on their way. But the man stopped them.

'That dog seems to be a friend of yours,' he said, in his curious monotone of a voice.

'Oh yes. He goes with us each morning now,' said Julian, politely. 'He quite thinks he's our dog! Nice fellow, isn't he?'

Block stared at Timmy, who growled. 'Mind you do not bring that dog into the house,' said Block. 'If you do, Mr Lenoir will have him killed.'

Julian saw George's face beginning to turn red with fury. He spoke hurriedly. 'Why should we bring him to the house, Block? Don't be silly!'

Block, however, did not appear to hear. He gave Timmy a nasty look, and went on his way, occasionally turning round to look at the little company of children.

'Horrid fellow!' said George, angrily. 'How dare he say things like that?'

When they got back to Marybelle's bedroom that morning, they pulled Timmy up from the pit, and let him out of the basket. 'We'll put him into the secret passage as usual,' said George, 'and I'll put some biscuits in with him. I got some nice ones for him this morning, the sort he likes, all big and crunchy.'

She went to the door – but just as she was about to unlock it and take Timmy into Sooty's room next door, Timmy gave a small growl.

George took her hand away from the door at once. She turned to look at Timmy. He was standing stiffly, the hackles on his neck rising up, and he was staring fixedly at the door. George put her hand to her lips warningly, and whispered:

'Someone's outside. Timmy knows. He's smelt them. Will you all talk loudly, and pretend to be playing a game? I'll pop Timmy into the cupboard where the rope-ladder is kept.'

At once the others began to talk to one another, while George swiftly dragged Timmy to the cupboard, patted him to make him understand he was to be quiet, and shut him in.

'My turn to deal,' said Julian loudly, and took a pack of snap cards from the top of the chest. 'You won last time, Dick. Bet I'll win this time.'

He dealt swiftly. The others, still talking loudly, saying anything that came into their heads, began to play snap. They yelled 'snap' nearly all the time, pretending to be very jolly and hilarious. Anyone listening outside the door would never guess it was all pretence.

George, who was watching the door closely, saw that the handle was gradually turning, very slowly indeed. Someone meant to open the door without being heard, and come in unexpectedly. But the door was locked!

Soon the person outside, whoever it was, realised that the door was locked, and the handle slowly turned the other way again. Then it was still. There came no other sound. It was impossible to know if anyone was still outside the door or not.

But Timmy would know! Signing to the others to carry on with their shouting and laughing, George let Timmy out of the cupboard. He ran to the door of the room, and stood there, sniffing quietly. Then he turned and looked at George, his tail wagging.

'It's all right,' said George to the others. 'There's no one there now. Timmy always knows. We'd better quickly take him into your room, Sooty, while the coast is clear. Who could it have been, do you think, snooping outside?'

'Block, I should say,' said Sooty. He unlocked the door and peered out. There was no one in the passage. Sooty tiptoed to the door at the end and looked out there also. He waved to George to tell her it was all right to take Timmy into his room.

Soon Timmy was safely in the secret passage, crunching up his favourite biscuits. He had got quite used to his peculiar life now, and did not mind at all. He knew his way about the passage, and had explored other passages that led from it. He was quite at home in the maze of secret ways!

'Better go and have our dinner now,' said Dick. 'And mind, Anne – don't go and say anything silly in front of that horrid Block, in case he reads your lips.'

'Of course I shan't,' said Anne, indignantly. 'I wouldn't have before, but I never thought of him reading my lips. If he does, he's very clever.'

Soon they were all sitting down to lunch. Block was there, waiting to serve them. Sarah was out for the day and did not appear. Block served them with soup, and then went out.

Suddenly, to the children's intense surprise and fright, they heard Timmy barking loudly! They jumped violently.

'Listen! That's Timmy!' said Julian. 'He must be somewhere near here, in that secret passage. How weird it sounds, his bark coming muffled and distant like that. But anyone would know it was a dog barking.'

'Don't say anything at all about it in front of Block,' said Sooty. 'Not a word. Pretend not to hear at all, if Timmy barks again. What on earth is he barking for?'

'It's the bark he uses when he's excited and pleased,' said George. 'I expect he's chasing a rat. He always goes right off his head when he sees a rat or a rabbit. There he goes again. Oh, dear, I hope he catches the rat quickly and settles down!'

Block came back at that moment. Timmy had again just stopped barking. But, in a moment or two, his doggy voice could be heard once more, very muffled. 'Woof! Woof-woof!'

Julian was watching Block closely. The man went on serving the meat. He said nothing, but looked round at the children intently, as if he wanted to see each child's expression, or see if they said anything.

'Jolly good soup that was today,' said Julian, cheerfully, looking round at the others. 'I must say Sarah is a wonderful cook.'

'I think her ginger buns are gorgeous,' said Anne. 'Especially when they are all hot from the oven.'

'Woof-woof,' said Timmy's voice from far away behind the walls.

'George, your mother makes the most heavenly fruit cake I ever tasted,' said Dick to George, wishing Timmy would be quiet. 'I do wonder how they're all getting on at Kirrin Cottage, and if they've started mending the roof yet.'

'Woof!' said Timmy, joyfully chasing his rat down another bit of passage.

Block served everyone and then silently disappeared. Julian went to the door to make sure he had gone and was not outside.

'I hope old Block *is* as deaf as a post!' he said. 'I could have sworn I saw a surprised look come into those cold eyes of his, when Timmy barked.'

'Well, if he *could* hear him, which I don't believe,' said George, 'he must have been jolly surprised to see us talking away and not paying any attention to a dog's barking at all!'

The others giggled. They kept a sharp ear for Block's return. They heard footsteps after a time, and began to pile their plates together for him to take away.

The schoolroom door opened. But it was not Block who came in. It was Mr Lenoir! He came in, smiling as usual, and looked round at the surprised children.

'Ah! So you are enjoying your dinner, and eating it all up, like good children,' he said. He always irritated the children because he spoke to them as if they were very small. 'Does Block wait on you properly?'

'Oh yes, thank you,' said Julian, standing up politely. 'We are having a very nice time here. We think Sarah is a wonderful cook!'

'Ah, that's good, that's good,' said Mr Lenoir. The children waited impatiently for him to go. They were so afraid that Timmy would bark again. But Mr Lenoir seemed in no hurry.

And then Timmy barked again! 'Woof, woof, woof!'

11 George is worried

Mr Lenoir cocked his head on one side almost like a startled dog, when he heard the muffled barking. He looked at the children. But they made no sign of having heard anything. Mr Lenoir listened a little while, saying nothing. Then he turned to a drawing-book, belonging to Julian, and began to look at the sketches there.

The children felt somehow that he was doing it for the sake of staying in the schoolroom a little longer. Into Julian's mind came the quick suspicion that somehow Mr Lenoir must have been told of Timmy's barking and come to investigate it for himself. It was the first time he had ever come to the schoolroom!

Timmy barked again, a little more distantly. Mr Lenoir's nose grew white at the tip. Sooty and Marybelle knew the danger-sign, and glanced at one another. That white-tipped nose usually meant a storm of temper!

'Do you hear that noise?' said Mr Lenoir, snapping out the words.

'What noise?' asked Julian, politely.

Timmy barked again.

'Don't be foolish! There's the noise again!' said Mr Lenoir. At that moment a gull called outside the window, circling in the sea-breeze.

'Oh – that gull? Yes, we often hear the gulls,'

said Dick, brightly. 'Sometimes they seem to mew
like a cat.'

'Pah!' said Mr Lenoir, almost spitting out the word.
'I suppose you will say they also bark like a dog?'

'Well, they might, I suppose,' agreed Dick, looking faintly surprised. 'After all, if they can mew
like cats, there's no reason why they shouldn't bark
like dogs.'

Timmy barked again very joyfully. Mr Lenoir faced
the children, in a very bad temper indeed now.

'Can't you hear that? Tell me what *that* noise is!'

The children all put their heads on one side, and
pretended to listen very carefully. 'I can't hear anything,' said Dick. 'Not a thing.'

'I can hear the wind,' said Anne.

'I can hear the gulls again,' said Julian, putting his
hand behind one ear.

'I can hear a door banging. Perhaps that's the
noise you mean,' said Sooty, with a most innocent
expression. His stepfather gave him a poisonous look.
He could really be very unpleasant.

'And there's a window rattling,' said Marybelle,
eager to do her bit too, though she felt very frightened
of her father, for she knew his sudden rages very well.

'I tell you, it's a dog, and you know it!' snapped Mr
Lenoir, the tip of his nose so white now that it looked
very strange indeed. 'Where's the dog? Whose is he?'

'What dog?' began Julian, frowning as if he were
very puzzled indeed. 'There's no dog here that I can
see.'

Mr Lenoir glared at him, and clenched his fingers. It
was quite clear that he would have liked to box Julian's
ears. 'Then listen!' he hissed. 'Listen and say what you
think could make that barking, if not a dog?'

They were all forced to listen, for by now they felt

scared of the angry man. But fortunately Timmy
made no sound at all. Either he had let the rat escape,
or was now gobbling it up. Anyway, there was not a
single sound from him!

'Sorry, but *really* I can't hear a dog barking,' said
Julian, in rather an injured tone.

'Nor can I!' said Dick, and the others joined in,
saying the same. Mr Lenoir knew that this time they
were speaking the truth, for he too could not hear
anything.

'When I catch that dog I will have him poisoned,' he
said, very slowly and clearly. 'I will not have dogs in
my house.'

He turned on his heel and went out quickly, which
was a very good thing, for George was quite ready to
fly into one of *her* rages, and then there would have
been a real battle! Anne put her hand on George's arm
to stop her shouting after Mr Lenoir.

'Don't give the game away!' she whispered. 'Don't
say anything, George!'

George bit her lip. She had gone first red with rage
and then white. She stamped her foot.

'How dare he, how dare he?' she burst out.

'Shut up, silly,' said Julian. 'Block will be back in a
minute. We must all pretend to be awfully surprised
that Mr Lenoir thought there was a dog, because, if
Block can read our lips, he mustn't know the truth.'

Block came in with the pudding at that moment, his
face as blank as ever. It was the most curious face the
children had ever seen, for there was never any change
of expression on it at all. As Anne said, it might have
been a wax mask!

'Funny how Mr Lenoir thought there was a dog
barking!' began Julian, and the others backed him up
valiantly. If Block could indeed read their lips he

would be puzzled to know whether there *had* been a
dog barking or not!

The children escaped to Sooty's room afterwards,
and held a council of war. 'What are we to do about
Timmy?' said George. 'Does your stepfather know
the secret way behind the walls of Smuggler's Top,
Sooty? Could he possibly get in and find Timmy?
Timmy might fly at him, you know.'

'Yes, he might,' said Sooty, thoughtfully. 'I don't
know if Father does know about the secret passages. I
mean, I expect he knows, but I don't know if he
guessed where the entrances are. I found them out
quite by accident.'

'I'm going home,' said George, suddenly. 'I'm not
going to risk Timmy being poisoned.'

'You can't go home alone,' said Julian. 'It would
look funny. If you do, we'd all have to, and then
we won't have a chance to solve this mystery with
Sooty.'

'No, for goodness' sake don't go and leave me just
now,' said Sooty, looking quite alarmed. 'It would
make my father furious, simply furious.'

George hesitated. She didn't want to make trouble
for Sooty, whom she liked very much. But, on the
other hand, she certainly was not going to risk danger
to Timmy.

'Well – I'll telephone my father and say I'm home-
sick and want to go back,' said George. 'I'll say I miss
Mother. It's quite true, I do miss her. You others can
stay on here and solve the mystery. It wouldn't be fair
of you to try and keep me and Timmy here when you
know I'd worry every moment in case someone got
into the secret passage and put down poisoned meat
for him to eat.'

The others hadn't thought of this. That would be

terrible. Julian sighed. He would have to let George
have her own way after all.

'All right. You telephone to your father,' he said.
'There's a phone downstairs. Do it now if you like.
There won't be anyone about now, I don't suppose.'

George slipped down the passage, out of the door
there, and down the stairs to where the telephone was
enclosed in a dark little cupboard. She dialled the
number she wanted.

There was a long wait. Then she heard the buzzing
noise – brr – brr – brr – that told her that the telephone
bell at Kirrin Cottage was ringing. She began to plan
what she should say to her father. She must, she really
must go home with Timmy. She didn't know how she
was going to explain about Timmy – perhaps she
needn't explain at all. But she meant to go home that
day or the next!

'Brr – brr – brr – brr' said the bell at the other end. It
went on and on, and nobody answered it. She did not
hear her father's familiar voice – only the bell that went
on ringing. Why did nobody answer?

The operator at the exchange spoke to her. 'I'm
sorry, there's no reply.'

George put down the receiver miserably. Perhaps
her parents were out? She would have to try again later
on.

Poor George tried three times, but each time with
the same result. No reply. As she was coming out of
the telephone cupboard for the third time, Mrs Lenoir
saw her.

'Have you been trying to telephone to your home?'
she said. 'Haven't you heard any news?'

'I haven't had a letter yet,' said George. 'I've tried
three times to telephone Kirrin Cottage but each time
there is no reply.'

'Well, we heard this morning that it is impossible to live in Kirrin Cottage while the men are hammering and knocking everywhere,' said Mrs Lenoir, in her gentle voice. 'We heard from your mother. She said that the noise was driving your father mad, and they were going away for a week or so, till things were better. But Mr Lenoir at once wrote and asked them here. We shall know tomorrow, because we have asked them to telephone a reply. We could not get them on the telephone today, of course, any more than you could, because they have gone away already.'

'Oh,' said George, surprised at all this news and wondered why her mother had not written to tell her too.

'Your mother said she had written to you,' said Mrs Lenoir. 'Maybe the letter will come by the next post. The posts are often most peculiar here. It will be a pleasure to have your parents if they can come. Mr Lenoir particularly wants to meet your clever father. He thinks he is quite a genius.'

George said no more but went back to the others, her face serious. She opened Sooty's door, and the others saw at once that she had had news of some sort.

'I can't go home with Timothy,' said George. 'Mother and Father can't stand the noise the workmen make, and they have both gone away!'

'Bad luck!' said Sooty. 'All the same, I'm glad you'll have to stay here, George. I should hate to lose you or Timmy.'

'Your mother has written to ask my mother and father to come and stay here too,' said George. 'What I shall do about Timmy I don't know! And they are sure to ask questions about him too. I can't tell a downright lie and say I left him with Alf the fisher-boy, or anything like that. I can't think *what* to do!'

'We'll think of something,' promised Sooty. 'Perhaps I can get one of the villagers to look after him for us. That would be a very good idea.'

'Oh yes!' said George, cheering up. 'Why didn't I think of that before? Let's ask someone quickly, Sooty.'

But it was impossible to do anything that day because Mrs Lenoir asked them to go down into the drawing-room after tea, and have a game with her. So none of them could go out to find someone to look after Timmy. 'Never mind,' thought George. 'He'll be safe tonight on my bed! Tomorrow will be soon enough.'

It was the first time that Mrs Lenoir had asked them down to be with her. 'You see, Mr Lenoir is out tonight on important business,' she explained. 'He has had to go to the mainland with the car. He doesn't like his evenings disturbed when he is at home, so I haven't been able to see as much of you all as I should have liked. But tonight I can.'

Julian wondered if Mr Lenoir had gone to the mainland on smuggling business! Somehow the smuggled goods must be taken across to the mainland and if all that signalling business the other night had to do with Mr Lenoir's smuggling then maybe he had now gone to dispose of the goods!

The telephone bell rang shrilly. Mrs Lenoir got up. 'I expect that is your mother or father on the phone,' she said to George. 'Maybe I shall have news for you! Perhaps your parents will be arriving here tomorrow.'

She went out into the hall. The children waited anxiously. Would George's parents come or not?

12   Block gets a surprise

Mrs Lenoir came back after a time. She smiled at George.

'That was your father,' she said. 'He is coming tomorrow, but not your mother. They went to your aunt's, and your mother says she thinks she must stay and help her, because your aunt is not very well. But your father would like to come, because he wants to discuss his latest experiments with Mr Lenoir, who is very interested in them. It will be very nice to have him.'

The children would very much rather have had Aunt Fanny instead of Uncle Quentin, who could be very difficult at times. But still, he would probably be talking with Mr Lenoir most of the time, so that would be all right!

They finished their game with Mrs Lenoir and went up to bed. George was to get Timmy to take him to her room. Sooty went to see that the coast was clear. He could not see Block anywhere. His stepfather was still away from the house. Sarah was singing in the kitchen and the little kitchen-maid, Harriet, was knitting there in a corner.

'Block must be out,' thought Sooty, and went to tell George that the coast was clear. As he went across the landing to the long passage that led to his own room, the boy noticed two black lumps sticking out at the bottom of the thick curtains drawn across the landing window. He looked at them in surprise, and then recognised them. He grinned.

'So old Block suspects we have a dog, and he thinks it sleeps in George's room or Julian's, and he's posted himself there to watch!' he thought. 'Aha! I'll give friend Block a nasty shock!'

He ran to tell the others. George listened, alarmed. But Sooty, as usual, had a plan.

'We'll give Block an awful shock!' he said. 'I'll get a rope, and we'll all go down to the landing. I'll suddenly yell out that there's a robber hiding behind the curtains and I'll pounce on Block, and give him a few good punches. Then, with your help, Julian and Dick, I'll fold him up well in the curtains – a good jerk will bring them down on top of him as well!'

The others began to laugh. It would be fun to play a trick on Block. He really was such an unpleasant fellow. A good lesson would do him no harm.

'While all the excitement is beginning I'll slip by with Timmy,' said George. 'I only hope he won't want to join in! He might give Block a good nip!'

'Well, hold on to Timmy firmly,' said Julian. 'Get him into your room quickly. Now – are we ready?'

They were. Feeling excited they crept down the long passage that led to the door which opened out on to the landing where Block was hiding. They saw the curtains move very slightly as they came along. Block was watching.

George waited with Timmy at the passage door, not showing herself at all. Then, with a yell from Sooty, a really blood-curdling yell that made both George and Timmy jump, things began to happen!

Sooty flung himself on the hidden Block with all his might. 'A robber! Help, a robber hiding here!' he shouted.

Block jumped, and began to struggle. Sooty got in two or three well-aimed punches. Block had often got him into trouble with his father, and now Sooty was getting a bit of his own back! Julian and Dick rushed to help.

A violent tug at the curtains brought them down on Block's head! Not only that, the curtain pole descended on him too, and knocked him sideways. Poor Block – he was completely taken by surprise, and could do nothing against the three determined boys. Even Anne gave a hand, though Marybelle stood apart, enjoying the fun though not daring to take part in it.

Just as it all began George slipped by with Timmy. But Timmy could not bear to miss the fun. He dragged behind George, and would not go with her.

She tried to force him, her hand on his collar. But Timmy had seen a nice fat leg waving about near him, protruding from the curtain. He pounced on it.

There was an agonised yell from Block. Certainly Timmy could nip hard with his sharp white teeth. He worried at the kicking leg for a few seconds, and then had a sharp slap from George. Shocked, Timmy let go of the leg and humbly followed his mistress. She never slapped him! She must indeed be angry with him. With tail well down Timmy followed her into the bedroom and got under the bed at once. He poked his head out and looked beseechingly at George with big brown eyes.

'Oh, Timmy – I *had* to slap you!' said George, and she knelt down by the big dog and patted his head. 'You see, you might have spoilt everything if you'd been seen. As it is I'm sure you bit Block and I don't know how we're going to explain that! Lie quietly now, old fellow. I'm going out to join the others.'

Timmy's tail thumped softly on the floor. George ran out of the room and joined the others on the landing. They were having a fine game with Block, who was yelling and wriggling and struggling for all he was worth. He was wrapped up in the curtains like a caterpillar inside a cocoon. His head was completely covered and he could see nothing.

Suddenly Mr Lenoir appeared in the hall below, with a very scared Mrs Lenoir beside him. 'What's all this?' thundered Sooty's stepfather. 'Have you gone mad? How dare you behave like this at this time of night?'

'We've caught a robber and tied him up,' panted Sooty.

Mr Lenoir ran up the stairs two steps at a time, amazed. He saw the kicking figure on the ground well-tied up in the heavy curtains. 'A robber! Do you mean a burglar? Where did you find him?'

'He was hiding behind the curtains!' said Julian. 'We managed to get hold of him and tie him up before he could escape. Could you call the police?'

An anguished voice came from inside of the curtains. 'Let me go! I've been bitten! Let me go!'

'Good heavens! You've got Block tied up there!' said Mr Lenoir, in amazement and anger. 'Untie him, quickly.'

'But – it can't be Block. He was hiding behind those curtains at the window,' protested Sooty.

'Do as you're told,' commanded Mr Lenoir, getting angry. Anne looked at the tip of his nose. Yes, it was turning white, as usual!

The boys reluctantly undid the ropes. Block angrily parted the curtains that enfolded him, and looked out, his usually blank face crimson with rage and fright.

'I won't stand this sort of thing!' he raged. 'Look

here, at my leg, sir! I've been bitten. Only a dog could have done that. See my leg?'

Sure enough there were the marks of teeth on his leg, slowly turning purple. Timmy had taken a good nip, and almost gone through the skin.

'There's no dog here,' said Mrs Lenoir, coming timidly up the stairs at last. 'You couldn't have been bitten by a dog, Block.'

'Who bit him, then?' demanded Mr Lenoir, turning fiercely on poor Mrs Lenoir.

'Do you think *I* could have bitten him, in my excitement?' suddenly said Sooty, to the enormous surprise of the others, and to their immense amusement. He spoke very seriously with a worried look on his face. 'When I lose my temper, I hardly know what I do. Do you think I bit him?'

'Pah!' said Mr Lenoir, in disgust. 'Don't talk nonsense, boy! I'll have you punished if I think you go about biting people. Get up, Block. You're not badly hurt.'

'My teeth do feel a bit funny, now I come to think of it,' said Sooty, opening and shutting his mouth as if to see if they were all right. 'I think I'd better go and clean them. I feel as if I've got the taste of Block's ankle in my mouth. And it isn't nice.'

Mr Lenoir, driven to fury by Sooty's impudence, reached out swiftly to box the boy's ears. But Sooty dodged and ran back up the passage. 'Just going to clean my teeth!' he called, and the others tried to keep from laughing. The idea of Sooty biting anyone was absurd. It was quite obvious, however, that neither Mr nor Mrs Lenoir guessed what had bitten Block.

'Go to bed, all of you,' ordered Mr Lenoir. 'I hope I shall not have to complain of you to your father tomorrow when he comes – or your uncle, as it may be. I don't know which of you are his children, and which not. I'm surprised at you making such a nuisance of yourselves in somebody else's house. Tying up my servant! If he leaves, it will be your fault!'

The children hoped fervently that Block *would* leave. It would be marvellous to have the deaf blank-faced fellow out of the house. He was on the watch for Timmy, they felt sure. He would snoop about till he got Timmy or one of them into trouble.

But Block was still there next morning. He came into the schoolroom with the breakfast, his face almost as blank as usual. He gave Sooty an evil look.

'You look out for yourself,' he said, in a curiously soft voice. 'You look out. Something's going to happen to you one of these days. Yes – and that dog too! I know you've got a dog, see? You can't deceive *me*.'

The children said nothing, but looked at one another. Sooty grinned, and rapped out a cheerful little tune on the table with his spoon.

'Dark, dire, dreadful threats!' he said. 'You look out for yourself too, Block. Any more snooping about, and you'll find yourself tied up again – yes, and I might bite you again too. You never know. My teeth feel quite ready for it this morning.'

He bared his teeth at Block, who made no reply at all, but merely looked as if he had not heard a word. The man went out, and closed the door softly behind him.

'Nasty bit of work, isn't he?' said Sooty. But George felt rather alarmed. She feared Block. There was something cold and clever and bad about those narrow eyes of his. She longed with all her heart to get Timmy out of the house.

She got a terrible shock that morning! Sooty came

to her, looking agitated. 'I say! What do you think? Your father's going to have *my* room. I've got to sleep with Julian and Dick. Block is taking all my things from my room to theirs this very minute, with Sarah. I hope we shall have a chance to get him out all right, before your father comes!'

'Oh Sooty!' said George, in despair. 'I'll go and see if I can get him at once.'

She went off, pretending to go to Marybelle's room for something. But Block was still in Sooty's room. And there he stayed, cleaning it all morning!

George was very worried about Timmy. He would wonder why she hadn't fetched him. He would miss his walk. She hovered about the passage all morning, getting into Sarah's way as she carried clothes from Sooty's old room to Julian's.

Block gave George some curious looks. He walked with a limp to show that his leg was bad from the bite. He left the room at last and George darted in. But Block returned almost at once and she dashed into Marybelle's room. Again Block left and went down the passage, and again the desperate little girl rushed into Sooty's room.

But Block was back before she could even open the cupboard door. 'What are you doing in this room?' he said, roughly. 'I haven't cleaned it all morning to have children in here messing it up again! Clear out of it!'

George went – and then once more waited for Block to go. He would have to see to the luncheon soon! He went at last. George rushed to the door of Sooty's room, eager to get poor Timmy.

But she couldn't open the door. It was locked – and Block had taken the key!

13 Poor George!

By now George was in despair. She felt as if she was in a nightmare. She went to find Sooty. He was in Julian's room, next to hers, washing his hands ready for lunch.

'Sooty! I shall have to get into the secret passage the way you first took us in,' she said. 'Through that little study-room of your father's – you know, where the sliding panels are.'

'We can't,' said Sooty, looking rather alarmed. 'He uses it now, and he'd half-kill anyone who went in there. He's got the records of all his experiments there, and he's put them ready to show your father.'

'I don't care,' said George, desperately. 'I've got to get in there somehow. Timmy may starve!'

'Not Timmy! He'll live on the rats in the passages!' said Sooty. 'Timmy could always look after himself, I bet!'

'Well, he'd die of thirst then,' said George, obstinately. 'There's no water in those secret passages. You know that!'

George could hardly eat any lunch because she was so worried. She made up her mind somehow to get into that little study-room, and see if she could open the entrance into the wall behind the panels. Then she would slip in and get Timmy. She didn't care what happened; she was going to get Timmy.

'I shan't tell the others, though,' she thought. 'They

would only try and stop me, or offer to do it themselves, and I don't trust anyone but myself to do this. Timmy's my dog, and *I'm* going to save him!'

After lunch, everyone went to Julian's room to discuss things. George went with them. But after a few minutes she left them. 'Back in a minute,' she said. They took no notice and went on discussing how to rescue Timmy. It really did seem as if the only way was to raid the study, and try and get into the secret passage without being seen.

'But my stepfather works there now,' said Sooty. 'And I shouldn't be surprised if he locks the door when he leaves the room.'

George didn't come back. After about ten minutes Anne grew puzzled.

'What can George be doing? It must be about ten minutes since she went.'

'Oh, she's probably gone to see if my old room is unlocked yet,' said Sooty, getting up. 'I'll peep out and see if she's about.'

She wasn't. She didn't seem to be anywhere! She wasn't in the passage that led to Sooty's old room; she couldn't be in that room because it was still locked, and she wasn't in Marybelle's room.

Sooty peeped in George's own room, the one she shared with Anne. But that was empty too. He went downstairs and snooped around a bit. No George!

He went back to the others, puzzled.

'I can't find her anywhere,' he said. 'Where can she be?'

Anne looked alarmed. This was such a strange house, with strange happenings. She wished George would come.

'She's not gone into that little study-room, has she?'

said Julian, suddenly. It would be just like George to try and get into the lion's den!'

'I didn't think of that,' said Sooty. 'Silly of me. I'll go and see.'

He went down the stairs. He made his way cautiously to his father's study. He stood quietly outside the shut door. There was no sound from inside. Was his father there or not?

Sooty debated whether to open the door and peep in or whether to knock. He decided to knock. Then, if his father answered he could rush back upstairs before the door could be opened, and his father would not know whom to scold for the interruption.

So he knocked, very smartly, rap-rap.

'Who's that?' came his stepfather's irritable voice. 'Come in! Am I to have no peace?'

Sooty fled upstairs at once. He went to the others. 'George can't be in the study,' he said. 'My stepfather's there, and he didn't sound in too good a temper either.'

'Then *where* can she be?' said Julian, looking worried. 'I do wish she wouldn't go off without telling us where she's going. She must be somewhere about. She wouldn't go very far from Timmy.'

They all had a good hunt over the house, even going into the kitchen. Block was there, reading a paper. 'What do you want?' he said. 'You won't get it, whatever it is.'

'We don't want anything from *you*,' said Sooty. 'How's your poor bad bitten leg?'

Block looked so unpleasantly at them that they all retreated from the kitchen in a hurry. Sooty put Julian and Dick on guard, and went up to the staff bedrooms to see if by any chance George had gone there. A silly idea, he knew, but George must be somewhere!

She wasn't there, of course. The children went back gloomily to Julian's room. 'This beastly house!' said Julian. 'I can't say I like it. Sorry to say so, Sooty, but it's a weird place with a funny feeling about it.'

Sooty was not hurt at all. 'Oh, I agree with you,' he said. 'I've always thought the same myself. So has Mother, and so has Marybelle. It's my stepfather that likes it.'

'Where *is* George?' said Anne. 'I keep on and on trying to think. There's only one place I'm certain she's not in – and that's your stepfather's study, Sooty. Even George wouldn't dare to go there while your stepfather was there.'

But Anne was wrong. The study was the very place where George was at that very moment!

The little girl had made up her mind that it was best to try and get in there, and wait for a chance to open the sliding panel. So she had slipped downstairs, gone across the hall, and tried the door of the study. It was locked.

'Blow!' said George, desperately. 'Everything is against me and Timmy. How can I get in? I must, I must!'

She slipped out of the side-door near the study and went into the little yard on to which the study-window looked. Could she get in there?

But the window was barred! So that was no good either. She went back again, wishing she could find the key to unlock the door. But it was nowhere to be seen.

Suddenly she heard Mr Lenoir's voice in the room across the hall. In a panic George lifted up the lid of a big wooden chest nearby, and climbed hurriedly into it. She closed the lid over her, and knelt there, waiting, heart beating fast.

Mr Lenoir came across the hall. He was going to his

study. 'I shall get everything ready to show my visitor when he comes,' he called to his wife. 'Don't disturb me at all. I shall be very busy indeed.'

George heard the sound of a key being put into the study door. It turned. The door opened and shut with a click.

But it was not locked again from the inside. George knelt in the dark chest and considered matters. She meant to get into that study. She meant to get through the entrance into the secret passage, where Tim was. That passage led from the study to Sooty's old bedroom, and somewhere in that passage was Timmy.

What she was going to do once she had Timmy she didn't quite know. Perhaps Sooty would take him to someone who could look after him for her, someone on Castaway Hill.

She heard the sound of Mr Lenoir coughing. She heard the shuffling of papers. Then she heard the click of a cupboard being opened and shut. Mr Lenoir was evidently busy!

Then he gave an exclamation of annoyance. He said something in an irritable voice that sounded like 'Now where did I put that?'

Then the door opened very suddenly and Mr Lenoir came out. George had just time to close down the lid, which she had opened to let in fresh air. She knelt in the chest, trembling, as Mr Lenoir passed there and went on across the hall.

George suddenly knew that this was her chance. Mr Lenoir might be gone for a few minutes and give her time to open that panel in the wall! She lifted the lid of the chest, and jumped out quickly. She ran into the study, and went to the place where Sooty had pressed the panelling.

But before she could even run her fingers over the

smooth brown oak, she heard returning footsteps! Mr Lenoir had hardly been half a minute. He was coming back at once.

In a panic poor George looked round for somewhere to hide. There was a large sofa against one wall. George crawled behind it, finding just room to crouch there without being seen. She was hardly there before Mr Lenoir entered the room, shut the door, and sat down at his desk. He switched on a big lamp over it, and bent to look at some documents.

George hardly dared to breathe. Her heart bumped against her ribs and seemed to make a terrible noise. It was very uncomfortable behind the sofa, but she did not dare to move.

She could not think what in the world to do. It would be terrible to be there for hours! What would the others think? They would soon be looking for her.

They were. Even at that moment Sooty was outside the study door, pondering whether to go in or to knock. He knocked smartly – rap-rap – and George almost jumped out of her skin!

She heard Mr Lenoir's impatient voice. 'Who's that? Come in! Am I to have no peace?'

There was no answer. No one came in. Mr Lenoir called again. 'Come in, I say!'

Still no answer. He strode to the door and flung it open angrily. No one was there. Sooty had fled upstairs at once.

'Those tiresome children, I suppose,' muttered Mr Lenoir. 'Well, if any of them comes and knocks again and goes away, I'll punish them properly. Bed and bread and water for them!'

He sounded fierce. George wished she was anywhere but in his study. What would he say if he knew she was only three or four feet away from him?

Mr Lenoir worked for about half an hour, and poor George got stiffer and stiffer, and more and more uncomfortable. Then she heard Mr Lenoir yawn, and her heart felt lighter. Perhaps he would have a nap! That would be good luck. She might creep out then, and try to get into the secret passage.

Mr Lenoir yawned again. Then he pushed his papers aside and went to the sofa. He lay down on it and pulled the rug there over his knees. He settled himself down as if for a good sleep.

The sofa creaked under him. George tried to hold her breath again, afraid that now he was so near to her he would certainly hear her.

Soon a small snore came to her ears. Then another and another. Mr Lenoir was asleep! George waited for a few minutes. The snores went on, a little louder. Surely it would be safe now to creep from her hiding-place?

George began to move, very cautiously and quietly. She crept to the end of the sofa. She squeezed out from behind it. Still the snores went on.

She stood upright and went on tiptoe to the panel that had slid aside. She began to press here and there with her fingers, trying to find the spot that would move the panel to one side.

She couldn't seem to find it. She grew red with anxiety. She cast a glance at the sleeping Mr Lenoir, and worked feverishly at the panel. Where was the spot to press, oh, where was it?

Then a stern voice came from behind her, making her jump almost out of her skin.

'And what exactly do you think you are doing, my boy? How dare you come into my study and mess about like this?'

George turned round and faced Mr Lenoir. He

always thought she was a boy! She didn't know what to say. He looked very angry indeed, and the tip of his nose was already white.

George was frightened. She ran to the door, but Mr Lenoir caught her before she opened it. He shook her hard.

'What were you doing in my study? Was it you who knocked and ran away? Do you think it is funny to play tricks like that? I'll soon teach you that it isn't!'

He opened the door and called loudly. 'Block! Come here! Sarah, tell Block I want him.'

Block appeared from the kitchen, his face as blank as usual. Mr Lenoir wrote something down quickly on a piece of paper and gave it to him to read. Block nodded.

'I've told him to take you to your room, lock you in, and give you nothing but bread and water for the rest of the day,' said Mr Lenoir, fiercely. 'That will teach you to behave yourself in the future. Any more nonsense and I'll whip you myself.'

'My father won't be very pleased when he hears you're punishing me like this,' began George in a trembling voice. But Mr Lenoir sneered.

'Pah! Wait till he hears from me how you have misbehaved yourself, and I am sure he will agree with me. Now go, and you will not be allowed out of your room till tomorrow. I will make your excuses to your father, when he comes.'

Poor George was propelled upstairs by Block, who was only too delighted to be punishing one of the children. As she came to the door of the room George shouted to the others who were in Julian's room next door.

'Julian! Dick! Help me! Quick, help me!'

14 A very puzzling thing

Julian, Dick, and the others rushed out at once, just in time to see Block shove George roughly into her room and shut the door. There was a click as he locked it.

'Here! What are you doing?' cried Julian, indignantly.

Block took no notice, but turned to go. Julian caught hold of his arm, and yelled loudly in his ear. 'Unlock that door at once! Do you hear?'

Block gave no sign whether he had or not. He shook off Julian's hand, but the boy put it back again at once, getting angry.

'Mr Lenoir gave me orders to punish that girl,' said Block, looking at Julian out of his cold, narrow eyes.

'Well, you jolly well unlock that door,' commanded Julian, and he tried to snatch the key from Block. With sudden vicious strength the man lifted his hand and struck Julian, sending him half across the landing. Then he went swiftly downstairs to the kitchen.

Julian looked after him, a little scared. 'The brute!' he said. 'He's as strong as a horse. George, George, whatever's happened?'

George answered angrily from the locked bedroom. She told the others everything, and they listened in silence. 'Bad luck, George,' said Dick. 'Poor old girl! Just as you were feeling for the opening to the passage too!'

'I must apologise for my stepfather,' said Sooty. 'He

has such a terrible temper. He wouldn't have punished you like this if he had thought you were a girl. But he keeps thinking you're a boy.'

'I don't care,' said George. 'I don't care about any punishment. It's only that I'm so worried about Timmy. Well, I suppose I'll have to stay here now, till I'm let out tomorrow. I shan't eat anything that Block brings me, you can tell him. I don't want to see his horrid face again!'

'How shall I go to bed tonight?' wailed Anne. 'All my things are in your room, George.'

'You'll have to sleep with me,' said little Marybelle, who looked very frightened. 'I can lend you a nightie. Oh dear – what will George's father say when he comes? I hope he will say that George is to be set free at once.'

'Well, he won't,' said George, from behind the locked door. 'He'll just think I've been in one of my bad moods, and he won't mind my being punished at all. Oh dear – I wish Mother was coming too.'

The others were very upset about George, as well as about Timmy. Things seemed to be going very wrong indeed. At tea-time they went to the schoolroom to have tea, wishing they could take George some of the chocolate cake set ready for them.

George felt lonely when the others had gone to tea. It was five o'clock. She was hungry. She wanted Timmy. She was angry and miserable, and longed to escape. She went to the window and looked out.

Her room looked straight down the cliff-side, just as Sooty's old room did. Below was the city-wall that ran round the town, going unevenly up and down as it followed the contours of the hillside.

George knew that she could not jump down to the wall. She might roll off it and fall straight down to the marsh below. That would be horrible. Then she suddenly remembered the rope-ladder that they used when they got down into the pit each day.

It had at first been kept in Marybelle's room, on the shelf in the cupboard, but since the children had been scared by knowing that someone had tried the handle of the door one morning, they had decided to keep the ladder in George's room for safety. They were afraid that perhaps Block might go snooping round Marybell's room and find it. So George had smuggled it to her own room, and hidden it in her suitcase, which she had locked.

Now, her hands shaking a little with excitement, she unlocked her suitcase and took out the rope-ladder. She might perhaps escape out of the window with it. She looked out again, the rope in her hands.

But windows overlooked the city-wall just there. The kitchen too must be just below, and maybe Block would see her climbing down. That would never do. She must wait till it was twilight.

When the others came back she told them what she was going to do, speaking in a low voice through the door.

'I'll get down on the wall, walk along it for some way, and then jump down and creep back,' she said. 'You get some food for me somehow, and I'll have it. Then tonight, when everyone has gone to bed I'll get into the study again and find the way through to the secret passage. Sooty can help me. Then I can get Timmy.'

'Right,' said Sooty. 'Wait till it's fairly dark before you go down the ladder, though. Block has gone to his room with a bad headache, but Sarah and Harriet are in the kitchen, and you don't want to be seen.'

So, when the twilight hung like a soft purple curtain

over the house, George slid down the rope-ladder out
of the window. She only needed to let about a quarter
of it out for it was far too long for such a short distance.

She fastened it to the legs of her heavy little oak bed.
Then she climbed out of the window and slid quietly
down the rope-ladder.

She passed the kitchen window, which fortunately
had its blinds drawn down now. She landed squarely
on the old wall. She had brought a torch with her so
that she could see.

She debated with herself what to do. She did not
want to run any risk of coming up against either Block
or Mr Lenoir. Perhaps it would be best to walk along
the wall till she came to some part of the town she
knew. Then she could jump off and make her way
cautiously back up the hill, looking out for the others.

So she began to walk along the broad top of the old
wall. It was very rough and uneven in places, and
many stones were missing. But her torch showed a
steady light and she did not miss her footing.

The wall ran round some stables, then round the
backs of some quaint old shops. Then it ran round a
big yard belonging to some house, and then round the
house itself. Then down it went, around some more
houses.

George could look into those windows that were
not curtained. Lights shone out from them now. It
was strange being able to see into the windows without being seen. A little family sat at a meal in one
room, their faces cheerful and happy. An old man sat
alone in another, reading and smoking.

A woman sat listening to a radio, knitting, as
George silently walked on the wall outside her
window. Nobody heard her. Nobody saw her.

Then she came to another house, a big one. The wall

ran close against it, for it was built where the cliff ran steeply down to the marsh just there.

There was a lit window there. George glanced in as she passed. Then she stood still in great surprise.

Surely, surely that was Block in there! He had his back to her, but she could have sworn it was Block. The same head, the same ears, the same shoulders!

Who was he talking to? George tried to see – and all at once she knew. He was talking to Mr Barling, whom everyone said was a smuggler – *the* smuggler of Castaway Hill!

But wait a minute – could it be Block? Block was deaf, and this man evidently wasn't. He was listening to Mr Barling, that was plain, and was answering him, though George could not hear the words, of course.

'I oughtn't to be snooping like this,' said George to herself. 'But it's very strange, very puzzling and very interesting. If only the man would turn round I'd know at once if it was Block!'

But he didn't turn. He just sat in his chair, his back to George. Mr Barling, his long face lit up by the nearby lamp, was talking animatedly, and Block, if it *was* Block, was listening intently and nodding his head in agreement every now and again.

George felt puzzled. If she only knew for certain that it was Block! But why should he be talking to Mr Barling – and wasn't he stone deaf after all then?

George jumped down from the wall into a dark little passage and made her way through the town, up to Smuggler's Top. Outside the front door, hiding in the shadows was Sooty. He laid his hand on George's arm, making her jump.

'Come on in. I've left the side door open. We've got a fine spread for you!'

The two slipped in at the side door, tiptoed past the

study, across the hall, and up to Julian's bedroom. Truly there was a spread there!

'I went and raided the larder,' said Sooty, with satisfaction. 'Harriet was out, and Sarah had run along to the post. Block has gone to bed for a rest, because, he said, he had such an awful headache.'

'Oh,' said George, 'then it couldn't have been Block I saw. And yet I'm as certain as certain can be that it was!'

'Whatever do you mean?' asked the others, in surprise. George sat down on the floor and began to gobble up cakes and tarts, for she was terribly hungry. Between her mouthfuls she told them how she had got out of the window, walked along the city-wall, and found herself unexpectedly by Mr Barling's house.

'And I looked into a lit window there, and saw Block talking to Mr Barling – and listening to him and answering him!' she said.

The others could not believe this. 'Did you see his face?' asked Julian.

'No,' said George. 'But I'm *certain* it was Block. Go and peep into his room and see if he's there, Sooty. He wouldn't be back yet from Mr Barling's, because he had a glass full of something or other, which would take him some time to drink. Go and peep.'

Sooty vanished. He came back quickly. 'He's in bed!' he said. 'I could see the shape of his body and the dark patch of his head. Are there *two* Blocks then? Whatever does this mean?'

15   Strange happenings

It certainly was very puzzling – most of all to George, who felt so certain it had been Block talking to the well-known smuggler. The others did not feel so certain, especially as George admitted that she had not seen his face.

'Is my father here yet?' asked George, suddenly, remembering that he was supposed to come that evening.

'Yes. Just arrived,' said Sooty. 'Just before you came. I nearly got run over by the car! Just hopped aside in time. I was out there waiting for you.'

'What are our plans?' asked George. 'I'll have to get Timmy tonight, or he'll be frantic. I think I'd better go and climb back through my window again now, in case Block comes along and finds I've disappeared. I'll wait till everyone is in bed and then I'll slip out of the window again, and you must let me into the house, Sooty, please. Then I'll go to the study with you and you must open the secret way for me. Then I'll find Timmy and everything will be all right.'

'I don't see that everything will be all right,' said Sooty, doubtfully. 'But anyway, your plan is the only one to follow. You'd better get back into your room now, if you've had enough to eat.'

'I'll take a few buns back with me,' said George, stuffing them into her pocket. 'Sooty, come and knock at my door when everyone is in bed and I'll know then that it's safe for me to slip out of the window, and come into the house again.'

It wasn't long before George was back in her room once more – just in time too, for Block appeared a little while after with a plate of dry bread and a glass of water. He unlocked the door and put them on the table.

'Your supper,' he said. George looked at his blank face and disliked it so much that she felt she must do something about it. So she took up the water and threw it deftly at the back of his head. It dripped down his neck and made him jump. Block took a step towards her, his eyes gleaming – but Julian and Dick were by the door, and he did not dare to strike her.

'I'll pay you back for that,' he said. 'See? You will never get that dog of yours back again!'

He went out and locked the door. Julian called through as soon as he had gone.

'What did you do that for, you idiot? He's a bad enemy to make.'

'I know. I just couldn't help it somehow,' said George, forlornly. 'I wish I hadn't now.'

The others had to go down to see Mr Lenoir. They left George feeling lonely. It was horrid to be locked up like this, even though she could escape through the window whenever she wanted to. She listened for the others to come back.

They soon did, and reported their meeting with George's father.

'Uncle Quentin is awfully tired and a bit cross, and frightfully annoyed with you for misbehaving,' said Julian, through the door. 'He said you were to be locked up the whole of tomorrow too, if you don't apologise.'

George didn't mean to apologise. She couldn't bear

Mr Lenoir, with his false smiles and laughter, and his sudden odd rages. She said nothing.

'We've got to go and have our supper now,' said Sooty. 'We'll save you some of it as soon as Block goes out of the room. Look out for a knocking on your door tonight. It'll be me, telling you everyone's in bed.'

George lay on her bed, thinking. Many things puzzled her. She couldn't get them straight somehow. The signaller in the tower – the peculiar man, Block – Mr Barling's talk to a man who looked so like Block; but Block was all the time in his bed at home. As she lay thinking, her eyes closed, and she fell asleep.

Anne went up to bed with Marybelle, and came to whisper good-night to her. The boys all went into the next room, for Sooty was now to share Julian's and Dick's bedroom. George woke up enough to say good-night and then slept again.

At midnight she awoke with a jump. Someone was knocking softly and impatiently on her door. It was Sooty.

'Coming!' whispered George through the door, and took up her torch. She went to the window and was soon safely down the rope-ladder. She jumped down from the wall, and went to the side door of the house. Sooty was there. She slipped in thankfully.

'Everyone's gone to bed,' whispered Sooty. 'I thought your father and my stepfather were never going. They stayed talking in the study for ages!'

'Come on. Let's go there,' said George, impatiently. They went to the study door, and Sooty turned the handle.

It was locked again! He pushed hard, but it wasn't a bit of good. It was well and truly locked!

'We might have thought of that,' said George, in

despair. 'Blow, blow, blow! What are we to do now?'

Sooty thought for a few moments. Then he spoke in a low voice, in George's ear.

'There's only one thing left to do, George. I must creep into your father's room – my old bedroom – when he is asleep – and I must get into the cupboard there, open the entrance to the secret passage, and slip in that way. I'll find Timmy and bring him back the same way, hoping that your father won't wake!'

'Oh! Would you really do that for me?' said George, gratefully. 'You *are* a good friend, Sooty! Would you rather I did it?'

'No. I know the way up and down that passage better than you do,' said Sooty. 'It's a bit frightening to be all alone there at midnight too. I'll go.'

George went with Sooty up the stairs, across the wide landing, to the door at the end of the passage that led to Sooty's old room, where George's father was now sleeping. When they got there, George pulled his arm.

'Sooty! The buzzer will go as soon as you open the door – and it will wake my father and warn him.'

'Idiot! I disconnected it as soon as I knew my room was to be changed,' said Sooty, scornfully. 'As if I wouldn't think of that!'

He opened the door that led into the passage. He crept up to his old room. The door was shut. He and George listened intently.

'Your father sounds a bit restless,' said Sooty. 'I'll wait my chance to creep in, George, and then, as soon as possible, I'll slip into the cupboard and open the secret passage to find Tim. As soon as I've got Timmy I'll bring him along to you. You could wait in Marybelle's room if you liked. Anne's there too.'

George crept into the room next door, where Anne and Marybelle lay fast asleep. She left the door open, so that she might hear when Sooty returned. How lovely it would be to have dear old Timmy again! He would lick her and lick her.

Sooty crept into the room where George's father lay, half-asleep. He made no sound. He knew every creaking board and avoided them. He made his way quietly to a big chair, meaning to hide behind it till he was certain George's father was sound asleep.

For some time the man in the bed tossed and turned. He was tired with his long journey, and his mind was excited with his talk with Mr Lenoir. He muttered now and again, and Sooty began to feel he would never be sound asleep! He grew sleepy himself, and yawned silently.

At last George's father grew quiet and peaceful. No more creaks came from the bed. Sooty cautiously moved out from behind the chair.

Then suddenly something startled him. He heard a sound over by the window! But what could it be? It was a very small sound, like a tiny creak of a door.

The night was rather dark, but the window, its curtains pulled right back, could easily be seen as a square of grey. Sooty fixed his eyes on it. Was someone opening the window?

No. The window did not move. But something strange was happening under it, near the sill.

A big window-seat was built in under the window, wide and comfortable. Sooty knew it well! He had sat on it hundreds of times to look out of the window. Now, what was happening to it?

It looked as if the top, or lid of the seat was slowly moving upwards, bit by bit. Sooty was puzzled. He had never known it could be opened like that. It had always been screwed down, and he had thought it was just a seat and nothing else. But now it looked as if someone had unscrewed the top, and had hidden himself inside, lifting up the top like a lid when he thought it was safe.

Sooty stared at the upward-moving lid, quite fascinated. Who was in there? Why had he hidden? It was rather frightening, seeing the lid move slowly, bit by bit.

At last the lid was wide open and rested against the window-pane. A big figure cautiously and slowly got out, not making the slightest sound. Sooty felt his hair rising up on his head. He was afraid, terribly afraid. He could not utter a sound.

The figure tiptoed over to the bed. He made a quick and sudden movement, and there was a stifled sound from George's father. Sooty guessed he had been gagged, so that he could not cry out. Still the boy could not move or speak. He had never been so scared in all his life.

The intruder lifted the limp body from the bed, and went to the window-seat. He put George's father into the darkness there. What he had done to make him unable to struggle Sooty didn't know. He only knew that poor George's father was being put down in the window-seat, and couldn't seem to move a hand to help himself!

The boy suddenly found his voice. 'Hi!' he yelled. 'Hi! What are you doing? Who are you?'

He remembered his torch and switched it on. He saw a face he knew, and cried out in surprise. 'Mr Barling!'

Then someone hit him a hard blow on the head and he remembered nothing more at all. He did not know that he was lifted into the window-seat too. He did not know that the intruder followed after him. He knew nothing.

George, awake in the next room, suddenly heard Sooty's voice crying out. 'Hi!' she heard. 'Hi, what are you doing? Who are you?' And then, as she slipped out of bed, she heard the next cry. 'Mr Barling!'

George was extremely startled. What was going on next door? She fumbled about for her torch. Anne and Marybelle were still asleep. George could not find her torch. She fell over a chair and banged her head.

When at last she had found her torch she tiptoed, trembling, to the door. She shone her torch and saw that the door next to hers was a little ajar, just as Sooty had left it, when he had crept inside. She listened. There was absolutely no sound at all now. She had heard a small bumping noise after Sooty's last cry, but she didn't know what it was.

She suddenly put her head round the door of her father's room, and shone her torch again. She stared in surprise. The bed was empty. The room was empty. There was no one there at all! She flashed her torch all round. She opened the cupboard door fearfully. She looked under the bed. She was, in fact, extremely brave.

At last she sank down on the window-seat, frightened and puzzled. Where was her father? Where was Sooty? Whatever had been happening here that night?

16 Next morning

As George sat by the window, on the very seat into which everyone had unaccountably disappeared, though she did not know it, she heard a faint sound from the passage.

Quick as lightning the girl slipped under the bed. Someone was creeping down the long passage! George lay silently on the floor, lifting the valance a little to try and see who it was. What strange things were going on tonight!

Someone came in at the door. Someone stopped there, as if to look and listen. Then someone crept over to the window-seat.

George watched and listened, straining her eyes in the darkness. She dimly saw the someone outlined against the grey square of the window. He was bent over the window-seat.

He showed no light at all. But he made some curious little sounds. First came the sound of his fingers tapping about on the closed lid of the seat. Then came the clink of something metallic, and a very faint squeaking. George could not imagine what the man – if it was a man – was doing.

For about five minutes the somone worked away at his task in the darkness. Then, as quietly as he had come, he went away. George couldn't help thinking it was Block, though his outline against the dark-grey of the window was too dim to recognise. But he had once given a little cough exactly like Block so often gave. It *must* be Block! But whatever was he doing in her father's room at night, on the window-seat?

George felt as if she was in a bad dream. The strangest things happened and kept on happening, and they didn't seem to make sense at all. Where was her father? Had he left his room and gone wandering over the house? Where was Sooty, and why had he called out? He wouldn't have shouted out like that, surely, if her father had been asleep in the room!

George lay under the bed, shivering, for a little while longer. Then she rolled out softly and went out of the door. She crept down the long passage to the end. She opened the door there and peeped out. The whole house was in darkness. Little sounds came to George's ears – a window rattling faintly, the creak of some bit of furniture – but nothing else.

She had only one thought in her mind, and that was to get to the boys' room and tell them the mysterious things that had happened. Soon she was across the landing, and had slipped through the door of Julian's bedroom. He and Dick were awake, of course, waiting for Sooty to come with Timmy and George.

But only George arrived. A scared George, with a very very curious story to tell. She wrapped herself in the eiderdown on Julian's bed, and told what had happened, in whispers.

They were amazed. Uncle Quentin gone! Sooty disappeared! Someone creeping into the room and fiddling about on the window-seat! What did it all mean?

'We'll come to Uncle Quentin's room with you, straight away now,' said Julian, pulling on a dressing-gown, and hunting about for his slippers. 'I've got a feeling that things are getting pretty serious.'

They all padded off to the other rooms. They went

into Marybelle's room and woke her and Anne. Both little girls felt scared. Soon all five children were in the next room, from which George's father and Sooty had so strangely vanished.

Julian shut the door, drew the curtains and switched on the light. At once they all felt better. It was so horrid to grope about in the dark with torches.

They looked round the silent room. There was nothing there to show them how the others had disappeared. The bed was crumpled and empty. On the floor lay Sooty's torch, where it had fallen.

George repeated again what she had thought she had heard Sooty call out, but it made no sense to anyone. 'Why call out Mr Barling's name, when there was only your father in the room?' said Julian. 'Surely Mr Barling wasn't hiding here – that would be nonsense. He has nothing to do with your father, George.'

'I know. But I'm sure it *was* Mr Barling's name that I heard Sooty call out,' said George. 'Do you think – oh yes, do you think Mr Barling could possibly have crept through the secret opening in the cupboard, meaning to do some dirty work or other – and have gone back the same way, taking the others with him because they discovered him?'

This seemed a likely explanation, though not a very good one. They all went to the cupboard and opened it. They groped between the clothes for the secret opening. But the little iron handle set there to pull on the stone at the back was gone! Someone had removed it – and now the secret passage could not be entered, for there was no way of opening it just there!

'Look at that!' said Julian in astonishment. 'Someone's been tampering with that too. No, George, the midnight visitor, whoever he was, didn't go back that way.'

George looked pale. She had been hoping to go and fetch Timmy, by slipping through the secret opening in the cupboard. Now she couldn't. She longed for Timmy with all her heart, and felt that if only the big faithful dog were with her things would seem much brighter.

'I'm sure Mr Lenoir is at the bottom of all this!' said Dick. 'And Block too. I bet that *was* Block you saw in here tonight, doing something in the dark, George. I bet he and Mr Lenoir are hand in glove with each other over something.'

'Well, then – we can't possibly go and tell them what has happened!' said Julian. 'If they are at the bottom of all these weird happenings it would be foolish to go and tell them what we know. And we can't tell your mother, Marybelle, because she would naturally go to your father about it. It's a puzzle to know what to do!'

Anne began to cry. Marybelle, frightened and puzzled, at once began to sob too. George felt tears pricking the backs of her eyelids, but she blinked them away. George never cried!

'I want Sooty,' wept Marybelle, who adored her cheeky, daring brother. 'Where's he gone? I'm sure he's in danger. I do want Sooty.'

'We'll rescue him tomorrow, don't you worry,' said Julian, kindly. 'We can't do anything tonight, though. There's nobody at Smuggler's Top we can possibly get advice or help from, as things are. I vote we go to bed, sleep on it, and make plans in the morning. By that time Sooty and Uncle Quentin may have turned up again. If they haven't, Mr Lenoir will have to be told by someone, and we'll see how he behaves! If he's surprised and upset, we'll soon know if he has had anything to do with this mystery or not. He'll have to do something – go to the police, or have the house turned upside down to find the missing people. We'll soon see what happens.'

Everyone felt a little comforted after this long speech. Julian sounded cheerful and firm, though he didn't feel at all happy, really. He knew, better than any of the others, that something very strange, and probably dangerous was going on at Smuggler's Top. He wished the girls were not there.

'Now listen,' he said. 'George, you go and sleep with Anne and Marybelle next door. Lock your door and keep the light on. Dick and I will sleep here, in Sooty's old room, also with the light on, so you'll know we are quite nearby.'

It was comforting to know that the two boys were so near. The three girls went at last into Marybelle's room, tired out. Anne and Marybelle got into bed again, and George lay down on a small but comfortable couch, pulling a thick rug over her. In spite of all the worry and excitement the girls were soon asleep, quite exhausted.

The boys talked a little, as they lay in Sooty's old bed, where their Uncle Quentin had been asleep some time before. Julian did not think anything more would happen that night. He and Dick fell asleep, but Julian was ready to wake at the slightest noise.

Next morning they were awakened by a most surprised Sarah, who had come in to draw the curtains and bring George's father a pot of early-morning tea. She could not believe her eyes when she saw the two boys in the visitor's bed – and no visitor!

'What's all this?' said Sarah, gaping. 'Where's your uncle? Why are you here?'

'Oh, we'll explain later,' said Julian, who did not want to enter into any details with Sarah, who was a.

bit of a chatterbox. 'You can leave the tea, Sarah. *We'd* like it!'

'Yes, but where's your uncle? Is he in *your* room?' said the puzzled Sarah. 'What's up?'

'You can go and look in our room if you like and see if he's there,' said Dick, wanting to get rid of the amazed woman. She disappeared, thinking that the household must be going mad. She left the hot tea behind, though, and the boys at once took it into the girls' room. George unlocked the door for them. They took it in turns to sip the hot tea from the one cup.

Presently Sarah came back, with Harriet and Block. Block's face was as blank as usual.

'There's nobody in your room, Julian,' began Sarah. Then Block gave a sudden exclamation and stared at George angrily. He had thought she was locked in her room – and here she was in Marybelle's room, drinking tea!

'How did you get out?' he demanded. 'I'll tell Mr Lenoir. You're in disgrace.'

'Shut up,' said Julian. 'Don't you dare to speak to my cousin like that. I believe you're mixed up in this curious business. Clear out, Block.'

Whether Block heard or not, he gave no sign of going. Julian got up, his face set.

'Clear out of this room,' he said, narrowing his eyes. 'Do you hear? I have a feeling that the police might be interested in you, Block. Now clear out!'

Harriet and Sarah gave little shrieks. The sudden mystery was too much for them. They gazed at Block and began to back out of the room. Fortunately Block went too, casting an evil look at the determined Julian.

'I shall go to Mr Lenoir,' said Block, and disappeared.

In a few minutes along came Mr and Mrs Lenoir to

Marybelle's room. Mrs Lenoir looked scared out of her life. Mr Lenoir looked puzzled and upset.

'Now, what's all this?' he began. 'Block has been to me with a most curious tale. Says your father has disappeared, George, and . . .'

'And so has Sooty,' suddenly wailed Marybelle, bursting into tears again. 'Sooty's gone. He's gone too.'

Mrs Lenoir gave a cry. 'What do you mean? How can he have gone? Marybelle, what do you mean?'

'Marybelle, I think I had better take charge of the telling,' said Julian, who was not going to let the little girl give away all the things they knew. After all, Mr Lenoir was probably at the bottom of everything, and it would be foolish to tell him what they suspected about him.

'Julian – tell me what has happened. Quickly!' begged Mrs Lenoir, looking really upset.

'Uncle Quentin disappeared from his bed last night, and Sooty has vanished too,' said Julian, shortly. 'They may turn up, of course.'

'Julian! You are keeping back something,' said Mr Lenoir, suddenly, watching the boy sharply. 'You will tell us *everything*, please. How dare you keep anything back at a moment like this?'

'Tell him, Julian, tell him,' wailed Marybelle. Julian looked obstinate, and glared at Marybelle.

The tip of Mr Lenoir's nose went white. 'I am going to the police,' he said. 'Perhaps you will talk to *them*, my boy. They will knock some sense into you!'

Julian was surprised. 'Why – I shouldn't have thought *you* would want to go to the police!' he blurted out. 'You've got too many secrets to hide!'

17 More and more puzzling

Mr Lenoir stared in the utmost amazement at Julian. There was a dead silence after this remark. Julian could have kicked himself for making it, but he couldn't unsay it now.

Mr Lenoir opened his mouth to say something at last, when footsteps came to the door. It was Block.

'Come in, Block!' said Mr Lenoir. 'There seem to have been peculiar happenings here.'

Block did not appear to hear, and remained outside the door. Mr Lenoir beckoned him in impatiently.

'No,' said Julian, firmly. 'What we have to say is not to be said in front of Block, Mr Lenoir. We don't like him and we don't trust him.'

'What do you mean?' cried Mr Lenoir, angrily. 'What do *you* know about my servants? I've known Block for years before he came into my service, and he's a most trustworthy fellow. He can't help being deaf, and that makes him irritable at times.'

Julian remained obstinate. He caught an angry gleam in Block's cold eyes, and glared back.

'Well, this is incredible!' said Mr Lenoir, trying not to lose his temper. 'I can't think what's come over everybody – disappearing like this – and now you children talking to me as if I wasn't master in my own house. I insist that you tell me all you know.'

'I'd rather tell it to the police,' said Julian, his eye on

Block. But Block showed no trace of expression on his face.

'Go away, Block,' said Mr Lenoir at last, seeing that there was no hope of getting anything out of Julian while the servant was there. 'You'd better all come down to my study. This is getting more and more mysterious. If the police have got to know, you may as well tell me first. I don't want to look a complete idiot in my own house in front of them.'

Julian couldn't help feeling a bit puzzled. Mr Lenoir was not behaving as he had thought he might behave. He seemed sincerely puzzled and upset, and he was evidently planning to get the police in himself. Surely he wouldn't do that if he had had a hand in the disappearances? Julian was lost in bewilderment again.

Mrs Lenoir was now crying quietly, with Marybelle sobbing beside her. Mr Lenoir put an arm round his wife and kissed Marybelle, suddenly appearing very much nicer than he had ever seemed before. 'Don't worry,' he said, in a gentle voice. 'We'll soon get to the bottom of this, if I have to get the whole of the police force in. I think I know who's at the bottom of it all!'

That surprised Julian even more. He and the others followed Mr Lenoir down to his study. It was still locked. Mr Lenoir opened it and pushed aside a great pile of papers that were on his desk.

'Now – what do you know?' he said to Julian quietly. The children noticed that the top of his nose was no longer white. Evidently he had got over his burst of temper.

'Well, I think this is a strange house, with a lot of strange things happening in it,' said Julian, not quite knowing how to begin. 'I'm afraid, you won't like me telling the police all I know.'

'Julian, don't speak in riddles!' said Mr Lenoir,

impatiently. 'You act as if I were a criminal, in fear of
the police. I'm not. What goes on in this house?'

'Well – the signalling from the tower, for instance,'
said Julian, watching Mr Lenoir's face.

Mr Lenoir gaped. It was clear that he was im-
mensely astonished. He stared at Julian, and Mrs
Lenoir cried out suddenly:

'Signalling! What signalling?'

Julian explained. He told how Sooty had discovered
the light-flashing first, and then how he and Dick had
gone with him to the tower when they had seen the
flashing again. He described the line of tiny, pricking
lights across the marsh from the seaward side.

Mr Lenoir listened intently. He asked questions
about dates and times. He heard how the boys had
followed the signaller to Block's room, where he had
disappeared.

'Got out of the window, I suppose,' said Mr Lenoir.
'Block's got nothing to do with this, you can rest
assured of that. He is most faithful and loyal, and has
been a great help to me while he has been here. I have
an idea that Mr Barling is at the bottom of all this. He
can't signal from his house to the sea because it's not
quite high enough up the hill, and is in the wrong
position. He must have been using *my* tower to signal
from – coming himself to do it too! He knows all the
secret ways of this house, better than I do! It would be
easy for him to come here whenever he wanted to.'

The children thought at once that probably Mr
Barling *had* been the signaller! They stared at Mr
Lenoir. They were all beginning to think that he really
and truly had nothing to do with the strange goings-
on after all.

'I don't see why Block shouldn't know all this,' said
Mr Lenoir, getting up. 'It's plain to me that Barling

could explain a lot of the odd things that have been happening. I'll see if Block has ever suspected anything.'

Julian pursed his lips together. If Mr Lenoir was going to tell everything to Block, who certainly must be in the plot somehow, he wasn't going to tell him anything more!

'I'll see what Block thinks about everything, and then if we can't solve this mystery ourselves, we'll get in the police,' said Mr Lenoir, going out of the room.

Julian did not want to say anything much in front of Mrs Lenoir. So he changed the subject completely.

'What about breakfast?' he said. 'I'm feeling hungry!'

So they all went to have breakfast, though Marybelle could eat nothing at all, because she kept thinking of poor Sooty.

'I think,' said Julian, when they were alone at the table, 'I rather think we'll do a little mystery-solving ourselves. I'd like a jolly good look round that room of your father's, George, to begin with. There must be some other way of getting out of there, besides the secret passage we know.'

'What do you think happened there last night?' said Dick.

'Well, I imagine that Sooty went there and hid, to wait until it was safe to try and get into the secret passage as soon as Uncle Quentin was asleep,' said Julian, thoughtfully. 'And while he was hiding, someone came into that room from somewhere, to kidnap Uncle Quentin. Why, I don't know, but that's what I think. Then Sooty yelled out in surprise, and got knocked on the head or something. Then he and Uncle Quentin were kidnapped together, and taken off through some secret way we don't know.'

'Yes,' said George. 'And it was Mr Barling who kidnapped them! I distinctly heard Sooty yell out "Mr Barling". He must have switched on his torch and seen him.'

'They are quite probably hidden somewhere in Mr Barling's house,' said Anne, suddenly.

'Yes!' said Julian. 'Why didn't I think of that? Why, that's just where they would be, of course. I've a jolly good mind to go down and have a look!'

'Oh, let me come too,' begged George.

'No,' said Julian. 'Certainly not. This is rather a dangerous adventure, and Mr Barling is a bad and dangerous man. You and Marybelle are certainly not to come. I'll take Dick.'

'You are absolutely *mean*!' began George, her eyes flashing. 'Aren't I as good as a boy? I'm going to come.'

'Well, if you're as good as a boy, which I admit you are,' said Julian, 'can't you stay and keep an eye on Anne and Marybelle for us? We don't want them kidnapped too.'

'Oh, don't go, George,' said Anne. 'Stay here with us.'

'I think it's mad to go, anyhow,' said George. 'Mr Barling wouldn't let you in. And if you did get in you wouldn't be able to find all the secret places in his house. There must be as many, and more, as there are here.'

Julian couldn't help thinking George was right. Still, it was worth trying.

He and Dick set out after breakfast, and went down the hill to Mr Barling's. But when they got there they found the whole house shut up. Nobody answered their knocking and ringing. The curtains were drawn across the closed windows, and no smoke came from the chimney.

'Mr Barling's gone away for a holiday,' said the gardener who was working in the next door flowerbeds. 'Went this morning, he did. In his car. All his servants have got a holiday too.'

'Oh!' said Julian, blankly. 'Was there anyone with him in the car – a man and a boy, for instance?'

The gardener looked surprised at this question, and shook his head.

'No. He was alone, and drove off himself.'

'Thanks,' said Julian, and walked back with Dick to Smuggler's Top. This was most odd. Mr Barling had shut up the house and gone off without his captives! Then what had he done with them? And why on earth had he kidnapped Uncle Quentin? Julian remembered that Mr Lenoir had not put forward any reason for that. Did he know one, and hadn't wanted to say what it was? It was all most puzzling.

Meantime George had been doing a little snooping round on her own. She had slipped into Uncle Quentin's room, and had had a really good look round everywhere to see if by chance there was another secret passage Sooty hadn't known about.

She had tapped the walls. She had turned back the carpet and examined every inch of the floor. She had tried the cupboard again, and wished she could get through into the secret passage there and find Timmy. The study door downstairs was again locked, and she did not dare to tell Mr Lenoir about Timmy and ask his help.

George was just about to leave the quiet room when she noticed something on the floor near the window. She bent to pick it up. It was a small screw. She looked round. Where had it come from?

At first she couldn't see any screws of the same size at all. Then her eyes slid down to the window-seat. There were screws there, screwing down the top oaken plank to the under ones that supported it.

Had the screw come out of the window-seat? Why should it, anyway? The others there were all screwed down tightly. She examined one. Then she gave a low cry.

'One's missing. The one in the middle of this side. Now just let me think.'

She remembered last night. She remembered how someone had crept in, while she had hidden under the bed, and had fiddled about by the window, bending over the polished window-seat. She remembered the little noises – the metallic clinks and the tiny squeaks. It was screws being screwed into the seat!

'Someone screwed down the window-seat last night – and in the darkness, dropped one of the little screws,' thought George, beginning to feel excited. 'Why did he screw it down? To hide something? What's in this window-seat? It sounds hollow enough. It never lifted up. I know that. It was always screwed down, because I remember looking for a cupboard under it, like the one we have at home, and there wasn't one.'

George began to feel certain there was some secret about the window-seat. She rushed off to get a screw-driver. She found one and hurried back.

She shut the door and locked it behind her in case Block should come snooping around. Then she set to work with the screwdriver. What would she find in the window-seat? She could hardly wait to see!

18   Curious discoveries

Just as she had unscrewed almost the last screw there came a tapping at the door. George jumped and stiffened. She did not answer, afraid that it was Block, or Mr Lenoir.

Then, to her great relief, she heard Julian's voice. 'George! Are you in here?'

The little girl hurried across to the door and unlocked it. The boys came in, looking surprised, followed by Anne and Marybelle. George shut the door and locked it again.

'Mr Barling's gone away and shut up the house,' said Julian. 'So that's that. What on earth are you doing, George?'

'Unscrewing this window-seat,' said George, and told them about the screw she had found on the floor. They all crowded round her, excited.

'Good for you, George!' said Dick. 'Here, let me finish the unscrewing.'

'No, thanks. This is *my* job!' said George. She took out the last screw. Then she lifted the edge of the window-seat. It came up like a lid.

Everyone peered inside, rather scared. What would they see? To their great surprise and disappointment they saw nothing but an empty cupboard! It was as if the window-seat was a box, with the lid screwed down for people to sit on.

'Well – what a disappointment!' said Dick. He shut

down the lid. 'I don't expect you heard anyone screwing down the lid, really, George. It might have been your imagination.'

'Well, it wasn't,' said George, shortly. She opened the lid again. She got right into the box-like window-seat and stamped, and pressed with her feet.

And quite suddenly, there came a small creaking noise, and the bottom of the empty window-seat fell downwards like a trap-door on a hinge!

George gasped and clutched at the side. She kicked about in air for a moment and then scrambled out. Everyone looked down in silence.

They looked down a straight yawning hole, which, however, came to an end only about eight feet down. There it appeared to widen out, and, no doubt, entered a secret passage which ran into one of the underground tunnels with which the whole hill was honeycombed. It might even run to Mr Barling's house.

'Look at that!' said Dick. 'Who would have thought of that? I bet even old Sooty didn't know about this.'

'Shall we go down?' said George. 'Shall we see where it goes to? We might find old Timmy.'

There came the noise of someone trying the handle of the door. It was locked. Then there was an impatient rapping, and a cross voice called out sharply:

'Why is this door locked? Open it at once! What are you doing in there?'

'It's Father!' whispered Marybelle, with wide eyes. 'I'd better unlock the door.'

George shut the lid of the window-seat down at once, quietly. She did not want Mr Lenoir to see their latest discovery. When the door was opened Mr Lenoir saw the children standing about, or sitting on the window-seat.

'I've had a good talk to Block,' he said, 'and, as I

thought, he doesn't know a thing about all the goings-on here. He was most amazed to hear about the signalling from the tower. But he doesn't think it's Mr Barling. He thinks it may be a plot of some sort against *me*.'

'Oh!' said the children, who felt that *they* would not believe Block so readily as Mr Lenoir appeared to.

'It's quite upset Block,' said Mr Lenoir. 'He feels really sick, and I've told him to go and have a rest till we decide what to do next.'

The children felt that Block would not be so easily upset as all that. They all suspected at once that he would not really go to rest, but would probably sneak out on business of his own.

'I've some work to attend to for a little while,' said Mr Lenoir. 'I've rung up the police, but unluckily the Inspector is out. He will ring me directly he comes back. Now can you keep out of mischief till I've finished my work?'

The children thought that was a silly question. They made no reply. Mr Lenoir gave one of his sudden smiles and little laughs, and went.

'I'm going to pop along to Block's room and see if he really *is* there,' said Julian, as soon as Mr Lenoir was out of sight.

He went to the wing where the staff bedrooms were, and stopped softly outside Block's. The door was a little ajar, and Julian could see through the crack. He saw the shape of Block's body in the bed, and the dark patch that was his head. The curtains were drawn across the window to keep out the light, but there was enough to see all this.

Julian sped back to the others. 'Yes, he's in bed all right,' he said. 'Well, he's safe for a bit. Shall we have a shot at getting down to the window-seat hole? I'd dearly like to see where it leads to!'

'Oh yes!' said everyone. But it was not an easy job to drop eight feet down without being terribly jolted! Julian went first and was very much jarred. He called up to Dick: 'We'll have to get a bit of rope and tie it to something up there, and let it hang down the hole – it's an awful business to let yourself drop down.'

But just as Dick went to find a rope, Julian called up again. 'Oh, it's all right! I've just seen something. There are niches carved into the sides of the hole – niches you can put foot or hand into. I didn't see them before. You can use them to help you down.'

So down went everyone, one after another, feeling for the niches and finding them. George missed one or two, clawed wildly at the air, and dropped down the last few feet, landing with rather a bump, but she was not hurt.

As they had thought, the hole led to another secret passage in the house, but this one went straight downwards by means of steps, so that very soon they went well below the level of the house. Then they came into the maze of tunnels that honeycombed the hill. They stopped.

'Look here – we can't possibly go any farther,' said Julian. 'We shall get lost. We haven't got Sooty with us now, and Marybelle isn't any good at finding the way. It would be dangerous to wander about.'

They could hear the hollow sound of footsteps coming from a tunnel to the left of them. They all shrank back into the shadows, and Julian switched off his torch.

'It's *two* people!' whispered Anne, as two figures came out of the nearby tunnel. One was very tall and long. The other – yes, surely the other was Block! If it wasn't Block it was someone the exact image of him.

The men were talking in low voices, answering one another. How could it be Block, though, if he could hear as well as that? Anyway, Block was asleep in bed. It was hardly ten minutes since Julian had seen him there. Were there two Blocks, then? thought George, as she had once thought before.

The men disappeared into another tunnel, and the bright light of their lanterns disappeared gradually. The muffled rumble of their voices echoed back.

'Shall we follow them?' said Dick.

'Of course not,' said Julian. 'We might lose them – and lose ourselves too! And supposing they suddenly turned back and found us following them? We should be in a horrid fix.'

'I'm sure the first man was Mr Barling,' said Anne, suddenly. 'I couldn't see his face because the light of the lantern wasn't on it – but he seemed just like Mr Barling – awfully tall and long everywhere!'

'But Mr Barling's gone away,' said Marybelle.

'*Supposed* to have gone away!' said George. 'It looks as if he's come back, if it *was* him. I wonder where those two have gone – to see my father and Sooty, do you think?'

'Quite likely,' said Julian. 'Come on, let's get back. We simply *daren't* wander about by ourselves in these old tunnels. They run for miles, Sooty said, and cross one another, and go up and down and round about – even right down to the marsh. We should never, never find our way out if we got lost.'

They turned to go back. They came to the end of the steps they had been climbing, and found themselves at the bottom of the window-seat hole. It was quite easy to pull themselves up by the niches in the sides of the hole.

Soon they were all in the room again, glad to see the sunshine streaming in at the window. They looked out. The marshes were beginning to be wreathed in mist once more, though up here the hill was golden with sunlight.

'I'm going to put the screws back into the window-seat again,' said Julian, picking up the screwdriver and shutting down the lid. 'Then if Block comes here he won't guess we've found this new secret place. I'm pretty certain that he unscrewed the seat so that Mr Barling could get into this room, and then screwed it down again so that no one would guess what had happened.'

He quickly put in the screws. Then he looked at his watch.

'Almost dinner-time, and I'm jolly hungry. I wish old Sooty was here – and Uncle Quentin. I do hope they're all right – and Timmy too,' said Julian. 'I wonder if Block is still in bed – or wandering about the tunnels. I'm going to have a peep again.'

He soon came back, puzzled. 'Yes, he's there all right, safe in bed. It's jolly funny.'

Block did not appear at lunchtime. Sarah said he had asked not to be disturbed, if he did not appear.

'He does get the most awful sick headaches,' she said. 'Maybe he'll be all right this afternoon.'

She badly wanted to talk about everything, but the children had decided not to tell her anything. She was very nice and they liked her, but somehow they didn't trust anyone at Smuggler's Top. So Sarah got nothing out of them at all, and retired in rather a huff.

Julian went down to speak to Mr Lenoir after the meal. He felt that even if the Inspector of police was not at the police-station, somebody else must be informed. He was very worried about his uncle and Sooty. He couldn't help wondering if Mr Lenoir had made up the bit about the Inspector being away, to put off time.

Mr Lenoir was looking cross when Julian knocked at his study-door. 'Oh, it's you!' he said to Julian. 'I was expecting Block. I've rung and rung for him. The bell rings in his room and I can't imagine why he doesn't come. I want him to come to the police-station with me.'

'Good!' thought Julian. Then he spoke aloud. 'I'll go and hurry him up for you, Mr Lenoir. I know where his room is.'

Julian ran up the stairs and went to the little landing up which the back-stairs went to the staff bedrooms. He pushed open Block's door.

Block was apparently still asleep in bed! Julian called loudly, then remembered that Block was deaf. So he went over to the bed and put his hand rather roughly on the hump of the shoulder between the clothes.

But it was curiously soft! Julian drew his hand away, and looked down sharply. Then he got a real shock.

There was no Block in the bed! There was a big ball of some sort, painted black to look like a head almost under the sheets – and, when Julian threw back the covers, he saw instead of Block's body, a large lumpy bolster, cleverly moulded to look like a curved body!

'*That's* the trick Block plays when he wants to slip off anywhere, and yet pretend he's still here!' said Julian. 'So it *was* Block we saw in the tunnel this morning – and it *must* have been Block that George saw talking to Mr Barling yesterday, when she looked through the window. He's not deaf, either. He's a very clever – sly – double-faced – deceitful ROGUE!'

19 *Mr Barling talks*

Meantime, what was happening to Uncle Quentin and Sooty? Many strange things!

Uncle Quentin had been gagged, and drugged so that he could neither struggle nor make any noise, when Mr Barling had crept so unexpectedly into his room. It was easy to drop him down the hole in the window-seat. He fell with a thud that bruised him considerably.

Then poor Sooty had been dropped down too, and after them had come Mr Barling, climbing deftly down by the help of the niches in the sides.

Someone else was down there, to help Mr Barling. Not Block, who had been left to screw down the window-seat so that no one might guess where the victims had been taken, but a hard-faced servant belonging to Mr Barling.

'Had to bring this boy, too – it's Lenoir's son,' said Mr Barling. 'Snooping about in the room. Well, it will serve Lenoir right for working against me!'

The two were half-carried, half-dragged down the long flight of steps and taken into the tunnels below. Mr Barling stopped and took a ball of string from his pocket. He tossed it to his servant.

'Here you are. Tie the end to that nail over there, and let the string unravel as we go. I know the way quite well, but Block doesn't, and he'll be coming along to bring food to our couple of prisoners tomorrow. Don't want him to lose his way! We can tie the string up again just before we get to the place I'm taking them to, so that they won't see it and use it to escape by.'

The servant tied the string to the nail that Mr Barling pointed out, and then as he went along he let the ball unravel. The string would then serve as a guide to anyone not knowing the way. Otherwise it would be very dangerous to wander about in the underground tunnels. For some of them ran for miles.

After about eight minutes the little company came to a kind of rounded cave, set in the side of a big, but rather low tunnel. Here had been put a bench with some rugs, a box to serve as a table, and a jug of water. Nothing else.

Sooty by now was coming round from his blow on the head. The other prisoner, however, still lay unconscious, breathing heavily.

'No good talking to him,' said Mr Barling. 'He won't be all right till tomorrow. We'll come and talk to him then. I'll bring Block.'

Sooty had been put on the floor. He suddenly sat up, and put his hand to his aching head. He couldn't imagine where he was.

He looked up and saw Mr Barling, and then suddenly he remembered everything. But how had he got there, in this dark cave?

'Mr Barling!' he said. 'What's all this? What did you hit me for? Why have you brought me here?'

'Punishment for a small boy who can't keep his nose out of things that don't concern him!' said Mr Barling, in a horrid sarcastic voice. 'You'll be company for our friend on the bench there. He'll sleep till the morning, I'm afraid. You can tell him all about it, then, and say I'll be back to have a little heart-to-heart talk with him!

And see here, Pierre – you do know, don't you, the foolishness of trying to wander about these old passages? I've brought you to a little-known one, and if you want to lose yourself and never be heard of again, well, try wandering about, that's all!'

Sooty looked pale. He did know the danger of wandering about those lost old tunnels. This one he was in he was sure he didn't know at all. He was about to ask a few more questions when Mr Barling turned quickly on his heel and went off with his servant. They took the lantern with them and left the boy in darkness. He yelled after them.

'Hi, you beasts! Leave me a light!'

But there was no answer. Sooty heard the footfalls going farther and farther away, and then there was silence and darkness.

The boy felt in his pocket for his torch, but it wasn't there. He had dropped it in his bedroom. He groped his way over to the bench, and felt about for George's father. He wished he would wake up. It was so horrid to be there in the darkness. It was cold, too.

Sooty crept under the rugs and cuddled close to the unconscious man. He longed with all his heart for him to wake up.

From somewhere there sounded the drip-drip-drip of water. After a time Sooty couldn't bear it. He knew it was only drops dripping off the roof of the tunnel in a damp place, but he felt he couldn't bear it. Drip-drip-drip. Drip-drip-drip. If only it would stop!

'I'll have to wake George's father up!' thought the boy, desperately. 'I *must* talk to someone!'

He began to shake the sleeping man, wondering what to call him, for he did not know his surname. He couldn't call him 'George's father'! Then he remembered that the others called him Uncle Quentin, and he began yelling the name in the drugged man's ear.

'Uncle Quentin! Uncle Quentin! Wake up! Do wake up! Oh, won't you please wake up!'

Uncle Quentin stirred at last. He opened his eyes in the darkness, and listened to the urgent voice in his ear feeling faintly puzzled.

'Uncle Quentin! Wake up and speak to me. I'm scared!' said the voice. 'UNCLE QUENTIN!'

The man thought vaguely that it must be Julian or Dick. He put his arm round Sooty and dragged him close to him. 'It's all right. Go to sleep,' he said. 'What's the matter, Julian? Or is it Dick? Go to sleep.'

He fell asleep again himself, for he was still half-drugged. But Sooty felt comforted now. He shut his eyes, feeling certain that he couldn't possibly go to sleep. But he did, almost at once! He slept soundly all through the night, and was only awakened by Uncle Quentin moving on the bench.

The puzzled man was amazed to find his bed so unexpectedly hard. He was even more amazed to find someone in bed with him, for he remembered nothing at all. He stretched out his hand to switch on the reading-lamp which had been beside his bed the night before.

But it wasn't there! Strange! He felt about and touched Sooty's face. What was this beside him? He began to feel extremely puzzled. He felt ill, too. What *could* have happened?

'Are you awake?' said Sooty's voice. 'Oh, Uncle Quentin, I'm so glad you're awake. I hope you don't mind me calling you that, but I don't know your surname. I only know you are George's father and Julian's uncle.'

'Well – who are you?' said Uncle Quentin, in wonder.

Sooty began to tell him everything. Uncle Quentin listened in the utmost amazement. 'But *why* have we been kidnapped like this?' he said, astonished and angry. 'I never heard of such a thing in my life!'

'I don't know why Mr Barling has kidnapped *you* – but I know he took me because I happened to see what he was doing,' said Sooty. 'Anyway, he's coming back this morning, with Block, and he said he would have a heart-to-heart talk with you. We'll have to wait here, I'm afraid. We can't possibly find our way to safety in the darkness, through this maze of tunnels.'

So they waited – and in due course Mr Barling did come, bringing Block with him. Block carried some food, which was very welcome to the prisoners.

'You beast, Block!' said Sooty, at once, as he saw the servant in the light of the lantern. 'How dare you help in this? You wait till my stepfather hears about it! Unless he's in it too!'

'Hold your tongue!' said Block.

Sooty stared at him. 'So you *can* hear!' he said. 'All this time you've been pretending you can't! What a sly fellow you are! What a lot of secrets you must have learnt, pretending to be deaf, and overhearing all kinds of things not meant for you. You're sly, Block, and you're worse things than that!'

'Whip him, Block, if you like,' said Mr Barling, sitting down on the box. 'I've no time for rude boys myself.'

'I will,' said Block, grimly, and he undid a length of rope from round his waist. 'I've often wanted to, cheeky little worm!'

Sooty felt alarmed. He leapt off the bench and put up his fists.

'Let me talk to our prisoner first,' said Mr Barling. 'Then you can give Pierre the hiding he deserves. It will be nice for him to wait for it.'

Uncle Quentin was listening quietly to all this. He looked at Mr Barling, and spoke sternly.

'You owe me an explanation for your strange behaviour. I demand to be taken to Smuggler's Top. You shall answer to the police for this!'

'Oh no, I shan't,' said Mr Barling, in a curiously soft voice. 'I have a very generous proposal to make to you. I know why you have come to Smuggler's Top. I know why you and Mr Lenoir are so interested in each other's experiments.'

'How do you know?' said Uncle Quentin. 'Spying, I suppose!'

'Yes – I bet Block's been spying and reading letters!' cried Sooty, indignantly.

Mr Barling took no notice of the interruption. 'Now, my dear sir,' he said to Uncle Quentin, 'I will tell you very shortly what I propose. I know you have heard that I am a smuggler. I am. I make a lot of money from it. It is easy to run a smuggling trade here, because no one can patrol the marshes, or stop men using the secret path that only I and a few others know. On favourable nights I send out a signal – or rather Block here does so, for me, using the convenient tower of Smuggler's Top . . .'

'Oh! So it *was* Block!' cried Sooty.

'Then when the goods arrive,' said Mr Barling, 'and again at a favourable moment I – er – dispose of them. I cover my tracks very carefully, so that no one can possibly accuse me because they never have any real proof.'

'Why are you telling me all this?' said Uncle Quentin scornfully. 'It's of no interest to me. I'm only interested in a plan for draining the marshes, not in smuggling goods across them!'

'Exactly, my dear fellow!' said Mr Barling, amiably. 'I know that. I have even seen your plans and read about your experiments and Mr Lenoir's. But the draining of the marsh means the end of my own business! Once the marsh is drained, once houses are built there, and roads made, once the mists have gone, my business goes too! A harbour may be built out there, at the edge of the marshes – my ships can no longer creep in unseen, bringing valuable cargoes! Not only will my money go, but all the excitement, which is more than life to me, will go too!'

'You're mad!' said Uncle Quentin, in disgust.

Mr Barling *was* a little mad. He had always felt a great satisfaction in being a successful smuggler in days when smuggling was almost at an end. He loved the thrill of knowing that his little ships were creeping in the mist towards the treacherous marshes. He liked to know that men were making their way over a small and narrow path over the misty marsh to the appointed meeting-place, bringing smuggled goods.

'You should have lived a hundred years or more ago!' said Sooty, also feeling that Mr Barling was a little mad. 'You don't belong to nowadays.'

Mr Barling turned on Sooty, his eyes gleaming dangerously in the light of the lantern.

'Another word from you and I'll drop you in the marshes!' he said. Sooty felt a shiver go down his back. He suddenly knew that Mr Barling really did mean what he said. He was a dangerous man. Uncle Quentin sensed it too. He looked at Mr Barling warily.

'How do I come into this?' he asked. 'Why have you kidnapped me?'

'I know that Mr Lenoir is going to buy your plans from you,' said Mr Barling. 'I know he is going to drain the marsh by using your very excellent ideas. You see, I know all about them! I know, too, that Mr Lenoir hopes to make a lot of money by selling the land once it is drained. It is all his, that misty marsh – and no use to anyone now except to me! But that marsh is not going to be drained – I am going to buy your plans, not Mr Lenoir!'

'Do *you* want to drain the marsh, then?' said Uncle Quentin, in surprise.

Mr Barling laughed scornfully. 'No! Your plans, and the results of your experiments, will be burnt! They will be mine, but I shall not want to use them. I want the marsh left as it is, secret, covered with mist, and treacherous to all but me and my men. So, my dear sir, you will please name your price to me, instead of to Mr Lenoir and sign this document, which I have had prepared, making over all your plans to me!'

He flourished a large piece of paper in front of Uncle Quentin. Sooty watched breathlessly.

Uncle Quentin picked up the paper. He tore it into small pieces. He threw them into Mr Barling's face and said, scornfully: 'I don't deal with madmen, nor with rogues, Mr Barling!'

20 Timmy to the rescue

Mr Barling went very pale. Sooty gave a loud crow of delight. 'Hurrah! Good for *you*, Uncle Quentin!'

Block gave a loud exclamation, and darted to the excited boy. He took him by the shoulder, and raised the rope to thrash him.

'That's right,' said Mr Barling, in a funny kind of hissing voice. 'Deal with him first, Block and then with this – this – stubborn – obstinate – fool! We'll soon bring them to their senses. A good thrashing now and again, a few days here in the dark, without any food – ah, that will make them more biddable!'

Sooty yelled at the top of his voice. Uncle Quentin leapt to his feet. The rope came down and Sooty yelled again.

Then there suddenly came the pattering of quick feet, and something flung itself on Block. Block gave a scream of pain and turned. He knocked the lantern over by accident, and the light went out. There was a sound of fierce growling. Block staggered about trying to keep off the creature that had fastened itself on to him.

'Barling! Help me!' he shouted.

Mr Barling went to his aid, but was attacked in his turn. Uncle Quentin and Sooty listened in amazement and fear. What creature was this that had suddenly arrived? Would it attack them next? Was it a giant rat – or some fierce wild animal that haunted these tunnels?

The fierce animal suddenly barked. Sooty cheered.

'TIMMY! It's you, Timmy! Oh, good dog, good dog! Go for him, then, go for him! Bite him, Timmy, hard.'

The two frightened men could do nothing against the angry dog. Soon they were running down the tunnel as fast as they could go, feeling for the string for fear of being lost. Timmy chased them with much enjoyment, and then returned to Sooty and George's father, rather pleased with himself.

He had a tremendous welcome. George's father made a great fuss of him, and Sooty put his arms round the big dog's neck.

'How did you come here? Did you find your way out of the secret passage you've been in? Are you half-starved? Look, here's some food.'

Timmy ate heartily. He had managed to devour a few rats, but otherwise had had no food at all. He had licked the drops that here and there he had found dripping from the roof, so he had not been thirsty. But he had certainly been extremely puzzled and worried. He had never before been so long away from his beloved mistress!

'Uncle Quentin – Timmy could take us safely back to Smuggler's Top, couldn't he?' said Sooty, suddenly. He spoke to Timmy. 'Can you take us home, old boy? Home, to George?'

Timmy listened, with his ears cocked up. He ran down the passage a little way, but soon came back. He did not like the idea of going down there. He felt that enemies were waiting for them all. Mr Barling and Block were not likely to give in quite so easily!

But Timmy knew other ways about the tunnels that honeycombed the hillside. He knew, for instance, the way down to the marsh! So he set off in the darkness, with Uncle Quentin's hand on his collar, and Sooty following close behind, holding on to Uncle Quentin's coat.

It wasn't easy or pleasant. Uncle Quentin wondered at times if Timmy really did know where he was going. They went down and down, stumbling over uneven places, sometimes knocking their heads against an unexpected low piece of roof. It was not a pleasant journey for Uncle Quentin, for he had no shoes on his feet, and was dressed only in pyjamas and rugs.

After a long time they came out on the edge of the marsh itself, at the bottom of the hill! It was a desolate place, and the mists were over it, so that neither Sooty nor Uncle Quentin knew which way to turn!

'Never mind,' said Sooty, 'we can easily leave it to Timmy. He knows the way all right. He'll take us back to the town, and once there we'll know the way home ourselves!'

But suddenly, to their surprise and dismay, Timmy stopped dead, pricking up his ears, whined and would go no farther. He looked thoroughly miserable and unhappy. What could be the matter?

Then, with a bark, the big dog left the two by themselves, and galloped back into the tunnel they had just left. He disappeared completely!

'Timmy!' yelled Sooty. 'Timmy! Come here! Don't leave us! TIMMY!'

But Timmy was gone; why, neither Sooty nor Uncle Quentin knew. They stared at one another.

'Well – I suppose we'd better try to make our way over this marshy bit,' said Uncle Quentin, doubtfully, putting a foot out to see if the ground was hard. It wasn't! He drew back his foot at once.

The mists were so thick that it was really impossible

to see anything. Behind them was the opening to the tunnel. A steep rocky cliff rose up about it. There was no path that way, it was certain. Somehow they had to make their way round the foot of the hill to the main-road that entered the town – but the way lay over marshy ground!

'Let's sit down and wait for a bit to see if Timmy comes back,' said Sooty. So they sat down on a rock at the entrance to the tunnel and waited.

Sooty began to think of the others. He wondered what they had thought when they had discovered that both he and Uncle Quentin were missing. How astonished they must have been!

'I wonder what the others are doing?' he said, aloud. 'I'd love to know!'

The others, as we know, had been doing plenty. They had found the opening in the window-seat where Mr Barling had taken the captives, and they had gone down it and actually seen Mr Barling and Block on their way to talk to Uncle Quentin and Sooty!

They had found out, too, that Block hadn't been in his bed – he had left a dummy there instead. Now everyone was talking at once, and Mr Lenoir was suddenly convinced that Block had been a spy, put in his house by Mr Barling, and not the good servant he had appeared!

Once Julian felt that he was convinced of this he spoke to him more freely, and told him of the way through the window-seat, and of how they had seen Mr Barling and Block that very day, in the under-ground tunnels!

'Good heavens!' said Mr Lenoir, now looking thoroughly alarmed. 'Barling must be mad! I've always thought he was a bit strange – but he must be absolutely mad to kidnap people like this – and Block must be, too. This is a plot! They've heard what I've been planning with your uncle – and they've made up their minds to stop it because it will interfere with their smuggling. Goodness knows what they'll do now! This is serious!'

'If only we had Timmy!' suddenly said George.

Mr Lenoir looked astonished.

'Who's Timmy?'

'Well, you might as well know everything now,' said Julian, and he told Mr Lenoir about Timmy, and how they had hidden him.

'Very foolish of you,' said Mr Lenoir, shortly, looking displeased. 'If you'd told me I would have had someone in the town look after him. I can't help not liking dogs. I detest them, and never will have them in the house. But I would willingly have arranged for him to be boarded out, if I'd known you'd brought him.'

The children felt sorry and a little ashamed. Mr Lenoir was an odd, hot-tempered person, but he didn't seem nearly as horrid as they had thought he was.

'I'd like to go and see if I can find Timmy,' said George. 'You'll get the police in now, I suppose, Mr Lenoir, and perhaps we could go and find Timmy? We know the way into the secret passage from your study.'

'Oh – so *that's* why you were hiding there in the afternoon yesterday,' said Mr Lenoir. 'I thought you were a very bad boy. Well, go and try and find him if you like, but don't let him come anywhere near me. I really cannot bear dogs in the house.'

He went to telephone the police-station again. Mrs Lenoir, her eyes red with crying, stood by him. George slipped away to the study, followed by Dick and Julian and Anne. Marybelle stayed beside her mother.

'Come on – let's get into that secret passage and try and find old Timmy,' said George. 'If we all go, and whistle and shout and call, he's sure to hear us!'

They found the way into the passage, by doing the things they had done before. The panel slid back, and then another, larger opening came as before. They all squeezed through it, and found themselves in the very narrow passage that led from the study up to Sooty's bedroom.

But Timmy was not there! The children were surprised, but George soon thought why.

'Do you remember Sooty telling us there was a way into this passage from the dining-room, as well as from the study and Sooty's bedroom? Well, I believe I saw a door or something there, as we passed where the dining-room must be, and it's likely Timmy may have pushed through it, and gone into another passage somewhere.'

They went back, one by one. They came to the dining-room – or rather, they walked behind the dining-room wall. There they saw the door that George had noticed as they passed – a door, small and set quite flat to the wall, so that it was difficult to see. George pushed it. It opened easily, and then flapped shut, with a little click. It could be opened from one side but not from the other.

'That's where Timmy's gone!' said George, and she pushed the door open again. 'He pushed against the door and it opened – he went through, and the door fastened itself so that he couldn't get back. Come on, we must find him.'

They all went through the small door. It was so low that they had to bend their heads to go through, even

Anne. They found themselves in a passage rather like the one they had just left, but not quite so narrow. It suddenly began to go downwards. Julian called back to the others.

'I believe it goes down to the passages where we used to take Timmy when we let him down into that pit to go for a walk! Yes, look – we've come to where the pit itself is!'

They went on, calling Timmy, and whistling loudly, but no Timmy came. George began to feel worried.

'Hallo! – Surely this is where we came out when we climbed down all those steps from the window-seat passage!' said Dick, suddenly. 'Yes, it is. Look, there's the tunnel where we saw Block and Mr Barling going!'

'Oh – do you think they've done something to Timmy?' said George, in a frightened voice. 'I never thought of that!'

Everyone felt alarmed. It was strange that Block and Mr Barling could go about unmolested by Timmy if Timmy was somewhere near! Could they have harmed him in any way? They had no idea that Timmy was at that very minute with George's father and Sooty!

'Look at this!' said Julian, suddenly, and he shone his torch on to something to show the others. 'String! String going right down this tunnel. Why?'

'It's the tunnel that Mr Barling and Block took!' said George. 'I believe it leads to where they've taken my father and Sooty! They're keeping them prisoners down here! I'm going to follow the string and find them! Who's coming with me?'

21   A journey through the hill

'I'm coming!' said everyone at once. As if they would
let George go alone!

So down the dark tunnel they went, feeling the
string and following it. Julian ran it through his
fingers, and the others followed behind, holding
hands. It would not do for anyone to get lost.

After about ten minutes they came to the rounded
cave where Sooty and George's father had been the
night before. They were not there now, of course –
they were on their way down to the marsh!

'Hallo, look! This is where they must have been!'
cried Julian, shining his torch round. 'A bench – with
tumbled rugs – and an over-turned lamp. And look
here, scraps of paper torn into bits! Something's been
happening here!'

Quick-witted George pieced it together in her
mind. 'Mr Barling took them here and left them. Then
he came back with some sort of proposal to Father,
who refused it! There must have been a struggle of
some sort and the lamp got broken. Oh – I do hope
Father and Sooty got away all right.'

Julian felt gloomy. 'I hope to goodness they haven't
gone wandering about these awful tunnels. Even
Sooty doesn't know a quarter of them. I wish I knew
what's happened.'

'Someone's coming!' suddenly said Dick. 'Snap out
the light, Ju.'

Julian snapped off the torch he carried. At once they were all in darkness. They crouched at the back of the cave, listening.

Yes – footsteps were coming. Rather cautious footsteps. 'Sound like two or three people,' whispered Dick. They came nearer. Whoever was coming was plainly following the tunnel where the string was.

'Mr Barling perhaps – and Block,' whispered George. 'Come to have another talk with Father! But he's gone!'

A brilliant light flashed suddenly round the cave – and picked out the huddled children. There was a loud exclamation of astonishment.

'Good heavens! Who's here? What's all this?'

It was Mr Barling's voice. Julian stood up, blinking in the bright light.

'We came to look for my uncle and Sooty,' he said. 'Where are they?'

'Aren't they here?' said Mr Barling, seeming surprised. 'And is that horrible brute of a dog gone?'

'Oh – was Timmy here?' cried George, joyfully. 'Where is he?'

There were two other men with Mr Barling. One was Block. The other was his servant. Mr Barling put down the lantern he was carrying.

'Do you mean to say you don't know where the others are?' he said, uneasily. 'If they've gone off on their own, they'll never come back.'

Anne gave a little scream. 'It's all your fault, you horrid man!'

'Shut up, Anne!' said Julian. 'Mr Barling,' he said, turning to the angry smuggler, 'I think you'd better come back with us and explain things. Mr Lenoir is now talking to the police.'

'Oh, *is* he?' said Mr Barling. 'Then I think it would

be as well for us all to stay down here for a while! Yes, you too! I'll make Mr Lenoir squirm! I'll hold you all prisoners – and this time you shall be bound so that you don't go wandering off like the others! Got some rope, Block?'

Block stepped forward with the other man. They caught hold of George first, very roughly.

She screamed loudly. 'Timmy! Timmy! Where are you? Timmy, come and help! Oh, TIMMY!'

But no Timmy came. She was soon in a corner with her hands tied behind her. Then they turned to Julian.

'You're mad,' Julian said to Mr Barling, who was standing nearby, holding the lantern. 'You *must* be mad to do things like this.'

'Timmy!' shouted George, trying to free her hands. 'Timmy, Timmy, Timmy!'

Timmy didn't hear. He was too far away. But the dog suddenly felt uneasy. He was with George's father and Sooty at the edge of the marsh, about to lead them round the hill to safety. But he stopped and listened. He could hear nothing of course. But Timmy knew that George was in danger. He knew that his beloved little mistress needed him.

His ears did not tell him, nor did his nose. But his heart told him. George was in danger!

He turned and fled back into the tunnel. He tore up the winding passages at top speed, panting.

And, quite suddenly, just as Julian was angrily submitting to have his hands tied tightly together, a furry thunderbolt arrived! It was Timmy!

He smelt his enemy, Mr Barling, again! He smelt Block. Grrrrrrrrrr-rrrrrr!

'Here's that awful dog again!' yelled Block, and leapt away from Julian. 'Where's your gun, Barling?'

But Timmy didn't worry about guns. He leapt at

Mr Barling and got him on the floor. He gave him a nip in the shoulder that made him yell. Then he leapt at Block, and got him down, too. The other man fled.

'Call your dog off; call him off, or he'll kill us!' cried Mr Barling, struggling up, his shoulder paining him terribly. But nobody said a word. Let Timmy do what he liked!

It wasn't long before all three of the men had gone into the dark tunnel, staggering about without a light, trying to find their way back. But they missed the string, and went wandering away in the darkness, groaning and terrified.

Timmy came running back very pleased with himself. He went to George and, whining with joy, he licked his little mistress from head to foot. And George, who never cried, was most astonished to find the tears pouring down her cheeks. 'But I'm glad, not sad!' she said. 'Oh, somebody undo my hands! I can't pat Timmy!'

Dick undid her hands and Julian's. Then they all had a marvellous time making a fuss of Timmy. And what a fuss he made of them too! He whined and barked, he rolled over and over, he licked them and butted them all with his head. He was wild with delight.

'Oh Timmy – it's lovely to have you again,' said George, happily. 'Now you can lead us to the others. I'm sure you know where Father is, Timmy, and Sooty.'

Timmy did, of course. He set off, his tail wagging, George's hand on his collar, and the others behind in a line, holding hands.

They had the lantern with them and two torches, so they could see the way easily. But they would never have taken the right tunnels if Timmy hadn't been with them. The dog had explored them all thoroughly, and his sense of smell enabled him to go the right way without mistake.

'He's a marvellous dog,' said Anne. 'I think he's the best dog in the world, George.'

'Of course he is,' said George, who had always thought that ever since she had had Timmy as a puppy. 'Darling Tim – wasn't it wonderful when he came racing up and jumped at Block just as he was tying Julian's hands? He must have known we needed him!'

'I suppose he's taking us to wherever your father and Sooty are,' said Dick. 'He seems certain of the way. We're going steadily downhill. I bet we'll be at the marshes soon!'

When they at last came to the bottom of the hill, and emerged from the tunnel in the mists, George gave a yell. 'Look! There's Father – and Sooty too!'

'Uncle Quentin!' shouted Julian, Dick and Anne. 'Sooty! Hallo, here we are!'

Uncle Quentin and Sooty turned in the greatest surprise. They jumped up and went to meet the dog and the excited children.

'How *did* you get here?' said George's father, giving her a hug. 'Did Timmy go back for you? He suddenly deserted us and fled back into the tunnel.'

'What's happened?' asked Sooty, eagerly, knowing that the others would have plenty of news to tell him.

'Heaps,' said George, her face glowing. It was so nice all to be together again, Timmy too. She and Julian and Dick began to tell everything in turn, and then her father told his tale, too, interrupted a little by Sooty.

'Well,' said Julian at last, 'I suppose we ought to be getting back, or the police will be sending out bloodhounds to trace us all! Mr Lenoir will be surprised to see us all turning up together.'

'I wish I wasn't in pyjamas,' said his uncle, drawing the rugs about him. 'I shall feel most peculiar walking the streets like this!'

'Never mind – it's awfully misty now,' said George, and she shivered a little, for the air was damp. 'Timmy – show us the way out of this place. I'm sure you know it.'

Timmy had never been out of the tunnel before, but he seemed to know what to do. He set off round the foot of the hill, the rest following, marvelling at the way Timmy found a dry path to follow. In the mist it was almost impossible to see which place was safe to walk on and which was not. The treacherous marsh was all around them!

'Hurrah! There's the road!' cried Julian, suddenly, as they came in sight of the roadway built over the marsh, running up the hill from the salty stretches of mud. They picked their way to it, their feet soaked with wet mud. Timmy tried to take a flying leap on to it.

But somehow or other he slipped! He fell back into the marsh, tried to find a safe foothold and couldn't. He whined.

'Timmy! Oh look, he's in the mud – and he's sinking!' screamed George, in panic. 'Timmy, Timmy, I'm coming!'

She was about to step down into the marsh to rescue Tim, but her father pulled her back roughly. 'Do you want to sink in, too?' he cried. 'Timmy will get out all right.'

But he wasn't getting out. He was sinking. 'Do something, oh, do something!' shouted George, struggling to get away from her father's hold. 'Oh, save Timmy, quick!'

22 Things come right at last

But what could anyone do? In despair they all gazed at poor Timmy, who was struggling with all his might in the sinking mud. 'He's going down!' wept Anne.

Suddenly there came the sound of rumbling wheels along the road to the hill. It was a lorry carrying a load of goods – coal, coke, planks, logs, sacks of various things. George yelled to it.

'Stop, stop! Help us! Our dog's in the marsh.'

The lorry came to a stop. George's father ran his eye over the things it carried. In a trice he and Julian were dragging out some planks from the load. They threw these into the marsh, and, using them as stepping-stones, the two reached poor sinking Timmy.

The lorry-driver jumped down to help. Into the marsh, crosswise on the other planks, went some more wood, to make a safe path. The first lot were already sinking in the mud.

'Uncle Quentin's got Timmy – he's pulling him up! He's got him!' squealed Anne.

George had sat down suddenly at the edge of the road, looking white. She saw that Timmy would now be rescued, and she felt sick with shock and relief.

It was a difficult business getting Timmy right out, for the mud was strong, and sucked him down as hard as it could. But at last he was out, and he staggered across the sinking planks, trying to wag a very muddy tail.

Muddy as he was, George flung her arms round him. 'Oh Timmy – what a fright you gave us all! Oh, how you smell – but I don't care a bit! I thought you were gone, poor, poor Timmy!'

The lorry-driver looked ruefully at his planks in the marsh. They were now out of sight beneath the mud. Uncle Quentin, feeling rather foolish in pyjamas and rugs, spoke to him.

'I've no money on me now, but if you'll call at Smuggler's Top sometime I'll pay you well for your lost planks and your help.'

'Well, I'm delivering some coal to the house next to Smuggler's Top,' said the man, eyeing Uncle Quentin's curious attire. 'Maybe you'd all like a lift? There's plenty of room at the back there.'

It was getting dark now, as well as being foggy, and everyone was tired. Thankfully they climbed up into the lorry, and it roared up the hill into Castaway. Soon they were at Smuggler's Top, and they all clambered down, suddenly feeling rather stiff.

'I'll be calling tomorrow,' said the driver. 'Can't stop now. Good evening to you all!'

The little company rang the bell. Sarah came hurrying to the door. She almost fell over in surprise as she saw everyone standing there in the light of the hall-lamp.

'Lands' sakes!' she said. 'You're all back! My, Mr and Mrs Lenoir will be glad – they've got the police hunting everywhere for you! They've gone down secret passages, and they've been to Mr Barling's, and . . .'

Timmy bounced into the hall, the mud now drying on him, so that he looked most peculiar. Sarah gave a scream. 'What's that? Gracious, it can't be a dog!'

'Come here, Tim!' said George, suddenly

remembering that Mr Lenoir detested dogs. 'Sarah, do you think you'd have poor Timmy in the kitchen with you? I really can't turn him out into the streets – you've no idea how brave he's been.'

'Come along, come along!' said her father, impatient with all this talk. 'Lenoir can put up with Timmy for a few minutes, surely!'

'Oh, *I'll* have him with pleasure!' said Sarah. 'I'll give him a bath. That's what he wants. Mr and Mrs Lenoir are in the sitting-room. Oh, shall I get you some clothes?'

The little party went in, and made their way to the sitting-room, while Timmy went docilely to the kitchen with the excited Sarah. Mr Lenoir heard the talking and flung open the sitting-room door.

Mrs Lenoir fell on Sooty, tears pouring down her cheeks. Marybelle pawed at him in delight, just as if she was a dog! Mr Lenoir rubbed his hands, clapped everyone on the back, and said: 'Well, well! Fine to see you all safe and sound. Well, well! What a tale you've got to tell, I'm sure!'

'It's a strange tale, Lenoir,' said George's father. 'Very strange. But I'll have to see to my feet before I tell it. I've walked miles in my bare feet, and they're very painful now!'

So, with bits of tales pouring out from everyone, the household bustled round and got hot water for bathing Uncle Quentin's feet, a dressing-gown for him, food for everyone, and hot drinks. It was really a most exciting time, and now that the thrills were all over, the children felt rather important to be able to relate so much.

Then the police came in, of course, and the Inspector at once asked a lot of questions. Everyone wanted to answer them, but the Inspector said that only

George's father, Sooty and George were to tell the tale. They knew most about everything.

Mr Lenoir was perhaps the most surprised person there. When he heard how Mr Barling had actually offered to buy the plans for draining the marsh, and how he had frankly admitted to being a smuggler, he sat back in his chair, unable to say a word.

'He's mad, of course!' said the Inspector of Police. 'Doesn't seem to live in this world at all!'

'That's just what I said to him,' said Sooty. 'I told him he ought to have lived a hundred years ago!'

'Well, we've tried to catch him in the smuggling business many and many a time,' said the Inspector, 'but he was too artful. Fancy him planting Block here as a spy, sir – that was a clever bit of work – and Block using your tower as a signalling place! Bit of nerve, that! And Block isn't deaf, after all? That was clever, too – sending him about, pretending he was stone-deaf, so that he could catch many a bit of knowledge not meant for his ears!'

'Do you think we ought to do something about Block and Mr Barling and the other man?' said Julian, suddenly. 'For all we know they're still wandering about in that maze of tunnels – and two of them are bitten by Timmy, we know.'

'Ah yes – that dog saved your lives, I should think,' said the Inspector. 'A bit of luck, that. Sorry you don't like dogs, Mr Lenoir, but I'm sure you'll admit it was a lucky thing for you all that he was wandering about!'

'Yes – yes, it was,' said Mr Lenoir. 'Of course, Block never wanted dogs here, either – he was afraid they might bark at his curious comings and goings, I suppose. By the way – where *is* this marvellous dog? I don't mind seeing him for a moment – though I do detest dogs, and always shall.'

'I'll get him,' said George. 'I only hope Sarah's done what she said, and bathed him. He was awfully muddy!'

She went out and came back with Timmy. But what a different Timmy! Sarah had given him a good hot bath, and had dried him well. He smelt sweet and fresh, his coat was springy and clean, and he had had a good meal. He was feeling very pleased with himself and everything.

'Timmy – meet a friend,' said George to him, solemnly. Timmy looked at Mr Lenoir out of his big brown eyes. He trotted straight up to him, and held up his right paw politely to shake hands, as George had taught him.

Mr Lenoir was rather taken aback. He was not used to good manners in dogs. He couldn't help putting out his hand to Timmy – and the two shook hands in a most friendly manner. Timmy didn't attempt to lick Mr Lenoir or jump up at him. He took away his paw, gave a little wuff as if to say 'How–do–you–do?' and then went back to George. He lay down quietly beside her. 'Well – he doesn't seem like a *dog*!' said Mr Lenoir, in surprise.

'Oh, he *is*,' said George, at once, very earnestly. 'He's a real, proper dog, Mr Lenoir – only much, much cleverer than most dogs are. Could I keep him, please, while we stay here, and get someone in the town to look after him?'

'Well – seeing he is such a very fine fellow – and seems so sensible – I'll let you have him here,' said Mr Lenoir, making a great effort to be generous. 'Only – please keep him out of my way. 'I'm sure a sensible boy like you will see to that.'

Everyone grinned when Mr Lenoir called George a boy. He never seemed to realise she was a girl. She grinned, too. She wasn't going to tell him she wasn't a boy!

'You'll never see him!' she said, joyfully. 'I'll keep him right out of your way. Thank you very much. It's awfully good of you.'

The Inspector liked Timmy, too. He looked at him and nodded across to George. 'When you want to get rid of him, sell him to me!' he said. 'We could do with a dog like that in our police force! Soon round up the smugglers for us!'

George didn't even bother to reply! As if she would ever sell Timmy, or let him go into the police force!

All the same, the Inspector had to call on Timmy for help before long. When the next day came, and no one had found Mr Barling and his companions in the maze of tunnels, and they hadn't turned up anywhere, the Inspector asked George if she would let Timmy go down into the tunnels and hunt them out.

'Can't leave them there, lost and starving,' he said. 'Bad as they are we'll have to rescue them! Timmy is the only one who can find them.'

That was true, of course. So Timmy once more went underground into the hill, and hunted for his enemies. He found them after a while, lost in the maze of passages, hungry and thirsty, in pain and frightened.

He took them like sheep to where the police waited for them. And after that Mr Barling and his friends disappeared from public life for quite a long time!

'The police must be glad to have got them at last,' said Mr Lenoir. 'They have tried to stop this smuggling for a long time. They even suspected *me* at one time! Barling was a clever fellow, though I still think he was half mad. When Block found out my ideas about draining the marsh, Barling was afraid that once the mists and the marsh were gone, that would be the end of all his excitement – no more smuggling! No more waiting for his little ships to come creeping up in the fog – no more lines of men slipping across the secret ways of the marsh – no more signalling, no more hiding away of smuggled goods. Did you know that the police had found a cave full of them inside the hill?'

It was an exciting adventure to talk about, now that it was all over. The children felt sorry about one thing, though – they were sorry that they had thought Mr Lenoir so horrid. He was a strange man in many ways, but he could be kind and jolly too.

'Did you know we're leaving Smuggler's Top?' said Sooty. 'Mother was so terribly upset when I disappeared, that Father promised her he'd sell the place and leave Castaway, if I came back safe and sound. Mother's thrilled!'

'So am I,' said Marybelle. 'I don't like Smuggler's Top – it's so weird and secret and lonely!'

'Well, if it will make you all happy to leave it, I'm glad,' said Julian 'But *I* like it! I think it's a lovely place, set on a hill-top like this, with mists at its foot, and secret ways all about it. I'll be sorry never to come here again, if you leave.'

'So will I,' said Dick, and Anne and George nodded.

'It's an adventurous place!' said George, patting Timmy. 'Isn't it, Timmy? Do *you* like it, Timmy? Have *you* enjoyed your adventure here?'

'Woof!' said Timmy, and thumped his tail on the floor. Of course he had enjoyed himself. He always did, so long as George was anywhere about.

'Well – now perhaps we'll have a nice peaceful time!' said Marybelle. 'I don't want any more adventures.'

'Ah, but *we* do!' said the others. So no doubt they will get them. Adventures always come to the adventurous, there's no doubt about that!

A complete list of the FAMOUS FIVE
ADVENTURES *by Enid Blyton*

A complete list of the SECRET SEVEN ADVENTURES *by Enid Blyton*

THE ENID BLYTON NEWSLETTER

Would you like to receive The Enid Blyton Newsletter? It has lots of news about Enid Blyton books, videos, plays, etc. There are also puzzles and a page for your letters. It is published three times a year and is free for children who live in the United Kingdom and Ireland.

If you would like to receive it for a year, please write to: The Enid Blyton Newsletter, PO Box 357, London WC2E 9HQ, sending your name and address. (UK and Ireland only)